PART I

Early Weavings

(New Standard Years   886–892)

1. The Planet Beyond

Umberto Phillips walked through the back streets of Landfall II on a chill autumn eve. He maintained a moderate pace, with his back straight, his step firm. *Don't look like a victim.* His eyes constantly scanned the street ahead of him, the doorways and alleys to either side. *Do look out for trouble.* The last thing he needed was to get mugged while visiting the planetary capital of Wehring's Stopover.

He could see the news bulletins: PHILLIPS MUGGED ON PERIPHERY; INCOGNITO ADJUDICATOR ASSAULTED ON SKID ROW; FROM TRIUNE ADJUDICATOR TO INTERPRETER—FAST FALL, HARD LANDING. Aldon Rizlov would not react favorably to such an incident. The Senior Triune Adjudicator for Sector Seven was not known for his sense of humor, nor for his tolerance of the unconventional.

Not that Phillips was particularly worried. He'd been to the Periphery often in the past and nothing untoward had ever happened. Still, there was no sense taking chances. It was after sunset and most of the shops in this part of the city had already closed for the night. The streetlights were infrequent, the shadows numerous and deep. Respectable citizens had by now abandoned this section of the city.

"Chin up, Umberto," he whispered. "Shoulders back. If you didn't want any danger at all, you should have stayed on Drinan IV and dozed your vacation away."

He skirted an oily puddle covering most of the sidewalk and nearly slipped on a discarded plastic liquor bottle. Balancing himself against a storefront window, he caught his reflection in the darkened glass. What he saw was an Inter-

stellar Interpreter with a casual attitude toward appearances
—the standard yellow uniform was faded and rumpled, and
the close-cropped hair and the mustache would both need a
trim to pass an official inspection.

"For a ninety-one-year-old guy, you don't look too bad,"
he told himself. *The miracle of rejuvenation*. He practiced a
raffish grin in the window and wondered whether Rizlov
would recognize him at this moment.

He watched his grin fade as he thought about the senior
member of his Triune. Aldon Rizlov was a competent man,
but conservative to an extreme. Phillips was fairly certain
that Rizlov knew about the yearly "sabbaticals" he took to
the planets of the Periphery, and that he disapproved. More
than once, Rizlov had hinted that he considered it inappro-
priate, perhaps even suspect, for a member of the Triune to
associate with people on the physical and legal fringes of the
Interstellar Union.

So what can he do? Phillips asked himself as he turned
away from the window. *Posing as an Interpreter isn't illegal, as long as I don't sign a contract for services. Mixing
anonymously out here recharges my batteries far better than
a trip to some resort planet. Rizlov may not like it, but he
takes issue with a lot of my legal opinions too. The man's
too traditional by half.*

Phillips resumed his walk back to his cheap hotel, step-
ping a little more firmly than before, defying anyone to
challenge his right to be there. But in the back of his mind a
doubt lingered. *What can he do?*

A few minutes at this quickened pace brought Phillips
within sight of his destination. The hotel announced its presence with a small, garishly lighted sign. It had no preten-
sions and did not boast of the fact that it had a human desk
clerk and maids—good automated equipment was far more
expensive than the local labor. Aldon Rizlov would never
stay in such a place, but Phillips found its dinginess and
careless atmosphere a welcome relief from the programmed,
sanitized luxury typical of hotels in the Inner Systems.
Crowded in between a disreputable pawnshop on one side
and a greasy cafeteria on the other, it exuded a shabby vitality that renewed Phillips's interest in life.

He entered the hotel and headed toward the stairway with the barest glance at the night desk clerk, who seemed engrossed in the evening tri-vid newscast. An hour's nap, a quick shower, maybe a bite to eat at the cafeteria, then he'd resume his search. He wasn't certain, but his unobtrusive inquiries had led him to believe that Kirowa was in the city. If so, Phillips thought he would probably find the Pilot in one of the bars or nightclubs on the Thoroughfare.

"Interpreter Tremira!" the clerk called in a thin, dry voice.

Phillips had taken two steps up the stairway before the words registered. *He* was Interpreter Tremira, to everyone out here.

He turned back quickly. "Yes, what is it?"

"Message for you." The clerk held up a small white envelope.

Now who . . . ? Phillips walked over to the desk and took the envelope.

"Came this afternoon while you was out." The small, balding man eyed the message curiously.

Phillips turned it over in his hands. It was sealed, and blank on both sides.

"Did you see who brought it?" he asked casually.

"Nope." The clerk shook his head, then added, "Just some messenger kid from the Spaceport."

"Well, thanks." Phillips slipped the message into his pocket and the clerk watched it disappear with a disappointed expression on his face.

"New assignment?" the clerk's voice wheedled in hopeful inquiry.

"Could be," Phillips replied and headed back to the stairway, determined to cut off further questions. To be fair, he admitted to himself, the seal had looked undisturbed, and the clerk's curiosity seemed genuine. *The real question*, he thought, fingering the envelope in his pocket, *is, Who knows I'm here?*

When he reached his third-floor room, Phillips entered quickly and slid the door shut behind him. He made sure the lock was activated, then crossed the room to pull the shade down over the one small window. Only then did he turn on the room's bedside lamp and take the envelope out of his pocket. He sat on the bed, pulled a thin pen out of his jacket pocket, and slit the envelope.

Inside was a single piece of paper folded into fourths. The typed message read: V'ANT TREMIRA: I AM TOLD YOU ARE LOOKING FOR ME. TRY THE STELLAR CELLAR TONIGHT AFTER EIGHT.

The note was unsigned, but Phillips was looking for only one person. The fact did not explain how Shardon Kirowa had known "V'ant Tremira" wanted to find him, and where the Interpreter was staying. And so soon after his arrival on Wehring's Stopover—Phillips as Tremira had come in on a commercial flight just that morning.

It was almost as if Kirowa had been waiting for him, Phillips thought, as he carefully returned the paper and envelope to his pocket. Phillips realized that the Pilot had extensive connections in the Periphery, but he doubted that they were *that* efficient. And yet, if that weren't the explanation for this message, then someone who knew Phillips's plans must have tipped Kirowa off. Someone who could have Phillips tracked and who had an interest in his trips to the Periphery. Someone like Aldon Rizlov. . .

Phillips brusquely halted such speculation. He could think of no reason for Rizlov to assist his efforts to contact Kirowa. Still, his mind whirled with possibilities, and he realized that his planned nap had become impossible. Instead, he stripped and stepped into the shower. As he adjusted the nozzle and steam began to fill the shower stall, the pulsating water relaxed his tense muscles, and the question of a link between Adjudicator Rizlov and Pilot Kirowa temporarily faded from his consciousness under the warm soothing spray.

Two hours later, Phillips stood on a busy sidewalk before the glittering entrance to the Stellar Cellar. A half-digested sandwich sat heavily in his stomach, hurrying pleasure-seekers jostled his elbows, and his thoughts raced along paths of conjecture, keeping pace with the flashing lights of the Thoroughfare. He was in the nighttime heart of the city, seven blocks long and two wide, pulsing with a concentration of the life that was dispersed throughout Landfall II during the day. In sharp contrast to the shabby district of his hotel, it nevertheless drew sustenance from the same fount of devil-may-care vitality typical of planets on the Periphery.

I'll never find out by standing here, Phillips thought, goading himself into action. He moved toward the flashing, multicolored arch, beneath which a flight of silvery stairs descended steeply. The exit was a smaller coal-black archway off to his right. Phillips noted with amusement that this latter was fitted with a slow-moving cushioned escalator, presumably for the comfort of customers who had enjoyed the establishment to excess. He reminded himself that he had to keep a clear head tonight, at least until he'd resolved his doubts about Kirowa.

At the foot of the stairway, Phillips hesitated momentarily before approaching the doorway roboguard. The guard was one of the newer models, nearly human in appearance, capable of detecting weapons and contraband and of identifying individuals passing before it.

On one of the Inner System planets, the machine would have been set to perform all those functions, ostensibly to apprehend fugitives and discourage criminal activity, though Phillips knew that less savory uses were sometimes made of the information. But here, on the Periphery, freedom was a basic principle, noninterference was standard operating procedure, and the reach of the authorities was far shorter. The club's owners had almost certainly installed the guard to protect their business and property, not to monitor the comings and goings of political malcontents or criminals, let alone incognito Triune Adjudicators.

"Please wait a moment before entering," the humanoid guard said in a pleasant anonymous voice, then added after a minute pause, "sir."

The robot made a show of giving Phillips the once-over with the appropriate head and eye movements, though he realized that most of the sensors were in its body or implanted in the walls, floor and ceiling of the entryway. Phillips thought he could hear the whir of scanning devices from inside the robot's bulky torso, but discounted that as the product of his imagination.

To ease his tension, Phillips studied the guard as it studied him. He saw a large manlike figure, well over two meters in height and very heavily built, incongruously dressed in bright formal attire—a red jumpsuit, white jacket, and matching pink hat and boots. Phillips supposed that the costume was intended to amuse customers, to distract them from the robot's mechanical scrutiny, but the effect was lost on him. He knew that the clownish appearance belied a deadly efficiency. Anyone trying to enter without the guard's permission would have to deal with nearly half a ton of fast, powerful, well-armed machinery.

"Thank you, sir. Please enter." The robot smiled in an almost natural way and gestured Phillips toward the doorway.

Phillips gave a polite nod to the guard, then smiled at having been caught up in the fiction after all. "Wake up, Tremira," he muttered to himself in gentle self-reproach. Still grinning, he walked through the doorway, which opened before him like the vertical black iris in a giant iridescent eye.

The sound hit him first, wild atonal music that had been alternately in and out of style several times since its first wave of popularity some sixty years ago. It was currently out of style on the Inner System planets, but Phillips didn't know which direction such trends took—inward from the Periphery or outward from the center. For all his chafing at the constraints of his official life and Rizlov's judicial and political conservatism, Phillips had always preferred the orderly chromatic music of his youth. He hoped the sounds now assaulting his ears represented the end of an old wave rather than the beginning of a new one.

With mixed anticipation and reluctance, Phillips pushed through the polarizing curtains that kept the doorway iris black. Inside, he saw that the curtains had been nearly superfluous. The place was not garishly lighted as the exterior had suggested. Instead, the huge oval room, bars at either end and booths along the walls, lay under a brightly starred nighttime sky. The holographic illusion was flawless. Philips knew that he was underground, with buildings overhead, but he felt as if he were outside on a perfectly clear, calm night.

He stood beside the entrance, near one of the bars, and surveyed the room, his eyes becoming accustomed to the subdued lighting. He noticed that the booths were illuminated dimly by small glowing bulbs, a different color for each booth, as far as he could see.

Phillips also began to catch flashes of color out of the corner of his eye, fleeting images that he took at first to be reflections from the unseen ceiling. Looking more carefully, he saw that they were holographic projections cavorting above the dance floor in the center of the room. Some human, some animal, some fantastic, they were mimicking loosely the movements of the dancers. He'd often seen such effects before, but he admired the unforced flair with which these particular phantoms performed.

Despite the music, this would be an entertaining place to spend an evening. Phillips hoped it wouldn't be too distracting.

He began walking toward the bar on the far end of the room, glancing at the booths he passed along the way. Most were occupied, but none by Kirowa. At the bar, he shouted over the music, ordering a foamy red wine produced on Wehring's Stopover and available elsewhere at exorbitant prices or not at all. Sipping his drink, he continued his stroll around the edge of the room. He was beginning to wonder if the message had been a hoax, and if his hearing would survive the experience.

"Tremira. V'ant Tremira!"

The harsh voice came faintly from the booth he'd just passed. Phillips turned around and saw a vaguely familiar heavyset man smiling up at him. He frowned slightly, then smiled back.

"Shardon Kirowa! It is you, isn't it?"

The other cupped his hand behind his ear and gestured Phillips into the red-lit booth. Phillips sat down opposite the Pilot and the music faded sharply into the background.

"Damn good sound damping, isn't it?" Kirowa said, correctly interpreting Phillips's surprised expression.

"Indeed." Phillips gave his companion an appraising look. "No wonder I didn't spot you. You've let your hair grow out and clipped your beard back to nothing. Are you still wearing Pilot's colors? In this light you look purplish black."

Kirowa leaned back and spread his arms dramatically.

"Ah, my friend, things are not always what they seem. Your Interpreter's yellow looks dusky orange in this light. Beneath this purple exterior lies a Pilot's blue uniform." He plucked at a spot on his sleeve and grinned. "Slightly soiled." The Pilot took a drink from his tall dark glass.

"And the hair? The beard?" By Central Council directive, civilian interstellar Pilots were to dress in light blue and to shave their heads. Male Pilots were to wear full beards. "Are the standards being changed?" Phillips asked in a tone of amused accusation.

"Standards? No." Kirowa ran his right hand over his close-cropped beard. "I regard this as a matter of personal preference. The hair too. I don't like myself bald."

"And you like sky blue?"

The Pilot grinned more broadly. "I wear the uniform because I've earned it and because it gives me credibility with some customers." He emphasized the last word in implied inquiry.

Phillips paused for another sip of his wine before responding. "Tell me, Shardon, how do you keep track of all your former customers?"

"I don't," Kirowa replied mildly. "There are so many, I couldn't if I tried."

"Am I special, then?" Phillips asked, trying to sound equally flattered and curious.

"Ah, I see," said Kirowa with an air of sudden enlightenment. "Yes, of course you're a special customer."

"How so?" Phillips felt a sudden coldness in the pit of his stomach.

"For one thing, you went to some trouble to find me." Kirowa smiled and held up his hand. "And don't ask me who passed the word along. To name one's contacts is to lose them."

Phillips waited for the Pilot to continue, his face blandly receptive.

"All right, the truth of the matter is, you interest me. You seem to have a deeper curiosity than the mere thrill-seekers I usually deal with. The last time we met, you mentioned the possibility of your coming out here again in about a year's time, so I let it be known here and there that if an Interpreter named V'ant Tremira were to inquire after me, I wouldn't mind meeting him." Kirowa downed the last of his drink and looked at Phillips. "So here you are," he said smugly. "Want other drink?"

Phillips nodded and Kirowa slid out of the booth.

On his last trip to the Periphery, one standard year before, Phillips had found himself at Landfall II's spaceport with credits to burn and no idea what to burn them on. A sympathetic bartender had introduced him to Shardon Kirowa, and Phillips and the Pilot had taken an immediate liking to each other. The rest of his vacation had consisted of a tour of out-of-the-way settlements that were nonconformist even by the loose standards of the Periphery. Kirowa had seemed to have an impressive number of connections among people who operated on the fringes of the law.

Watching Kirowa head toward the bar in back, Phillips had to admit that the man's explanation was plausible. Plausible, but not convincing. He still couldn't believe that an informal network of contacts would have been able to get word to the Pilot so quickly and keep track of himself so thoroughly.

What possible ulterior motive could Kirowa have for contacting me? Phillips asked himself. And if Kirowa were acting for someone else (say it—*Rizlov*), what could that person (*Rizlov!*) hope to gain? Even granted that Rizlov would like to see him discredited and dismissed, how could his contacts with Shardon Kirowa further such an end? Phillips was puzzled, but more determined than ever to be wary.

He let his eyes follow the floating holographic images above the dance floor, more distinct now, more solid than when he'd first noticed them. The figures had become more clearly sexual, their movements wilder and more suggestive, and the dancers beneath them were gyrating and intertwining with similarly heightened intensity. Phillips became aware of a faintly exciting musky scent in the air, and wondered whether it came from the dancers or from pheromone pumps installed somewhere in the club.

"They'll get even more interesting before the night's over," Kirowa said with a sly grin, slipping back into the booth with the drinks. "Not for those with weak hearts or rigid morals. Here's to life." He raised his glass and took a large swallow. Phillips sipped his wine.

Kirowa let out a sigh of satisfaction. "So, here we are. What can I do for you, V'ant?"

Phillips set his glass down and gestured toward the dance floor. "This is amusing, of course, but nothing you can't find in the Inner Systems. I was hoping maybe you could show me something a little more adventurous, a little more out of the ordinary."

The Pilot sat still for a moment, as if in thought, then asked, in one of the Ergon dialects, "Isn't an Interpreter's life exciting enough, flying from planet to planet, serving as the go-between for important people throughout the Union?"

"Not really," Phillips replied in the same dialect, accepting the challenge. "It's mostly boring business deals between dull executives."

"I'm sorry." Kirowa laughed. "Just a childish little test I couldn't resist." He leaned closer, arms resting on the table-top. "I'll bet this is one you haven't heard before," and he continued in a sibilant language unlike any Phillips had ever come across. When he'd finished, he looked at Phillips, his eyes sparkling with excitement, and asked, "Well?"

Indeed Phillips hadn't heard it before, and he knew a good many languages, and recognized many more, even though he was not the Interpreter he was pretending to be. He worked to keep his voice calm as he replied, "No, that doesn't sound familiar. Of course, there are many languages across the Union, and no one knows all of them."

"No need to be so wary, my friend," Kirowa reassured him. "That's not a language found in the Union. It's from a planet called Seelzar, far out from the Periphery, beyond Morin's World. It would be astounding indeed if you had recognized it."

"Morin's World?" Phillips asked, unable to hide his surprise.

Kirowa nodded. "Light-years farther out than that."

Morin's World marked the edge of the Interstellar Union in Sector Seven. Lifeless but capable of sustaining life, it held the only alien artifacts ever discovered by mankind. Either that or the oddest natural formations—green crystal wells twelve meters wide extending down into the planet's interior as far as they could be traced and beyond. The Union maintained a scientific base on the planet and forbade settlement or travel beyond.

And yet here was Kirowa claiming to know of a populated planet farther out.

Phillips shook his head. "You can't mean that."

"Why not?"

"You realize what you're saying?" This was a dangerous joke.

Kirowa raised his glass and took a long drink. He set it down and looked at Phillips. "I do indeed." He sounded uncharacteristically serious.

"Well." Phillips raised his own glass, sorting his thoughts. *Beyond the Periphery.*

Space was divided into three zones: the Inner Systems—well settled, well regulated, largely developed and explored; the Periphery—the rough, young, frontier edge of humanity's expansion; and Beyond—the rest of the universe. The Interstellar Union maintained strict controls on ventures beyond the Periphery. Exploration was carefully regulated and monitored, and settlement was only allowed in cases where the authorities (the Central Council) felt that the Union's reach would not exceed its grasp.

To Phillips, the Council's concern bordered on paranoia. Punishment for violations was severe in the extreme, usually reconditioning or death. For an entire settled planet to exist out there, unknown to the Central Council!

It wasn't possible.

And yet, Kirowa must have some reason for spinning such a tale. What was he really leading up to?

Despite the booth's sound damping, Phillips lowered his voice. "How can you know of such a place?" He fought an urge to reach across and grab the Pilot by the arm.

A brief flicker of irritation passed across Kirowa's face. Chagrined, Phillips realized the magnitude of the disclosure he had just demanded.

"Sorry," he added quickly, with an apologetic smile. "Wrong question. Why tell me about Seelzar?"

"I've already told you," the Pilot replied patiently.

"You're a special customer. I think your curiosity is more genuine than that of most of the people I deal with. They collect experiences the way others collect rare works of art —with no appreciation for their real worth, but solely to impress others. You seem to value knowledge and new experiences for their own sake." He looked directly at Phillips, almost as if challenging him to deny the description.

Phillips took a drink of his wine. "You flatter me."

Kirowa laughed. "Not at all. I'm a good judge of character."

Phillips looked out toward the dancers, paying little attention to the contortions of the humans on the floor or to their airborne counterparts. The sound dampers kept the music down to an irritating whisper. *He's taking too big a risk,* Phillips thought. *He's only seen me a few times before. If he were the operator he seems to be, he'd never be so trusting.*

"Maybe I'm not so good a judge," Phillips said cautiously, looking back to Kirowa. "How do I know you're not just pulling a gullible Interpreter's leg with this tale of an unlisted planet?"

"You want proof? Excellent!" Kirowa reached across to clap Phillips on the shoulder. "I thought you would. I dislike doing business with people who take on faith everything they're told." Kirowa leaned closer. "I could take you there," he said with a conspiratorial grin, "but that would take a few days' preparation. How about if I showed you a sample of Seelzar's wares and introduced you to one of its inhabitants?"

"You mean here, on Wehring's Stopover?" The story was becoming more improbable rather than less.

"Where else?" Kirowa smiled. "Wouldn't that be sufficiently out of the ordinary for you?"

"I'm just surprised that you'd risk such a thing. The Union's grip is weaker out here, but it's not nonexistent. How did you manage to avoid the spaceport inspectors?"

"I didn't, but what they don't know won't hurt me," Kirowa replied. The slightest edge to his voice warned Phillips against pursuing the matter.

It was, Phillips realized, no small matter. The Interstellar Union bowed to reality and asserted little of its authority on the Periphery. However, it was the Union's firm policy to maintain control of travel across its boundary, so the spaceports of the frontier worlds were watched at least as closely as those on the Inner Systems. Maybe more so. Every arrival and departure from Landfall II would be checked scrupulously, and the inspectors were notoriously unbribable. Either Kirowa was lying or he had found a way to fool some very well-trained and well-equipped Union agents.

Phillips decided to call the Pilot's bluff.

"Very well," he said with a brisk nod. "I'll take you up on that offer. When and where do we meet?"

"Here, tomorrow night, nine o'clock. If you aren't here by ten, I'll assume you've changed your mind."

"I won't."

"Good." Kirowa finished his drink in one gulp and rose. "I have to be going now. Give me at least ten minutes before you leave."

He laughed at Phillips's startled look. "No, I don't think we're being watched, and I don't think you're going to follow me. But why take chances? You want to keep your record clean, don't you?"

The blue-suited Pilot disappeared through the exit long before his question stopped echoing in Phillips's mind. *You want to keep your record clean, don't you?* Was it just an innocent remark? A warning? A challenge? By the time Phillips left the Stellar Cellar, the lights were nearly all out, the music was a low, rhythmic pulsation felt more than heard, and most of the dancers had settled to the floor under half-concealing privacy sheets. The musky odor was nearly overwhelming.

Phillips slept fitfully that night. Shardon Kirowa and Aldon Rizlov kept spinning through his dreams, accompanied by loud, grating music. Faster they spun, and faster, until their faces became a single blur, pulsing with the music, threatening to engulf him.

He awoke abruptly, his heart pounding, reverberating in the small room. The nightmare's tension slowly faded, leaving Phillips clammy with sweat in the cool darkness. He lay that way for some time, staring at the blank gray ceiling and forcing himself to weigh the possibilities calmly, carefully, as if he weren't personally involved; as if this were just another case before the Triune, and he one of three impartial judges.

Gradually Phillips relaxed, emotionally and physically, as he constructed an interpretation that fit what he knew of Kirowa, Rizlov, and himself. Lying naked under thin sheets in his cramped hotel room, he finally made his decision. Aldon Rizlov would have to set a subtler trap than this if he hoped to snare Adjudicator Umberto Phillips.

Confidently, he put the matter aside and closed his eyes. Within two minutes he was sound asleep.

When Phillips awoke for the second time that morning, the sun was well up and his mood was correspondingly bright. He took a quick shower and donned the yellow uniform of V'ant Tremira. Downstairs, the day clerk was stationed behind the hotel desk. She was large and round and had a leer that could rout any man. Phillips approached her cautiously.

"Morning, Delia."

She looked up and smiled. Phillips noticed with horror that her makeup matched her pantsuit—purple and green. He doubted that the combination had ever been fashionable anywhere.

"Good morning, V'ant. Sleep well?" Her voice seemed to take on a suggestive tone automatically. Phillips tried to ignore it.

"Uh, yes. Say, I'm going to be out for most of the day. Would you please hang onto any messages that come for me?"

"Why, V'ant," she breathed, leaning toward him, "I'd be glad to hang onto anything for you."

"Thanks, Delia." He began backing toward the doorway. "I'll be by later to pick them up."

Her large blue eyes met his and she winked. "You can pick up anything you want, anytime, dear."

Delia's husky laughter followed Phillips through the door and out to the sidewalk. He wondered if anyone had ever been sufficiently brave or desperate to take the woman up on one of her unsubtle offers, but the thought faded quickly as he studied the scene outside his hotel.

The neighborhood was no longer the deserted backwater it had been the night before. Today it was a bustling swirl of humanity. All around him people were opening shops, making deliveries, buying and selling, and just conversing idly in groups of two or three. The street was thick with vehicles of all sorts, from large multifan trucks to sporty solo floaters. A smattering of two- and three-wheeled pedcycles darted along the streets and sidewalks, threatening drivers and pedestrians alike.

Phillips stepped aside to avoid a small boy wobbling along uncertainly on what must have been his first two-wheeler. He paused to look back at the struggling youngster, and for just a moment he was a child again, riding his first and only cycle along a bumpy forest trail on Norhaven. Even then they had been anachronisms on the Inner Planets, but his father had been a man to whom convention had been a challenge rather than a guide.

"Depend on yourself," his father had said, presenting the young Umberto with a pedcycle instead of the floater he'd hoped for. "Use your own strength, test your own balance! Leave motors and gyros for the sick and lame." The words had been stern, but a hint of reassurance, of confidence lurked in his father's gray eyes.

With a boost onto the seat and a firm push, Umberto had been sent along a path among the thick trees. He'd pedaled several meters, then struck a root and fell, skinning his arm. It had stung fiercely, but he looked back to see Gregor Phillips standing tall and straight at the start of the path, waiting. *You can do it, son*, he read in his father's strong weathered face. The thought of crying died aborning. How could he cry with such a father? It was impossible.

So he struggled back onto the cycle and tried again. And fell. And tried again, until he could ride the paths around his house without once faltering, dodging roots and bumps and branches effortlessly.

Now the boy disappeared around a corner and Phillips was back on a busy street in Landfall II. He began walking in the general direction of the spaceport. It was several kilometers away, beyond the factory district on the extreme southern edge of the city, but Phillips took his time. He paused to look in shop windows and studied the people and vehicles passing by. He entered two cafeterias, exiting by their back doorways, before stopping to eat in a third. He realized he couldn't shake or even spot a professional tail, but he felt compelled to go through the motions.

When he finally reached the spaceport, Phillips headed for the crew area. He had no desire to attract official attention by consulting the port supervisor's office, so he used his Interpreter's guise to discover Kirowa's dock number through more informal channels.

From the crews' belowground lounge, locker room and sleeping space, Phillips took a lift to the terminal's third-story observation deck, from which he studied Kirowa's ship.

He saw a standard Class R cruiser—designed for passengers and small loads of cargo. It was a dull gray ellipsoid some thirty meters high, resting on a flattened circular base four meters thick. There were no insignia, no serial numbers on its hull. As with all Union ships, it was identified by an ultrawave code broadcast continuously by a transmitter in the ship's hull, sealed in during the manufacturing process. Only official Space Traffic Monitors could receive and decipher the code.

To all appearances, it was an outstandingly normal ship. There were no guards around it, no unusual piles of cargo nearby, no movement of any kind into or out of it. It didn't look like a ship that had run Beyond and brought back forbidden cargo. Phillips shrugged. He hadn't expected to see anything out of the ordinary.

He turned from the expanse of glass and went over to one of the vidphones on the opposite wall. Canceling the video function, he punched in a number known to only the highest Security officials in the Sector. Perhaps one or two other people on Wehring's Stopover had clearance to use it.

After a moment's silence, the h-wave connections clicked on and a woman's voice came through. "Internal Affairs." Very businesslike.

"This is Adjudicator Phillips. Listen carefully."

"Yes, sir?" Very military.

"I am on Wehring's Stopover, Landfall II." He spoke in a hushed tone, hurriedly. "An acquaintance of mine, Interpreter V'ant Tremira, has just informed me of a possible border violation by a Pilot named Shardon Kirowa. Tremira suspects that the Pilot is planning to entice him into helping finance an illicit trip Beyond."

"Sir, do you have any . . . ?"

"I have no time to explain. I believe I'm being followed. The Pilot has set up a meeting with Tremira tonight at a nightclub called the Stellar Cellar."

"But . . ."

"Nine o'clock local time." Phillips severed the connection.

He knew that matters were now out of his own hands, but he had a pretty good idea about what would happen from here on out. His message would reach Rizlov or his Director of Security, John Caulston, who would in turn contact Kirowa and cancel the whole charade.

Phillips strolled down to the restaurant on the second floor and ate a quick meal. For the next four hours, he wandered around the terminal area, keeping his eye on Kirowa's ship and on the spaceport entrance gates. He returned frequently to the observation deck. Everything remained normal, as he had suspected it would. At six o'clock, he took an autocab back to his hotel.

When he reentered the shabby, sparsely furnished lobby, Phillips noticed with mixed feelings that the lecherous day clerk had been relieved by the inquisitive night clerk. He approached the wizened fellow casually.

"Any messages today, Gandy?"

"Eh?" The clerk looked up from his tri-vid screen. "Oh, it's you, Interpreter Tremira. What was that?"

"Any messages today?" Phillips repeated, keeping his voice carefully neutral.

The little man turned slowly to study the row of mail slots. "Nope. Nothin' for anybody." He gave Phillips a sly glance. "Expectin' somethin'?"

"No. Just checking." Phillips began to move toward the stairs.

"Oh," Gandy paused, momentarily deflated. Then he brightened. "If any messages do come in, you want me to let you know?"

"Sure," Phillips said absently. *No messages? Strange.* He knew that Kirowa must have gotten word of his call to the authorities by now. If the Pilot had decided to cancel their meeting, the message should already be here. But since it wasn't, did that mean the meeting was still on? If so, why?

Preoccupied, Phillips wandered up the stairs to his room, heedless of the night clerk's attempts to prolong their conversation. He tapped his room code into the door lock, getting the combination right after two tries. The door slid open with a slight squeal, a sign of poor maintenance he'd scarcely noticed.

Once in his room, Phillips dropped into the lone plastifoam chair and closed his eyes. *Relax and wait,* he told himself. There was still a wait of over two hours before he was to meet Kirowa. Perhaps the Pilot was simply trying to string him along, play on his uncertainties, exact a small measure of revenge for Phillips's having seen behind Rizlov's gambit. Very well. He could wait.

An hour and a half later, Phillips began pacing around the confines of the room. He was feeling claustrophobic; the air seemed stale, stagnant. He glanced at the wall clock: *8:30*. *Kirowa's carrying this too far.* A deep frown line scored his forehead. His hands were clasped tightly behind his back. Finally, he stepped over to the window and twisted its control knob all the way to the right. The clear plastic panels folded into recesses on either side of the window frame, rather like the furling of gossamer flitters' translucent wings in the evening on Norhaven, he thought, before the chill of the night immobilized the delicate creatures.

Resting his hands on the windowsill, Phillips leaned out and sniffed the crisp autumn air. It was fresh, but it was not clean and pure—the slight breeze was heavy with the odors of Landfall II. He breathed in deeply and appreciatively. They were rough honest odors, the odors of people living intensely. From cheap liquor and uncollected garbage to factory emissions and starship exhausts, the city drew together a myriad of aromas, some pungent, some subtle, to create its own heady perfume.

Phillips looked out over the city, parts shut down for the night, parts just beginning to stir, parts blocked from view by nearby taller buildings. He watched thin hazy clouds being pushed across the thick-starred moonless sky and felt the same breeze reviving him.

The evening air suggested possibilities. In a place such as this, anything could happen. An unconventional rogue like Shardon Kirowa could even form an alliance with Senior Triune Adjudicator Aldon Rizlov, conservative to the core. And if their plan to discredit one of Rizlov's younger, more liberal colleagues had been discovered, and had therefore failed, so what?

Phillips knew Kirowa well enough to realize that the man might still want to have some fun with the situation. Why begrudge him that? Phillips could afford to be a gracious winner. He would go to their rendezvous at the Stellar Cellar as planned. If Kirowa wanted to observe from some darkened corner while Phillips drank wine, watched the dancers and waited in vain for the Pilot, what did it matter?

In a cheery mood, Phillips stepped briskly down the stairs to the lobby. He smiled at the night clerk. "Hey, Gandy! I'm going out for a while. Hang onto all my messages, will you?"

The clerk bobbed his shiny head, then looked up in delayed puzzlement as Phillips fairly skipped out the door.

Phillips hurried the few blocks to an autocab call station, where he summoned one of the small bubble-topped vehicles. Now that he had figured out the game, he was going to enjoy it to the hilt. Maybe he would even try dancing, if he could find a suitable partner. As he waited for the cab, he hummed an old drinking song he had learned thirty years ago and had forgotten until now.

He didn't notice the two figures standing in the shadows of an alleyway a half block down the street. And when his cab arrived and he entered and it sped him toward the bus-

tling thoroughfare, he didn't notice the two figures join a
third in their own floater. Their opaque, silvered bubble reflected first darkened and ill-kept buildings, then more respectable shops on lighted streets, and finally the garish
entertainment district, as they followed Phillips at a discreet
distance.

2. Death on the Periphery (887)

When the autocab pulled up at the station nearest the Stellar
Cellar, Phillips inserted a fifty-credit voucher into its fare
meter, the counter deducted the charge from the voucher's
value, and the cab's top levered open. He pocketed the slip,
stepped out onto the crowded sidewalk, and wended his way
toward the nightclub's arched entrance.

Several cab-lengths away from the station, the silver-
topped floater sat, reflecting the faces of the passersby. As
Phillips descended the Cellar's stairway, the floater's gleaming top opened and its three riders emerged. They walked
deliberately, heading directly for the Cellar's entrance, cutting across the flowing pedestrian traffic. Despite the hurry
and congestion, no one jostled them, no one berated them,
no one gave them more than a glance, quickly averted.

At the base of the stairway, Phillips jovially greeted the
red-clad roboguard. While it inspected him for weapons, he
told a classic joke about three Antarean water-worshippers
and a lecherous cephalopod.

The guard's pink hat bobbed as it moved its head up and
down and from side to side, scanning Phillips carefully. Its
round blue eyes never blinked, even when he came to the
punch line.

"Thank you, sir. Please enter," the guard said in an una-
mused monotone.

"But don't you get it?—'I'm putting my feet down.'"

Phillips stared up at the metal giant in its red and white outfit. "This is funny," he declared firmly.

"Thank you, sir. Please enter," it repeated, its lips remaining in a pleasant half-smile that was far short of a laugh.

"No sense of humor," Phillips commented with mock pity. Shaking his head, he turned and sauntered through the black iris of the doorway. He grimaced momentarily when the club's music hit him, but he squared his shoulders and told himself to enjoy even that. If everyone else there could do it, so could he.

Phillips glanced at his watch. It was a few minutes past nine. *A reasonable time,* he decided. *Kirowa will think I expect him to be here.* He parted the inner curtains and stepped into the starlit room beyond. He bought a drink at the near bar and walked slowly around the perimeter of the dance floor, casually scanning the booths. *Might as well go through the motions of looking for him, in case he's watching,* Phillips thought. He was rapidly losing interest in Kirowa as he surveyed the prospects for an evening's companionship.

He finished his drink at the club's second bar and got a refill, all the while sizing up the few solo female dancers. One in particular caught his eye. She was small and slender with short dark hair, and wore a gauzy translucent skirt and skin-tight blouse, modestly opaque. Phillips watched her flitting on bare feet between the couples and the other singles, as light as the holograms floating above. She seemed so graceful that he wondered half-seriously whether she might actually *be* a hologram.

Phillips resumed his walk along the circle of booths surrounding the dance floor. He was no longer concerned about the aborted plot between Rizlov and Kirowa, nor did he care whether or not the Pilot was observing him surreptitiously. Let him gloat if he wanted to. Phillips kept watching the sleek little figure gliding and swirling amongst the other dancers, lumbering hulks by comparison. He was hoping she would glance his way, but she seemed to be in a world of her own, serenely unaware of everyone else, as she translated the raucous music into sublime, fluid motion.

He felt a tug on his sleeve and heard a harsh, familiar voice. "She's really something, isn't she?"

It can't be. He froze momentarily, then forced himself to turn slowly toward the booth directly behind him. The same booth as the night before. The same blue uniform turned purplish by the red bulb. Kirowa's smile faded into a puzzled frown as Phillips stared numbly at him.

"Are you all right? Come, sit down, sit down!" He motioned Phillips into one of the seats opposite him in the booth.

"What are . . ." Phillips started, then caught himself. "I'm a little surprised to see you here." He managed to get the words out in a semblance of his normal voice. What was Kirowa doing here if the game was over? Surely Rizlov or Caulston would have gotten word to Kirowa by now?

"Where else would I be?" the Pilot asked with an air of forced joviality, lifting a squat glass of some blackish liqueur. "We had a deal, didn't we?"

"Well, yes, I suppose so," Phillips stammered, still trying to collect his thoughts.

"Say, you aren't having second thoughts about this, are you?" Kirowa's voice carried a note of disapproval.

"No, no." How could Rizlov and Kirowa possibly trap him now that he had made an official report of the fictitious off-limits planet and Kirowa's bogus offer to take him to one of its inhabitants? To buy some time, Philips replied, "I was just wondering how long we'll be gone. If your Seelzaran is hidden far from the city, perhaps I should leave word at my hotel in case a work assignment comes in."

"When you're on vacation?" Kirowa reached across the shiny black table and grasped Phillips's wrist tightly. His face was ruddy in the light of the booth's glow bulb. "My friend, I believe you are losing your nerve."

Phillips stiffened in feigned indignation. "Not at all. But I have an on-call clause in my agency contract. Recall from a vacation is worth a lot of bonus credits, and there's a hefty penalty if I'm unreachable." He looked at Kirowa with a hurt expression. "Surely you don't begrudge me the chance for some extra income, or at least the protection of what I already have?"

Kirowa looked intently into Phillips's eyes for a moment longer, then relaxed his grip. "You've got me there," he laughed. "Don't worry about your agency contract. We won't be leaving the city. In fact, we won't have to leave this booth."

"What?" *He couldn't be serious, could he?*

The Pilot smiled broadly, clearly enjoying Phillips's confusion. "Surely you've noticed her. She's quite good-looking and a remarkable dancer." He shifted his eyes briefly toward the dance floor, then back to Phillips.

Phillips tried to catch a glimpse of the small lithe woman who had fascinated him already that night. He finally saw her on the far side of the dance floor, sailing through a mid-air pirouette as if she were in freefall.

"That one?" Phillips looked sharply at Kirowa. "She's your Seelzaran?"

Kirowa nodded.

This is becoming an awfully elaborate joke. "Why bring her to such a public place, and why let her be so conspicuous?"

"That?" Kirowa gestured toward the dance floor with his glass. "She's actually being rather restrained. Her true abilities are quite remarkable." He set his glass down and added, "Besides, she's an independent adult capable of making her own decisions, and she wanted to come here. Isn't that right, Niala?"

"Indeed it is, Shardon."

The voice, so near, startled Phillips. He jerked around, almost knocking over his glass. There she was, two feet away, standing absolutely still and relaxed, as if she had always been there and could stay forever. She was not sweating nor even breathing heavily from her dancing. Her face was still calm, with the merest suggestion of amusement around the eyes.

"Shall I stand here all night, or will one of you invite me to sit?" Her voice was light, with a slight lisp, but there was a sense of composure and authority in it that belied her small size. Kirowa moved over to make room for her on his side of the booth while Phillips continued to stare.

Niala's accent was one Phillips had not heard before. He

thought it fit perfectly the sibilant language with which Kirowa had tantalized him the night before. A worm of doubt began to twist slowly in his mind. Could Kirowa's claim be entirely on the level? If so, how would Rizlov and Caulston respond to his own report earlier in the day?

The woman sat down next to Kirowa, and it seemed to Phillips as if that were what she had been born to do. So graceful. So natural. She was barely half the Pilot's size, and yet Phillips knew that she was, in some indefinable way, much the stronger of the two. Power radiated from her wide pale eyes, crouched in the slight quirk of her lips and lay easily in her small hand resting on the tabletop.

"You realize, Shardon, that this V'ant Tremira is not what he claims to be?" More than the words themselves, the assurance behind them made Phillips shiver. Niala's steady gaze, cool and unchallenging, spoke of an indifference that he found unnerving. He nearly missed Kirowa's reply in the tumult of his emotions.

"An Interpreter? Of course not. I've known that all along. But despite his masquerade, I think he's a man we can trust."

Kirowa too? Phillips was beginning to feel like a tissue sample under a microscope. He was about to protest this cold-blooded analysis when Niala fired a question at him.

"What are you afraid of?"

Afraid? Phillips thought. *Afraid that you are a Seelzaran. Afraid that Kirowa has nothing to do with Rizlov. Afraid of what my notification through Security channels may lead to. Afraid that I've made a tragic mistake.* As he tried to formulate an answer to her question, Niala turned to Kirowa.

"Something is happening outside, Shardon!" There was a slight edge to her voice that gave it the urgency of a shout.

Before Kirowa could reply, a muffled explosion sounded from the club's entrance area, followed by the piercing evacuation siren cutting through the music, the conversation, and the booth's sound damping.

The people on the dance floor froze, then looked around frantically for directions or explanations. The music died out; the siren continued. The holographic figures began careening around the room, the projector running wildly on its own. Some people sitting in booths began to get up and mill around, joining the confused dancers. A few headed for the exit near the club's second bar, then more followed in a rush.

Phillips thought he smelled a faint acrid taint in the air. He turned to his companions. "Shouldn't we be leaving too?"

Kirowa was looking at Niala, who seemed to be listening intently to something.

"What are we waiting for?"

Kirowa shot him an impatient glance and Niala said, "There is no fire. The front guard has been disabled. You may need your weapon, Shardon."

"What weapon?" Phillips demanded. "The guard won't pass anyone who's armed."

"The Cellar's owner owes me a favor or two," Kirowa replied, pulling an energy pistol from inside his jacket.

"What do you need that for?"

"There they are," Niala said in an intense whisper.

Two figures appeared in the entrance doorway, one a woman of above-average height with a slender build, the other a man several centimeters shorter and nearly as broad as he was tall. Both were bald and each seemed to be unarmed. They stood together for a moment, surveying the room. Then the man began walking to his right, along the far line of booths. The woman moved to the left, toward the booth in which Phillips and his companions sat.

"Special Operatives!" Phillips gasped. So *that* was the response to his report! This was bigger than Rizlov. Only the Central Council had access to the Operatives.

"Speed and strength," Kirowa muttered to Niala, hefting his pistol. "Which should I go for?"

"Neither. They would have needed a weapons carrier to take out the roboguard." She nodded toward the exit, where a large crowd had gathered. "I think that's who's blocking the exit. They can't let anyone leave until they find us."

The Pilot slipped his pistol back inside his jacket. "Right. With all the pushing and shoving over there, I should be able to get close enough for at least one good shot."

"And I'll deal with the woman and try to get back out the

entrance," Niala said in a matter-of-fact tone. "We'll meet at my ship in two hours."

Phillips listened to this conversation incredulously. "Do you realize what you're saying? Those aren't just local police, they're the I.U.'s cyborg agents!"

"Go quickly, Shardon, before she gets any closer," Niala said, ignoring Phillips. She grasped his left hand for just a moment, gazing deep into his eyes. Then she moved aside and Kirowa slipped out of the booth, moving with the other, confused patrons through the swirling holograms toward the exit doorway.

The Seelzaran turned to Phillips. "Ready?"

"Ready for what?" he asked tersely. "These aren't ordinary people you're up against. They've been trained and conditioned from birth for fighting and killing. Their reflexes have been chemically enhanced. They have microaugmenters in their joints and alloy reinforces woven into their muscle tissue." He wanted to shout as he saw no wavering in her determination, but he kept his voice low. "You'll both be killed, don't you understand? You don't stand a chance."

Before Niala could respond, a pair of figures suddenly appeared next to the booth. Phillips jerked involuntarily; his breath caught in his throat. The two yellow and orange dancers spun around each other for a few moments, then shot toward the ceiling. "Damn holograms," Phillips mumbled shakily as his heart started beating again.

Niala caught his wrist in a grip that was painfully strong. "Listen to me, Tremira or whatever your name is. Shardon and I will both be killed or worse if we *don't* fight, and you may be too for associating with us. Unless . . ." She paused and studied his face intently. "No, whatever else you are, you aren't working with them." She released his wrist and added, "Besides, we have a better than average chance of winning. Shardon is no Operative, but he's very good with his gun, and they won't expect anyone to be armed."

Phillips shook his head in exasperation. "Shardon? What about you? You aren't even armed." He saw the muscular Operative making steady progress checking booths across the room. *The woman must be almost here*, he thought.

"Don't worry." She smiled grimly. "I can manage. Just stay out of the way until I've taken care of the woman, then run for the entrance. The man may try to head us off, unless he's distracted by Shardon. He's built for strength but he'll still be pretty fast, so don't wait for me—I can keep up. If he gets there before we do, let me handle it. Don't try to do anything heroic." There was no ridicule or humor in her voice, just a deadly earnestness.

Niala's intensity was amplified by the unnatural quiet in the Cellar itself, with the music silenced and everyone massed over 100 meters away at the exit. The booth's sound damping was off, but all Phillips could hear was a low muttering from the crowd. And something else. He listened intently and could just make out the regular tapping of footsteps approaching from behind him. They were quiet but not stealthy; he knew the Operative would have no reason to be cautious. Phillips had to fight the urge to lean out of the booth to see how close she actually was.

He was about to whisper a warning to Niala when suddenly the bald woman was standing at their booth. She looked at Phillips, then at Niala. "Where is Pilot Kirowa?" she asked in a flat thin voice.

Phillips waited for Niala to do something, but she remained seated and said nothing.

The tense silence lasted only a few moments. To Phillips, it seemed like hours. The Operative glanced dispassionately from Phillips to Niala and back. Niala looked at the Operative with wide innocent eyes, and Phillips churned inside wondering if he should identify himself and try to prevent Niala from doing anything rash.

"Very well," the Operative said without inflection. "You will both come with me."

Phillips decided that things had gone far enough. "Look," he started to say, meaning to pull rank on the Operative, or at least try to, but he never finished the sentence. When the Operative turned her attention on him, Niala moved.

One minute the Operative was standing at the open end of the booth, leaning slightly forward and reaching toward Phillips, the next she was lying face down across the table with blood oozing from her nose and the back of her skull.

Fragments of thick glass were scattered about. Niala was still seated but the palm of her right hand was bleeding slightly.

"Don't stare, move!" Niala hissed at him.

"But what happened?" Phillips asked, knowing but not believing the only possible explanation.

"Later. The other hasn't noticed yet, but he will." Niala stood and pulled Phillips to his feet. "Run for the entrance. Now!"

Phillips thought about the penalty for border violations, then about the penalty for killing a Special Operative (a crime rare in the extreme). He thought about the woman's muscular companion and about the armed Operative blocking the exit. Not even his Adjudicator's status would protect him in this situation. He began to run.

Behind him, he heard the sharp discharge of an energy pistol on full power, then another. He wondered whether it was Kirowa or the armed Operative. The people around the exit began shouting and screaming. Phillips risked a glance over his shoulder and saw that many of them were rushing back toward him, toward the entrance. The heavily muscled Operative was pushing his way toward the exit against the flow of the crowd.

Just then a purple and blue goat-man came flying through the air directly at Phillips. He shut his eyes instinctively and crashed into a chair.

"We have more to fear than holograms," Niala said in exasperation. "Come, we're nearly at the entrance."

Phillips got to his feet and immediately collapsed, pain lancing through his right knee.

"Go on. I'll be all right," he said through gritted teeth.

"Ridiculous. You can't even stand up." She lifted him up and, with one of his arms over each of her shoulders, half-dragged and half-carried him through the polarized curtains of the inner entrance.

The entryway was not dark, as Phillips had expected. Bright light shone through the doorway iris, jammed half open by a body lying across its threshold. The body was tall and rangy and bald. It had fallen backward into the doorway, head first. Half of its left side had been burned away, and it held a heavy laser rifle in its right hand.

Phillips gasped in pain as Niala pulled him across the dead Operative. The air was thick with the odor of charred flesh. He swallowed desperately against a wave of nausea.

Beyond the doorway, the roboguard stood immobilized. Its bright costume hung in blackened tatters and its control circuits had been ruined by a shaped-charge explosive. A laser burst had punched neatly through its left eye. Its blaster still pointed at the Operative's body.

Niala carried Phillips quickly to the far side of the entry-way, away from the roboguard and the iris-door. A few moments later the first of the panicked crowd came rushing through the door and tripped over the dead Operative. The rest followed close behind, trampling on those who had fallen or falling themselves under the crush of people from behind.

Gradually the swirling mass of people thinned out as those who could made their way up the stairs to the sidewalk and away. Niala waited until the bulk of the crowd had passed, with only a few stragglers still emerging from the entrance. Then she leaned Phillips against the wall, still holding him up on his right side.

"We don't want to be the last ones here. Can you walk with my help?"

"I think so," he said tightly, keeping all his weight on his left leg.

"Good." She smiled encouragingly. "Pretend you're drunk and we won't attract as much attention."

He leaned heavily on her and held back a groan. The pain was bearable, but the walk was going to be rough. "Couldn't we wait a while, give my knee a little more of a rest?" he asked, trying not to sound too plaintive.

"We can't afford any more delays," she said briskly. "Shardon will be waiting for us at my ship."

They went up the stairway one agonizing step at a time, paused for a moment at the top, then wandered down the sidewalk away from the Stellar Cellar—to all appearances a seriously tipsy Interpreter and his beautiful, supportive companion. A few long blocks later, they arrived at an inconspicuous private floater. Niala pressed her palm against the lock plate and the dull blue-gray bubble lifted open. She helped Phillips into the passenger's seat, then moved around to the driver's side.

When the bubble closed over them, Niala left it opaque. She spoke a few sibilant phrases into the floater's dimly lighted control console. The blue and green indicators brightened as dials shifted from the zero position and the floater began to move.

Phillips was in a daze. This small, seductively graceful woman couldn't have killed a Special Operative, but he had just seen her do precisely that. It sent a chill through him. His earlier attraction became tinged with fear. Who or what was she, anyway?

Niala reached into a side compartment and pulled out a small, thin cylinder. "For the pain," she explained as she pressed it against the side of Phillips' neck. He felt a mild warmth spread down through his body. When it reached his knee, it rolled gently over the pain, wrapping it in a soft, smooth blanket. He let his head fall back against the floater's cushioned seat and slowly relaxed.

When Phillips came to, the floater had stopped and Niala was just raising the bubble. He felt remarkably alert and his knee was no longer stiff, nor even sore. "Are we at the spaceport?" he asked, feeling as if he'd ridden much farther.

"No, we're at my ship," Niala responded.

"Well, where is that, then?" Phillips began to ask, but Niala was already out of the floater and running over to a similar vehicle parked a short distance away.

Phillips flexed his knee experimentally, but there was no pain, so he got out of the floater and looked around. He saw that they were indeed at her ship, or at least *a* ship. It was unlike any he had seen before. A pearly fifteen-meter sphere, it was supported over the center of a dull black ring by a series of struts, also dull black. The ring was a half-meter thick, and dipped and twisted to fit the contours of the ground on which it rested.

Niala had disappeared behind the other floater. Phillips followed, still favoring his right leg, just in case.

Judging by the terrain—a twenty-degree slope with scat-

tered rocky outcroppings and thick multitrunked conifers—
Phillips guessed they were as far away from the spaceport as
possible, in the foothills of the Nabor Mountains north of
Landfall II. As he walked over to the other floater, he wondered how the ship could have landed undetected, and just
what he'd gotten himself into.

He found Niala kneeling on the ground near the second
floater, Kirowa's head resting in her lap. The Pilot was
alive, but horribly injured. His right shoulder had been
burned to the bone, and the energy beam had scored deeply
into his chest. His face was deathly pale. Kirowa's eyes
flickered open and seemed to focus on Phillips. He whispered something to Niala.

She looked up at Phillips. "He wants to tell you something." There was a tension in her voice, as of emotions held
tightly in check.

Phillips squatted down next to her. "What is it, Shardon?"
He concentrated on Kirowa's face.

Kirowa struggled for each word. "Not your fault. I've told
her. You didn't know." His breath was a painful rasping.
"Not your fault," he whispered, barely audible.

"Quiet. Don't talk any more," Niala said softly, her voice
shaking. Even as she said it, Kirowa's eyes closed. His
breathing slowed, then stopped.

Phillips stood slowly, a heavy lump forming in his chest.

Niala sat there for several minutes, head bowed. Then she
looked up at Phillips. Her eyes glinted moistly in the starlight. "I know you're more than an Interpreter, just as Shardon was more than a Pilot. Why did my son have to die?"

"Your son?" Phillips asked, stunned. "How could he be?"

"He's been away from home for a long time." Niala laid
the Pilot down on the ground and stood up, facing Phillips.
The top of her head came up to his chin, but he was the one
who felt intimidated, as much by his own sense of guilt as
by her strength.

"What is your real name?" she demanded.

"Phillips. Umberto Phillips," he replied, avoiding her
eyes. He had betrayed Shardon earlier that evening, and he
had fantasized about seducing Shardon's mother. How could
he face Niala now?

"Well, Umberto Phillips, people aren't always as young as they seem. You, for instance, are considerably older than your thirty apparent years. That suggests possibilities."

Phillips frowned. *How does she know that?*

"It isn't obvious, but it shows," Niala continued, seeming to read his mind. She looked at him appraisingly. "Why don't we trust each other a little? I think we have some interests in common."

"All right," he said after a short pause. "But first tell me something." Phillips looked up at the star-filled sky. He had to know. "Is there really a planet called Seelzar out there?"

"It's my home." She gestured toward Kirowa's body. "He was born there."

After what he'd seen tonight, Phillips had trouble *not* believing what the Pilot had told him, but that just raised more questions. They came in a torrent. "How did you get here without being detected? What do you want? Why did Shardon tell me about Seelzar?"

Niala held up her hand to silence him. "Please! One at a time. As to how I got here undetected, I can't explain the details. Essentially my ship absorbs detector beams instead of reflecting them, so it doesn't show up on the monitors' screens. What do I want? I want what Shardon and all our people want—to keep Seelzar from being discovered and absorbed by the Interstellar Union."

Phillips looked at Niala, then at Kirowa's body. He felt sick. "And my third question?" He forced himself to continue. "Why did Shardon tell me?"

She turned away and stared off into the twisted trees. "Well, he seemed to think you would be sympathetic, and he knew you were more than an Interpreter." After a long pause, Niala turned back to look into his eyes. "Was he right? Would you protect a planet full of people from being overrun by your own Union?"

A Triune Adjudicator working against the Union? He considered the situation. He wasn't sure there was much he could do even if he wanted to. And yet, didn't these people only want what he himself had been trying to find—freedom to live their lives as they chose?

Phillips sighed deeply. Adjudicator Bakhtaswani might understand his position. Rizlov would call him a traitor.

"I'll try," he told Niala softly. "There may be little I can do, but I'll try." *I owe Shardon that, at least*.

(New Standard Year 887—Drinan IV)

3. One Adjudicator Down

John Caulston crept along, staying deep within the shadow of a tall, unkempt hedge. Darkly camouflaged from head to toe, he bent low, sweating profusely. He cursed himself silently for having put off this operation until the hottest night of the summer. He'd stalled and delayed and planned, and now he was paying for it. He blinked the sweat out of his eyes and moved on.

Although secrecy was of the essence, Caulston found the sheltering hedge to be a decidedly mixed blessing. Twice already he'd had to stifle a curse as he'd brushed up against the thorn-laden branches. He wondered why anyone would import such foul plants to Drinan IV in the first place. So what if they were from the man's home planet? On a good day Rajnesh was only a tolerable world, and Janglar bushes were far from its best feature. *The bastard could at least trim the damned things*, Caulston thought viciously as he got snagged for the third time. He extricated himself silently and proceeded.

This was not the sort of job he would ordinarily do. In fact, he hadn't actually been in the field for over two decades. Not that he wasn't up to it. His rejuvenations kept him fit enough and his mind was as sharp as ever. It was just that he was in charge now, the Sector's Director of Security, and his subordinates were supposed to be the ones getting their hands dirty. But in this case he couldn't trust anyone else.

He couldn't even trust Rizlov, who would be the most direct beneficiary. Caulston wasn't at all sure Rizlov would approve of his method of taking out Adjudicator Bakhtaswani. And even if he did approve, the Senior Adjudicator would certainly sacrifice his Security Director to save himself and his career if the plot began to come undone. Rizlov had probably been aiming at a seat on the Central Council his entire adult life. His sympathies might be with Caulston, but over 100 years of ambition were hard to ignore. No, Caulston knew he had to do this alone.

And it did have to be done.

He reached the spot where the hedge came closest to the estate's garage. He had to cover about thirty meters of open ground, but it was quite dark. A heavy overcast blocked the starlight and Drinan City was far enough away to keep its lights from brightening the clouds overhead. Moreover, Caulston knew the security layout as well as anyone, and it was laughable. No guards. No security barrier. No hidden sensors—visual, infrared, auditory, or anything else. Only a metal fence easily scaled, basic electronic locks on the doors and windows that a SecFor trainee could crack, and a distress hotline that was pointless if no one knew anything was wrong. And Kaswan Bakhtaswani lived here alone except for occasional guests.

Caulston scanned the area carefully for observers, signs that anybody at all was up and about. As he'd expected, the place was dead. No sound, nothing moving. A quick dash and he was crouching at the side of the garage, next to an out-of-style oval slide window. He pulled a multifrequency synchronizer from a pouch on his belt and set it against the window's locking mechanism. In less than a minute there was a muted *click* and the window slid sideways into its housing. One cautious peek, then he pulled himself up and through the window, which he closed behind him.

Ridiculously easy, he thought scornfully.

To be fair, Caulston admitted, Bakhtaswani was neither stupid nor ignorant, despite his disregard for security. Quite the opposite, in fact. He was brilliant in arguing his position in Triune hearings; a genius at legal reasoning. But he was incredibly naive in some ways. He seemed to think that the only threat he needed to consider was the casual, rare, bumbling burglar, whom his fence and locks just might discourage. He apparently had no idea that a person in his position necessarily made enemies. Powerful enemies. In particular, Bakhtaswani's enemies were those who valued the integrity of the Union, who didn't want to see its authority flouted, especially by someone sworn to uphold the principles of law and order that held the Union together.

The Security Director surveyed the large garage. Light coming in through three small windows and a large skylight revealed two floaters and spaces for two more. One of the floaters was an expensive oversized model suitable for conveying passengers and equipment through rough country where roads were poor or nonexistent. Bakhtaswani was an avid outdoorsman and often spent the entire between-sessions break camping in the Baelric Forest or some other still unsettled area of Drinan IV. However, the current Triune session had just begun, so the heavy-duty floater would remain idle for some time to come. It wasn't the one.

Caulston was interested in the other, nearer vehicle. In the dim light, three interlocking rings of silver glinted on each side, identifying it as the Adjudicator's official floater. That was the one he'd be using to commute daily between his estate and the Justice Building in Drinan City. For years he'd been easing along in this smooth black machine, for years collecting admiring and envious stares from his lesser fellow travelers. Caulston glared at the silver insignia, the rounded bubble top, with hatred and contempt. For years this clever lawyer from the backwoods planet of Rajnesh had enjoyed the prestige and privileges of one of the highest positions in the Union, and for years he had defended the malcontents, the revolutionaries, the would-be destroyers of the system.

The Security Director clenched his gloved fist convulsively. He wanted badly to smash his heavy service boot into the side of Bakhtaswani's floater, to shout out "Fraud! Traitor!" for all the world, all the Sector to hear.

But he didn't. Instead, he took two deep breaths to calm down and unhooked a small hand light from his belt. Guided by its narrow red beam, he opened the back hatch on the official floater. Quietly, carefully. For a moment he studied the power plant in the dim ruddy glow, tracing the control cables, scrutinizing the connections to confirm what he already knew.

Yes, there was the spot, on the right side, as far down as he could reach, where the main power lead entered the heavy metal housing. Caulston pulled a small plastic cube out of a pouch on his belt. Dull gray like the power plant itself, no one would notice unless looking specifically for it. And Bakhtaswani certainly wouldn't be looking. Why should he? He had no enemies. He was the voice of freedom and mercy on the Triune.

Caulston grinned as he attached the compact shaped explosive to the underside of the joint between the main power lead and the metal housing. In the morning, Bakhtaswani would complacently start up his floater and head toward the Government Complex for another day of confronting Rizlov and confounding justice at the pinnacle of the Sector's governmental structure. Two minutes later, the vibration-sensitive timer in the small plastic cube would go off, and there would be an opening on the Sector's Triune.

Caulston tugged on the cube to make sure its metal-adhesive side had firmly bonded to the power plant, then he straightened up and closed the floater's hatch. Carefully, quietly. Hand light resheathed, he stepped cautiously through the dark to the oval window, slid it open, waited a moment, then scrambled out, resealing the window behind him.

Shortly after sunrise, Kaswan Bakhtaswani would be history, blown across hundreds of meters of highway by a faulty power plant. Regrettable, but these things happen. And with Bakhtaswani out of the way, Rizlov would be able to reestablish some sanity, some order to the Sector's affairs. The third Adjudicator, Phillips, had been giving Rizlov some problems too, but Caulston was convinced that most of his inspiration and determination came from Bakhtaswani, and would vaporize along with the Rajneshi Adjudicator.

Satisfied with his night's work, Caulston retraced his steps back to and along the Janglar hedge. A quick leap and a sharp pull got him over the estate's fence. He sat there for a few minutes in the untrimmed summer-long grass, catching his breath and listening for anything like the sounds of discovery. All he heard were the almost subliminal noises of small night creatures hunting, mating, proclaiming their territories. Overhead the clouds were thinning and an occasional star peeked through.

"Time to be heading home, John," he whispered to himself. He felt suddenly light-headed, released from tension he hadn't noticed until it was gone. He jogged a kilometer back toward Drinan City, following but keeping his distance from the highway, to where his floater was hidden behind a stand of trees. Breathing easy in the dark warm air, he didn't notice the deep scratches on one leg, where the hedge thorns had torn through the fabric of his camouflage suit.

Back home, sitting on the edge of his bed, he winced as he eased out of his sweat-soaked, skintight clothing. "The damn things are sharper than I thought," he muttered, but decided that a long hot shower and a mild antiseptic spray would repair the damage. The suit itself would go into his home's disposal unit, along with the rest of the night's equipment. No harm done.

Across the street from his house, in the cover of a neighbor's flowering shrubs, a person ostensibly in Caulston's employ as a SecFor agent finished making an entry on a recorder pad and slipped quietly away.

On an estate to the far southwest of the city, a small strip of dark cloth hung from a thorny branch. In the garage of that same estate, three small drops of blood dried slowly on the floor beneath a sliding oval window.

Caulston took his shower and had a quick drink before going to bed. He slept soundly.

About an hour after sunrise, on the perimeter highway southwest of the city, a violent explosion destroyed one floater, killing its driver instantly and blocking traffic for some time. Five other floaters were damaged, and two people injured slightly. It was quickly ascertained that the vehicle was Adjudicator Bakhtaswani's, and he was the driver and sole occupant of the vehicle.

Security Director Caulston heard about the incident almost

immediately, of course, but there was no reason for him to become involved. Bakhtaswani's name gave it a high profile, but it was nonetheless simply a tragic accident.

The Traffic Safety Division began the official investigation at the accident site, interviewing witnesses and analyzing the debris. However, very little debris remained, and the witnesses could add nothing. One woman did claim to have heard two explosions instead of one, but no one else could corroborate that. She received a mere footnote in the final report.

Finding little at the scene, the investigators shifted their attention routinely to the vehicle's maintenance and repair records, and from there to the manufacturer, but there was no clear, definite explanation for the malfunction. Metal does fatigue and occasionally develop flaws that cause it to give way under stress. More than that, the investigators could not say without entering the realm of pure speculation, and that was not their job. They completed their inquiries and turned in their report three days after the accident. Director Caulston commended them for their efficiency.

The incidental reports of someone prowling around the deceased Adjudicator's estate the night after the accident were filed under "Curiosity Seekers" and dismissed as inconsequential. Certainly not worth forwarding to the SecFor Director himself.

Four days after Bakhtaswani's death, the Adjudicator's personal attorney arrived from Rajnesh to begin settling his affairs and disposing of his assets.

A week after the fatal explosion, the accident was out of the public eye and mind, and officially a closed case. Attention was directed instead to the question of Bakhtaswani's successor. Did Rizlov have someone in mind? Would the Central Council become involved in the selection, or simply approve whomever Rizlov chose? How would this affect the general direction and specific decisions of the Triune? Even that speculation was low-keyed and short-lived, since people found it hard to maintain interest for long in something over which they had no influence.

During all of this, Director Caulston went about his business as usual, attempting to enforce the rules and regulations of the Union to the best of his abilities. He spent his days in his office high atop the Security Headquarters building, administering and planning. Through the one-way glass walls he could look down on the entire Government Complex, all in a sense his responsibility.

With Bakhtaswani out of the way, his job would be, had already become easier. For one thing, without the dissident-loving Adjudicator to worry about, he could make freer use than before of the Special Security Compounds, where he dealt with cases beyond the reach of official judicial channels.

Every system has its flaws, he realized. The evidence of some crimes against the Union was inherently ambiguous, some counselors were extremely adept at pulling their clients through the cracks in the laws, and even traitors occasionally had very influential friends. Caulston saw his role as being in part to correct the system's mistakes, to catch those sneaking through the cracks. Such people were invited to spend some time at one of the four Special Security Compounds within a few hundred kilometers of Drinan City. There the severity of their offenses was made graphically clear to them, and they were often engaged in stimulating conversations about their past activities, future plans, and their like-minded associates. A few guests chose not to talk at all, most talked before their visits were over, and nearly all eventually ended up at the bottom of Ahlwadden's Slough northeast of Drinan City or buried in the waste fields north of Brinktown far to the west. A few genuinely saw the error of their ways and agreed to work as spies for the system instead of against it.

Not a perfect answer, Caulston admitted, sitting in his office and revising, adding to his guest list, but one that Adjudicator Rizlov would at least tolerate, especially now with his chief rival gone. It was a sad comment that he had to be so circumspect in his diligence. Caulston was convinced that if people knew their crimes would be punished and how severely, they would be less likely to entertain dangerous ideas in the first place, and the Union would be dramatically more secure.

It was so clear, so reasonable, yet even his own people

couldn't be trusted to see the truth. He had to keep his guest list in his head, in case some junior officer or clerk somehow stumbled upon it and revealed it to somebody with connections.

The possibility of disclosure had certainly diminished with Bakhtaswani's death, but there was still the Central Council to consider, and who knew precisely where that body would draw the line between loyalty and abuse?

Fortunately, Caulston did have some people he could count on, people whose true allegiances he'd discovered in various ways—a chance remark here, behavior under pressure there, recommendations from others he trusted. So he could send out his invitations and maintain his Compounds, as long as he was careful.

Still, he regretted the inefficiency of his covert system, and the waste of some excellent resources. His current Deputy Director, for instance. Grestahk Malvasian was extremely bright and a tireless worker, but impossible to read. He would be an excellent addition to Caulston's secret network, but the Director simply couldn't take the chance. How could he trust a man who didn't even have the sense to accept rejuvenation status when it was offered to him?

Maybe one day, he mused, still working on his list.

4. A Midnight Abduction

John Caulston was eighty-eight years old. The rejuvenation process worked very well for him. Standing in front of his bedroom mirror, wearing nothing but a pair of briefs, he was pleased by what he saw. He had the slim, well-muscled body of a man one-fourth his age. Deeply tanned, with thick blond hair cut short to fit his profession, he looked every inch the first-class soldier, which was what he was and had been nearly his entire life.

His mother had been a member of the Sector Council, and had arranged for Caulston to be admitted to a Security training program when he was sixteen. After that, young John's natural talent and his determination took over. He excelled in the five years of intensive classroom and field work, and upon graduation advanced quickly through the officers' ranks, helped only occasionally by his mother. By the age of forty, he had risen to the position of Chief Assistant Deputy Director of Security for Sector Seven, one of the youngest SecFor members ever to hold that office. His new status was a source of great pride for his parents; to Caulston it was satisfying recognition that he was excellent at his work, which was his top priority, though he was pleased by his parents' reaction as well.

Caulston settled into his new role, continuing to be an outstanding field man as well as becoming an able administrator. Six years after his promotion, his parents were killed in an outburst of Purist violence on his home planet Verdancy. The then Director of Security mishandled the affair so seriously that he was removed from office, dragging his Deputy along with him.

The forty-six-year-old Caulston was named acting Director, with his first order of business to crush the rebellion that had taken his parents' lives. He carried out the assignment ruthlessly, driven by grief, anger, and professional pride. He succeeded so well that his promotion was made permanent and he was granted rejuvenation status at the same time.

The memories were still with him, over forty years later, and had lost none of their immediacy. He no longer cried for his parents, but his tears were still there, crystalline shards stuck in his heart.

A pair of hard old eyes stared out at Caulston from his mirror. Their yellowish brown depths still carried the bittersweet memories of that time so long ago. He had vowed then never to give a centimeter to those who'd murdered his parents, and he had honored that vow, protecting the Interstellar Union from all who would threaten its stability. Even, especially those of high status who threatened from within.

It was a vow he renewed daily, whenever he gazed into his one personal memento: a palm-sized holocube over seventy-five years old. It was a portrait in three dimensions of a tall, stately woman in a flowing official gown. She was looking straight forward with a small but confident smile. Next to her stood a shorter, slightly paunchy man with a vague, scholarly look about him. Alive, they had pointed him in the right direction, and their deaths still fueled his determination to protect the Union from its enemies.

And so much of your service goes unrewarded, unrecognized, he commiserated with his reflection.

His ruminations were interrupted by a muted chime. He stepped quickly over to the home systems terminal in his bedroom. A small red light indicated that someone was at the front gate.

She's here already? Caulston wondered as he called up the visuals from the gate. A small woman stood there, dressed in Security gray, faded brown hair cut short.

"You're early," he said with false severity in his dry voice.

"But Director Caulston," the woman said in apologetic tones and with a gleam in her eye, "we did say eight-thirty, didn't we?" She looked into the camera and smiled. It was an unextraordinary smile in a plain face, but it had fascinated Caulston from the first time she'd come into his office.

He pressed two keys on his terminal and a set of numbers blinked on in the lower right-hand corner of his screen. Eight-thirty-two. Where had the time gone?

"My mistake," he replied. "You're actually about two minutes late. But I'll forgive you this time. Come in." He tapped in a command and the front gate slid open, closing quickly behind the woman as she entered.

That gate and the larger one in back for vehicles were the only two entrances to Caulston's property. The place was surrounded by a solid metal wall loaded with sensors and devices intended to discourage trespassers. It wasn't quite the level of protection Rizlov had, but it was sufficient.

No sensible, sane person had ever even tried to break in,

and the few crazies who had, political nuts or genuine mental cases, had been shipped away to anonymous graves without ever peeking over the wall. Anyone trying to bypass the wall by coming over it in a flyer would find some unpleasant surprises installed in the roof of Caulston's house. Sensible precautions for a man in his position.

When the woman entered the yard, the security system shifted automatically to the tracking camera covering the front path. Caulston watched her approach for a minute or so. She was short and a little on the heavy side, but she walked lightly, more like a trained dancer than the Security Communications Officer she actually was. He felt a pleasant anticipatory arousal beginning and he pulled on a robe as he went downstairs to meet her at the door. His rejuvenation treatments gave him not only the body but also the sex drive of a man a quarter his age.

Not that sex was the only or even the primary attraction she had for him. He'd known women, professionals and amateurs, who had been more sexually exciting, but the relationships had never developed beyond that. With Comm Officer Genesse Eurlis, there had been something more from that very first meeting.

Caulston pressed the door's dispersal control button just as she reached the front step. The built-in sensors turned on the chimes announcing her presence, and they continued to ring as the door became thinner and thinner. When it became transparent, she stepped through into his arms.

"John, you needn't have dressed up for me," she whispered into his ear, standing on her toes and pressing against him.

He held her tightly and rocked slowly from side to side. "I just didn't want you to feel ill at ease with all those clothes on."

She pushed away from him enough to look into his face. "That can be easily corrected." She reached up to her collar and began undoing the snaps on the front of her uniform.

"Ah, well," Caulston said, grinning, "let's at least keep the public at large out." He reached over and reactivated the door control, causing it to solidify once more.

"Prude," she chided, nearly finished with the snaps. "Besides, no one's going to see us through that wall."

"Exhibitionist," he rejoined, reaching inside her uniform, moving his hands down and behind. "You never can tell," he added, pulling her to him once more.

"Uh huh." She raised her hands to his face and urged him down to meet her parted lips. They kissed gently at first, then with increasing urgency. Eventually they loosened their embrace and leaned away from each other.

"Sir, I don't mean to spoil the mood, but have any arrangements been made for dinner?"

He raised his eyebrows in feigned amazement. "How could you possibly eat at a time like this?"

"You shouldn't have to ask me that," she replied, pushing one of her hands inside his briefs.

"I mean food," he said, giving her nose a gentle tweak.

"Oh, that!" She removed her hand slowly. "A girl has to keep up her strength, you know."

He laughed. "Hah! If you were any stronger, I'd be worried about protecting my virtue." He wasn't entirely kidding. She sometimes surprised him with how well conditioned she was. There didn't seem to be an ounce of fat on her.

"Well, if you don't think you can trust me, perhaps I should leave." She began refastening the snaps on her uniform.

"Now Gen, don't be that way." He began undoing the snaps again. "Dinner will be served in five minutes unless my kitchen unit breaks down. We have fresh local greens, broiled silverside steaks from the oceans of Coelinth, just-baked bread, and a startling white wine from Wehring's Stopover. And, if you behave yourself,"—he paused and pulled his robe tightly around himself—"an extravagant dessert concoction, the name of which escapes me, accompanied by marvelous fresh-ground coffee from someplace in Sector Two."

"Behave myself!" she snorted. "I'll behave myself after we eat. Let's go make sure nothing malfunctions in the kitchen. I'd hate to miss out on this feast because of some glitch in the programming."

"After you, my dear." He stepped aside and bowed her toward the dining room, beyond which was the kitchen.

Caulston followed close behind her, marveling for the thousandth time at his luck in finding such a woman. She excited his young body sexually and his older mind emotionally. Just as important, he felt safe with her. She was one of the few people he trusted, and with reason.

Wary from hard experience, he had not immediately pursued a closer association with her after that first encounter nearly three years ago. Instead, he had carefully reviewed her official history from birth to her promotion from Communications Clerk to Communications Officer. He had also conducted a discreet informal inquiry into her personality and her political beliefs. To his surprise and relief, she seemed to be excellent "inner circle" material, and his indirect offer to join his small group of loyalists met with a careful but sincere acceptance.

That had been over two years ago. Since then, she had developed into an important part of his covert network, her official position making her a valuable source of information and an ideal communications link among the other members. As for their personal relationship . . .

His thought was interrupted by a poke in the ribs.

"Huh? What?"

"I said, Could you wipe that silly grin off your face and help me with the dinner? Here," Genesse thrust two covered trays at him. "You take the food in and I'll get the wine."

The meal was as good as he'd hoped, and the companionship better. He felt more relaxed with this woman than with anyone he could remember. Caulston could almost forget he was Director of Security for Sector Seven, sitting beside Genessee, exchanging glances and caresses. Thoughts of rebels and criminals, plans for protecting the system in spite of itself, worries about who knew what were all submerged under the gentle flow of her voice, pushed aside by her smile, banished by her touch. How had he survived all those years without her?

As the evening proceeded through the coffee and dessert, they became less dressed and less verbal. Eventually they dimmed the lights and made their way upstairs to the bedroom. Two bodies with a single mind, they came together on Caulston's large cool bed and made slow love, unhurried, savoring each other. This world they shared with no one else.

The image John Caulston carried with him into sleep was her plain, wonderful face smiling down at him.

In the middle of the night something, an odd noise, an unfamiliar stirring of the air, woke Caulston instantly from a sound sleep. Eyes closed, he lay very still, listening, *feeling*. Was Genesse there? The bed felt half-empty. Where was her breathing? He heard a pounding silence. He opened his eyes to minute slits, but he could make out nothing. The room was pitch-black. The last he remembered, the wall panels had been glowing a warm dim orange. She could have turned them off, but where was she?

The grounds and the house were well protected and thoroughly monitored. Even a successful break-in would set off alarms sufficient to wake the dead. Something much more subtle had awakened Caulston just now. Logically, there could be no intruder in the room. And yet . . .

Slowly, with excruciating care, he began to slide his right hand over toward the left edge of the bed. If he could reach far enough without alerting whoever might be in here with him, he would roll off onto the floor, making a quick grab underneath the bed in the same motion. An energy pistol was fastened magnetically to the bottom of the bed on that side. Once he had that, he could take some action.

Of course, Genesse could be in the kitchen having a late-night snack. She might wander back upstairs and turn the lights on to find Caulston pointing his gun at an empty room. Embarrassing, to be sure, but he much preferred to take a chance on being embarrassed than on being dead.

Nearly there. He kept his breathing as calm and regular as he could, tensed his muscles without actually moving. *Now!*

Caulston pushed with all his strength, nearly flying off the bed. Before he hit the floor, his hand was under the bed, closing around his energy pistol. Or on where it should have been. The magnetic plate was there, but the pistol was gone. He felt along the floor, but it wasn't there either.

Now what? Had Genesse taken it to investigate some noise downstairs? He clearly remembered placing the gun there earlier in the evening, before she had arrived.

He crouched motionless next to the bed, straining to hear anything—Genesse moving around downstairs, some telltale breathing or stealthy footfalls upstairs, anything. Breathing silently through his mouth, all he heard was his own heartbeat. Caulston was about to risk a dash for the door when the room's lights suddenly came on at full illumination.

"The gun isn't there, Director Caulston," said a deep emotionless voice.

Squinting against the glare from the wall panels, Caulston could barely make out a figure seated in the chair next to the home systems terminal. He was on Caulston's side of the bed, but in the far corner about twelve meters away.

"Who are you?" he demanded with considerably more confidence than he felt. Naked, unarmed and half-blind, he nevertheless saw no reason to admit his weakness.

"A man with an errand," the voice said, unchanging.

"Where's Genesse?" Caulston covered his worry under an angry promise. If she were hurt, this man would pay, whoever he was.

"Concerned, eh?" He thought he heard a hint of amusement in the voice. "Don't worry. She left over an hour ago. Unharmed."

As his eyes adjusted to the light, Caulston began to resolve some details of the man sitting in his bedroom. A shiny blue-black uniform. Short and very heavyset. A dark brown complexion, tanned nearly black. Flaming red hair and blue eyes. A gun in his right hand. The gun was pointed directly, unwaveringly in Caulston's direction. It was Caulston's gun.

"We don't have all night, Director Caulston." Without turning his head or shifting the gun a millimeter, the intruder reached down to his left and picked up a black satchel from the floor. He threw it onto the bed. "Please put those clothes on so we can leave."

"Any point in asking where we're going?"

"Not much. You'll find out when we get there." The man's eyes never left Caulston. He didn't even seem to blink. "Get dressed."

Caulston stood up and reached for the satchel. He considered throwing it at the man and either jumping him or trying to reach the door, but just as quickly dismissed the plan. Whoever he was, he was clearly a professional. Trying something now would be a good way to keep from getting any older, and Caulston wanted to add considerably to his eighty-eight years. He opened the satchel and pulled out a drab green one-piece uniform with attached boots.

Who is this guy? Who sent him? Caulston wondered as he pushed his feet down into the boots. They fit perfectly. *How did he get in here?* He slid his arms into the jacket sleeves and sealed the uniform's front strip. Just the right size. It could have been tailored for him. *Is Genesse involved with this somehow? Is she an accomplice or another victim?*

"I can't say much for your taste," he said to his still-seated abductor, "but you certainly got my measurements right." That wasn't much of a clue, he realized, although it did probably narrow the field to those with access to the Sector's personnel records. There was something vaguely familiar about the man, but Caulston couldn't figure out what it was.

"Thanks," replied the red-haired man, standing. "Let's go. And bring the satchel along," he added, almost as an afterthought.

Caulston picked up the black plastic bag and walked toward the door. The hallway was dark, and he could see no sign of light coming up from the downstairs rooms.

As good a time as any, he decided. He passed through the doorway, perhaps two meters in front of the other man. He took two slow, unsuspicious steps down the hallway, then flung the satchel back toward the stocky man and raced for the stairway only three or four meters ahead. If he could just make it downstairs, he thought, he might be able to reach his other hidden energy pistol, the one not even Genesse knew about.

He got to the stairway, more than a little surprised that no shots had been fired. Surely the man hadn't been so distracted that he couldn't even *try* to shoot? Caulston turned to leap down the stairs, prepared to risk an injured ankle for the sake of speed, when he was caught suddenly in an iron grip. Someone or something held him tightly around the waist, pinning his arms to his sides. He tried to wriggle free, but he couldn't move a centimeter. All he could do was kick his captor's legs, which seemed to have no effect at all.

"Very good, very good, Director Caulston." A deep chuckle followed the words down the hallway. "You had to try something sooner or later, and now that that's out of the way, we can proceed in an orderly manner." The hall light came up to moderate levels. "You might even have some doubts about my capabilities, but I think even you will admit you're no match for my companions." The man walked casually toward Caulston, stopping just beyond arm's reach, aiming the gun as steadily as ever. "Release him, but don't let him dash off again," he said to whoever was holding Caulston.

The pressure vanished, and Caulston flexed his arms to see if they were still functioning. They were, so he turned around cautiously to see who had caught him so neatly. What he saw put any thoughts of further resistance out of his mind.

He was looking into a grotesque face, one that had once been human and still almost was. The eyes, slightly below the level of his own, were light brown and completely expressionless. They stared at him without shifting or blinking. The skin was extremely pale. There were no eyebrows, no whiskers, no hair at all. The entire head looked as smooth as a polished stone bust, and its features as flexible. The body it surmounted was a humanoid boulder, impossibly broad, but not at all fat, stretching its oversized uniform to the limits, with each bulge a muscle.

Functionally enhanced human. Cyborg. Special Operative. That meant the Council.

"Ah, so they want to see me," Caulston said, feeling a little numb at the prospect. Special Operatives worked solely under the direction of the Central Council or their assigned agents. Even though a meeting with the Central Council in itself didn't worry him, the manner in which he was being summoned did. An armed abduction in the middle of the night was unlikely to culminate in an award for outstanding service to the Union. Had someone found out about his role in Bakhtaswani's death?

"Lights, please," the man with the gun said loudly, ignoring Caulston's remark. The downstairs lighting came on, but remained dim. Still, it was bright enough for Caulston to see a woman standing at the foot of the stairs, aiming a needle gun at him. She had an energy pistol attached to her belt and what looked like a microbomb rifle slung over her shoulder. She was disturbingly similar to the giant who'd caught him at the top of the stairs. Not as large, but still very sturdy-looking, she was also bald and had the same empty face, as if there were no person behind it. A companion Special Operative, one who was especially proficient with weapons, judging from her armament.

"After you?" Caulston asked, turning to look at the red-haired man.

The stocky team leader merely shook his head and gestured every so slightly with the gun.

Caulston walked down the stairs, through the house, and out the back door, following the muscular Operative, followed by the man with Caulston's gun. The armed Operative stayed to one side, covering the entire procession.

There was little to no chance of escape, the SecFor Director realized, but things could certainly have been worse. For one thing, he was still alive. It would have been easier and neater to kill him in his bedroom than anywhere else, so the Council probably had something other than execution in mind. Maybe they were divided and open to persuasion. Maybe he was being taken this way by an agent overly concerned with speed and secrecy, and the clandestine abduction didn't imply a negative outcome at all.

Right. Maybe they want to appoint you to the Council itself. Let's be realistic, John, he chided himself.

Also on the plus side, realistically, Genesse was safe. The red-haired Agent would have had little reason to lie about that. Caulston was thankful that she had not been hurt. Still, it puzzled him that she was not here. Objectively, it looked as if she had betrayed him. It was the simplest explanation. But he couldn't accept that. He knew her better than he'd known anybody in a long, long time. Their personal revelations had been mutual, their warmth genuine. Caulston had dealt his entire life with secretive people, and he'd learned how to read evasion in their eyes, dissemblance in their tone of voice. He would stake his life that Genesse was not one of them, that her love for him was sincere.

So where was she? How had the team gotten in without setting off any alarms? How had the man found the gun Caulston hid beneath his bed? The questions whirled around Caulston's brain, picking at his attention, distracting him. And they had free rein, since there was nothing he could do at the moment except follow orders. The smaller, more immediate questions had temporarily pushed into the background a larger, more basic question: What did the Central Council want with him?

The trio and Caulston reached the end of the back path. A silver floater was parked there, just inside the closed rear gate. On its side, a seven-pointed gold star gleamed in the bright moonlight. It looked like a small personnel transport, with space for two in the driver's compartment and room for perhaps six more in the passenger section. The male Operative slid open the floater's rear door and squeezed through with little room to spare.

Caulston hesitated momentarily. He looked back at the team leader.

"Go on, Director Caulston." The man took a small step forward. Tiny sparks of moonlight glinted off his blue-black uniform. It looked as if a piece of deep space, stars and all, had wrapped itself around him. His voice was of the same material, deep, dark, cold. "Don't make us use force this late in the game. You'll find it quite comfortable inside."

"I'm sure I will," Caulston replied without a gram of conviction. In seventy years of Security work, he'd yet to see a transport that could be described as comfortable in even the loosest sense of the word. He stepped through the doorway and saw immediately that "comfortable" was indeed the wrong word. "Luxurious" was more appropriate. The interior was lighted by a soft yellow glow from the walls, ceiling, even the floor. Instead of the usual side benches and functional safety straps, there were four swivel-mounted form-adjusting plastifoam recliners. Very expensive. Hardly designed for ordinary soldiers. Or ordinary prisoners.

The male Operative was standing just inside the door, eyes fixed on Caulston. A massive finger pointed to the chair farthest from the door. Caulston walked over to it and sat down. He sank a few centimeters into the material as it molded itself around him. The muscular guard sat in the chair directly behind his, and the armed Operative came into the compartment, taking the chair nearest the door.

When they were all seated, the stocky agent looked in, nodded once as if satisfied by what he saw, and slid the door shut, all without a word. Caulston glanced at his two companions, who stared back at him alertly, impersonally. He resigned himself to a silent trip, however long it might be.

Shortly after the door closed, Caulston felt a slight jerk, and assumed that they were on their way. There was no other indication that they were moving. He felt no vibration, heard none of the hum typical of an operating power plant. So in silence, in a shadowless yellow glow with companions no more talkative than rocks, Caulston left his once secure home, heading for he knew not where. His guess was the spaceport, but he had no way of knowing until the door was opened again.

He closed his eyes and tried to relax, hoping to clear his mind of the worries he could do nothing about. If he were indeed to meet the Council, he would have to be sharp, to have a well-reasoned defense of his policies. His breathing slowed, became deep and regular. The covert actions would be especially open to question, he assumed. But they were the ones only he or someone in his position could carry out, and they were essential in shoring up the weak points of the system. Surely the Council could be made to see that. He sank deeper into the soft support of his chair as his thoughts became vague and trailed off into darkness.

5. The Council's Offer

Caulston gave a start and opened his eyes suddenly, for a moment disoriented, wondering where he was. Then he remembered. The two Special Operatives were gone and the door of the floater was open.

Drugged? No—gassed!

He struggled out of the chair's enveloping comfort and stumbled over to look out the door, still feeling a little blurry from sleeping. What he saw outside the door made him pause to squeeze his eyes shut before opening them again.

The floater was parked in a cargo bay of an interstellar freighter. Huge supporting beams arched overhead. Gray metal walls curved off to the left and right, following the curve of the ship. Tall rows of sealed crates filled much of the available space.

Just a small part of a routine shipment, John?

"Ah, Director Caulston. I was hoping you'd be awake by now." It was the red-haired Agent, and he sounded almost friendly. "You'd have been quite a load to carry up to your cabin." The barest hint of a smile tugged at the corners of his mouth. "Come on out. I'll show you the way." He beckoned with his right hand, which still held Caulston's gun.

So much for friendly, Caulston thought wryly. He stepped out of the floater and immediately felt the subsonic rumble of the starship's engines through the soles of his feet. They were already under way! He glanced back at the Council floater and saw that it was anchored to the floor by large magnetic clamps. He wondered how long he'd been out and what sort of soporific they'd used on him.

"Down this aisle and to your left," the agent said, pointing.

Caulston preceded him over to a lift shaft, which they took up several levels. They stopped at what Caulston estimated to be the upper level of the living quarters, or very near to it. A short walk along a curved corridor past several closed, unmarked doors, and they had arrived. The muscled Operative was standing in front of the door. He stepped aside, pressed a small panel on the wall, and the door slid open.

"Make yourself at home, Director Caulston. The accommodations should be quite adequate." The black-clad agent gestured him into the room. "Bed, bath, food service, entertainment tapes. If you need anything else, just call. We'll do what we can to make your trip a pleasant one."

"Will you let me choose my destination?" Caulston asked as the door slid shut. He got no response and the door didn't reopen. He stood facing it for a minute or so, then turned and examined his room. Rooms, actually. It was more a first-class suite than a cabin. There was a bedroom, bathroom, and combination sitting and dining room. Every necessity seemed to be provided for, and several nonessentials were included too. The food dispenser had an array of choices suitable for a gourmet. The entertainment terminal could provide hardcopy, sound, 2-D video, and holoprojection. The bathroom's shower stall included a sonic massager, as well as UV and infrared lamps.

There was even a small closet with a robe and two changes of clothing, stylish and of good quality.

Seeking to boost his spirits, Caulston first used the shower and massager, then slipped into the robe and ordered a light but exotic meal, which he ate while watching a classic comic adventure in 2-D mode.

The story was one of his favorites, though he'd be ashamed to admit it to his colleagues. It involved a high sector official and his combat-duty clone, who agree to trade places to add variety to their lives and gain a new perspective on the universe. After much confusion and many misadventures, they trade back, each realizing that the air isn't necessarily cleaner on the next planet. A bit of fluff, with a ludicrous plot and improbable characters. But Caulston always found it quite diverting, and diversion was what he needed very badly at the moment.

When the show was finished, and he'd drunk the last of a liter of excellent wine, he felt much better. He decided to get some sleep first and then, when he was rested, begin seriously assessing his situation regarding the Council.

Caulston was still feeling very confused. His initial apprehension was beginning to fade in light of the VIP treatment he was being given aboard ship. Why would the Council do this if their motives were hostile? And yet, why kidnap him if they were friendly? And finally, where did Genesse fit into all of this?

Just one day ago they had been lovers and allies, he and his small bright Comm Officer. What had happened to them? What had happened to her? Was she really unharmed, as the Agent had said? If only he could see her again, to know at least that she was all right.

He dimmed the dining room lights and went into the bedroom, to which he had given only a cursory glance before. The bed was a good-sized single, form-adjusting with built-in massager. He slipped out of his robe and pulled back the covers. And stopped. On the bed next to the pillow was a small object, a palm-sized holocube. He let his breath out slowly and then reached down to pick up the cube. He knew what it was, but he forced himself to look anyway.

There, in its depths, was a tall woman in a gown, smiling, standing next to a shorter, paunchy man. It took another half-liter of wine and twenty minutes of the bed's massaging for Caulston to fall asleep, and his sleep was not an untroubled one.

Caulston was in the suite three and a half standard days before he was notified that the ship had arrived. During that time, he saw no one. No one came by to check on him and he made no effort to communicate with anyone. He assumed the suite was monitored, but that didn't concern him. Under the present circumstances, he had nothing to hide. All he could do was think and they couldn't see into his brain.

Finding the holocube had removed one of his doubts

about Genesse—she was alive and had some connection with his abductors. But it had raised another. She had almost certainly either left it in his room herself or had someone leave it there. No one else knew its significance for him. What he hadn't decided, what the holocube's mere presence couldn't answer, was why she'd done it. Was it a final expression of regret for having betrayed him, or was it her way of telling him that she had not betrayed him at all, despite appearances?

In his three and a half days alone, he came no closer to finding the answers. What he did find was a growing anger at being played with in this way and at having Genesse used against him. He also found a determination not to bow to the Council no matter what—he'd stand his ground and let them do their worst. He was beginning to think that their worst wouldn't be very bad at all. Let them read that in their monitors if they could!

Caulston estimated the flight time at around three days, but it was only an estimate. The ship's landing was so smooth that Caulston wasn't aware of exactly when it occurred. The artificial gravity masked acceleration and deceleration, and adjusted at an unnoticeably gradual rate from the level of Drinan IV to that of Bandura, the Council's planet. (Caulston couldn't imagine that they were taking him anywhere else.) For all Caulston knew, the ship could have been on the ground with its gravity off for hours by the time the red-haired Agent opened the door to his suite.

"We've arrived, Director Caulston," the man announced simply.

Caulston looked up with feigned nonchalance. He'd be damned if he'd let them get a rise out of him. "Where?" It almost had to be Fortuity, the only city on Bandura and the Capital of the Union, but the question was a reminder not to let himself assume anything.

"Very good," the Agent nodded soberly. "We'll have to hurry. They wanted to see you as soon as you arrived."

"Okay. Let's go." Caulston stood up. There was no sense in arguing or stalling—they could always stun him and carry him out. Packing was likewise out of the question—

the holocube was in his pocket, and there was nothing else he needed or wanted to take with him.

The muscular Operative was still standing guard outside the door. Caulston wondered if he'd been there the entire trip.

All three took the lift down to the cargo bay, where they were met by the female Operative. There the Council floater was waiting, unclamped and ready to drive down the loading ramp. Caulston got in the back along with the two Operatives, and the team's leader closed the door on them.

Things were much as they had been when he'd been abducted on Drinan IV. Except that he was now dressed in a stylish blue and silver suit instead of a prison-green uniform. And, thanks to Genesse, his parents' portrait was in his pocket instead of being left behind.

Caulston swayed slightly as the floater took off, then the sense of motion disappeared. He smiled and nodded at his two companions, ignoring their conditioned impassivity. They weren't going to gas him this time. Fortuity was so tightly controlled that even if he tried to escape, he would have nowhere to go.

On other planets a Sector Security Director could pull rank on most functionaries, military and civilian, overriding orders, passing through security checks unhindered, blustering his way onto ships ready for departure, going wherever he liked whenever he liked. Not on Bandura. Here if an order to stop John Caulston were issued by the Council or in the Council's name, John Caulston would be stopped.

So he couldn't escape. That wasn't why he was smiling at the transformed man and woman guarding him. He was smiling because events were moving toward a resolution. From what he knew and could guess, that resolution was going to be in his favor.

The Council wanted something from him, which gave him bargaining power. What they wanted and what they would offer in exchange were mere details. They were human, they were part of the system, and therefore he could cope with them. And in the floater's enveloping yellow glow, a conviction surfaced that he felt had somehow been with him all along. He clasped the holocube portrait of his parents in one hand, and an image came to him of a plain, sleepy, loving smile. He knew, no matter what the Council said or did, that Genesse was on his side.

The trip to Council Hall was short, and Caulston was conscious and alert during every minute of it, reviewing what he knew of where he was.

Bandura was largely a desert planet, with a surface almost completely devoid of water except for small amounts locked in permafrost at the poles. There was, however, one enormous underground pocket of water near the equator. It was the only one ever found on the planet and it was the size of a small sea. Fortuity had been built directly above it. Domed to prevent water loss due to evaporation, the city had an elaborate system for recycling all of its water. It was connected to its spaceport by a multilane underground tunnel and drew its power from vast arrays of solar collectors spreading out from the city in all directions.

The planet was surrounded by defensive satellites and manned military space stations. The city was likewise heavily guarded, though there was no indigenous life even remotely dangerous to a human being. All traffic into and out of the city was closely monitored, as was movement between the various sections of the city itself.

Although the Council floater in which Caulston was riding was opaque, he knew the city from previous visits. Fortuity consisted of five concentric circles. The outer, largest circle was devoted to agriculture, including both the growing and processing of food for the city's inhabitants. It was a broad belt of fields and vineyards and orchards that was both farm and park. Citizens could stroll through it to relax and recharge their batteries. Provided, of course, they first got a permit to do so.

The next circle in was where the majority of the populace lived and where they shopped for most of their goods and services, both the necessities and luxuries. Packed tightly side by side and piled high one atop the other, their living units reminded Caulston of an insect colony. He could well appreciate the need for access to the green spaces of the first circle.

The third circle contained the few manufacturing plants of

the city, plus the maintenance and transportation facilities. Crowded, loud, metallic, and dirty, it was the essential but negative counterpart of the farmland.

The fourth circle was where the water pumps, recycling operations, and power distribution functions were centered. Few people were evident here. Most of the operations were highly automated and of necessity extremely reliable. Huge pipes and massive cables dominated the scene.

The fifth and innermost circle was the reason for the satellites and the other security precautions. It was the governmental center for the Interstellar Union, where the Central Council met, where Unionwide policies were formulated and from whence directives were issued to all the Sector capitals.

The people in that final circle had ordered him kidnapped, Caulston knew. Soon he would find out why.

Caulston had been to Fortuity twice before, on official business as Security Director of Sector Seven. Each time it had taken him over two hours to get from the outside entrance of the city to the fifth circle, despite the fact that his visits had been prearranged and that he'd been provided with all the documentation he needed. This time, locked inside the Council floater, he estimated that the trip took about fifteen or twenty minutes.

When the rear door opened and the red-haired Agent asked/ordered him out, Caulston was not only inside the fifth circle, but just a few meters away from the entrance to Council Hall, at the very center of the city. And the massive mirror-polished golden doors, impressive but impractical, were being swung open slowly and silently by two muscular Operatives. He'd never been inside before, but the Agent led the way and Caulston followed without hesitation.

Down a long hallway with a high vaulted ceiling they went—the Agent, Caulston, and his two guards. At the end was a smaller door of clear thick crystal with a gold seven-pointed star embedded in its depths. The Agent pointed to a half-meter silver circle on the floor directly in front of the star.

"This is where we part. Stand in that circle, look straight ahead, and announce yourself." He seemed about to add something, but stepped back to stand beside the two Operatives. All three watched Caulston as he stepped into the circle.

"John Caulston, Director of Security for Sector Seven, to see the Council." He was pleased to hear that his voice matched his determination—clear and firm.

Caulston saw the briefest flicker of red light and assumed that a laser had done a retinal scan on him. His voice pattern was probably being analyzed too, he figured, along with his overall physical appearance. Less than a minute passed before the crystal door lifted up into the ceiling with the merest whisper of sound.

"Enter, Director Caulston." The voice came from the darkness on the other side of the doorway. It was soft and distinct, not unpleasant and yet somehow not quite right to Caulston's ear.

He walked forward into the unlighted chamber. The crystal door slid closed behind him. No light came through it from the hallway outside. He could make out nothing at first, then an area straight ahead of him began to lighten, and soon there was an island of light where seven silver- and gold-robed individuals sat in a semicircle facing him. They were sitting on a raised platform on heavy black chairs with thick white cushions and armrests. Everything else in the room, including floor, ceiling and walls, remained invisible. The light did not seem to disperse at all.

"Come closer, into the circle," said the same voice. Caulston could not tell which Council member was speaking. A line of yellow light appeared on the floor and led from where Caulston stood to a white circle just at the edge of the Council's patch of light, equidistant from all of them. He followed the line to the white circle, then studied the seven Councilors as thoroughly as he could without being too obvious.

He was immediately struck by their similarity to one another. They all looked to be around thirty years old with shoulder-length dark-brown hair and smooth olive-tinted skin. Their loose-fitting robes disguised their bodies to the extent that Caulston could not distinguish males from females. As far as he could tell, they all had slender builds and were nearly the same height. Even their faces were so alike that he would have been hard-pressed to distinguish one from another. He thought briefly of the Special Operatives, then discarded the comparison. These faces weren't expressionless or dead—they were alive with interest, confidence, and an overriding tranquility. But it was the same for each of them. There was no sense of individuality.

The soft, slightly askew voice addressed him again.

"John Caulston, Director of Security for Sector Seven, you have been accused of abusing the powers and privileges of your office to the detriment of the Sector and of the Union as a whole. This hearing is being officially recorded as evidence of the justice of the Union."

It was the center Councilor who spoke, though his/her face changed expression no more than did those of the other six Council members. Caulston wondered if their similarity of appearance and manner was by design, a ploy to keep people off balance.

"Following is a list of the charges, with particulars. You will be given the opportunity to respond at the conclusion of the presentation."

There was a slight pause, then a voice from no identifiable direction began reciting a list of indictments, some dealing with events several years back but most arising from the past two or three years. Citizens illegally detained, funds misdirected, citizens abused, personnel improperly assigned, citizens murdered. Bakhtaswani's murder was at the top of the list.

The indictments were what he'd expected, but he was more than a little surprised to hear Genesse Eurlis listed as a co-conspirator on many of the more recent charges. She *must* have been working with the Council! Were they afraid he'd bring her name up if they didn't, to confuse matters or to get some revenge? What difference would that make? They could simply deny any connection with her if they needed, and he had no proof.

When the litany ended, there was another brief pause before the central Councilor spoke. "Such are the charges brought against you, Director Caulston. They cannot be taken lightly. You should know that the penalty for such crimes can be as harsh as reconditioning or death. We have already considered the case against Communications Officer Eurlis, and the appropriate measures have been taken. You now have the opportunity to reply to these charges." The Councilor shifted in his/her chair. Caulston noticed several others rearranging themselves likewise. "Consider well your response. What do you have to say in your own defense?"

Caulston was still trying to make sense out of their actions against Genesse. She must have helped gather evidence for their case against him, just as she must have let the Agent and two Operatives through his security system.

He clenched his jaw and stared at each of the Councilors in turn. Whatever game these subtle bastards were playing, John Caulston wanted no part of it. He'd been stretching the rules, even breaking them, to save the system that kept these seven in power. Now they were going to turn on him, and on the woman he loved, and for what? To appease a few powerful friends of some of the traitors he'd acted against? To establish that the Council was in charge, and that no one else could act independently, not even a Sector Security Director?

The fools, he thought. *The smug, shortsighted fools.* In each pair of dark brown eyes he saw the conviction that they were handling the problem appropriately. In fact, they didn't even know what the problem was! Instead of sending their Agent-Operative teams out to arrest dedicated I.U. officials, the Council should have been devising plans to locate and neutralize the traitors seeking to undermine the Union. The Council's open support for Caulston's efforts would have been a strong deterrent to those with seditious tendencies. Even their covert aid would have been invaluable. What he could have done with a few Special Operatives to command! Instead, here he stood, accused, with an opportunity to defend himself that was a mere formality.

And Genesse had already been sentenced.

Caulston directed his reply to the Councilor at the end of the semicircle to his right. *If that offends the others, too bad. They're all the same—why look at more than one?*

"With all due respect, these proceedings are a sham and a disgrace." He kept his voice low, but his tone matched his words. "You seven sitting here in your dark chamber under your dome on your desert planet don't know what's going on out there, on the real worlds. Do you think you can ignore the forces bent on destroying the Union? Do you think your defenses here will protect you if the rest of the system falls?"

He raised his voice as he proceeded, still staring at the one Councilor. "Do you think sacrificing me is going to appease your enemies? They don't care about one man, they hate the system. They hate its order, its necessary regulations. They'll sacrifice its security for total license, its prosperity for aimless deterioration, its peace for anarchic violence."

He was shouting in the darkened chamber. The Councilors remained placid observers in their pool of light. "I saved your Union over forty years ago. It cost an entire planet and thousands of lives on two others, and you applauded me then. Now I'm trying to control the destroyers before they become so strong, before all-out war breaks out. And you condemn me. Have you become gutless over the years, too soft to do what is necessary? Are you incapable of making the hard choices required to protect the trillions of orderly, peaceful citizens?"

He paused, then turned toward the Councilor in the middle. In a lowered voice, he continued. "Then condemn me. I admit that I've done what I am charged with. More than that, I am proud of it and would do it again. It had to be done, to protect the Union from its enemies and perhaps from itself. I am guilty of that. But Communications Officer Eurlis had nothing to do with it. I used her without her knowledge of my intentions or activities. Do what you will with me, but let her go. Don't punish her simply for being associated with me."

Silence. The seven Councilors exchanged glances with one another. They all turned back to look at Caulston. That quickly, without a word being spoken, the decision had been made. *What a farce,* Caulston thought, despising the Council's concern for appearances, its dishonesty, its stupidity.

The middle Councilor pronounced the verdict and the sentence. "John Caulston, Director of Security for Sector Seven, we find you guilty of the offenses with which you have been charged. Your intentions are irrelevant to the question at hand. Your protestation of innocence on behalf of Officer Eurlis was expected and will have no effect on her case. In light of the seriousness of your offenses and the position of trust from which you engaged in them, this Council has only one possible sentence to impose." The Councilor paused.

I'm not going to wince, you bastard. Caulston continued to stare at the Councilor scornfully.

"That sentence is death. It is to be carried out with all due expedition. Let this be a reminder to all, no matter how powerful: The Interstellar Union's laws will be enforced and justice will be served. Hearing adjourned."

The lights in the Council Chamber went out. Caulston looked around, and saw only the path of yellow lights he'd followed upon entering the room. The Councilors were undoubtedly already gone or protected from anything he could possibly do, unarmed and alone. Caulston didn't particularly admire futile gestures, so he turned and walked back along the lighted path. At its end, a line of white light appeared across his path of yellow. It grew swiftly as the crystal door slid silently upward.

Caulston's eyes adjusted quickly to the hallway's relative brightness. Waiting for him were the red-haired Agent and the two Special Operatives.

"Are you going to do the job yourself?"

"What?" The Agent looked momentarily taken aback. "Ah, I see. No, that's not my job. But there is someone who wants to see you. I'm to take you there."

"Here, in Fortuity?" Caulston couldn't think of anyone he knew in the city. Except Genesse. She must be here. Was this to be a poetic last meeting? Had they sentenced her to death too?

"Here, in this building. Come on, I'll show you."

Keeping prisoners in Council Hall? This made no sense at all to Caulston.

The Agent led the way, with the two Operatives flanking Caulston. They walked back along the hallway several meters, then turned down a side corridor on the left. Caulston couldn't remember it being there when he'd first entered the building. The light dimmed as a door materialized behind them to block off the corridor from the main hallway.

The corridor was short. At its end was a lift tube barely large enough to hold Caulston and the other three. They entered and the tube platform descended quickly. Caulston could only guess at how far they dropped, since there were no indicators of any kind inside the tube. He thought they went down at least a hundred meters, well into the bedrock under the sand.

Why keep prisoners so far down? Caulston wondered. The city was so well guarded and so carefully monitored that no one could escape, even if they got out onto the streets.

When the platform finally stopped, the tube's door slid open to reveal a solid wall only a few centimeters away. On the wall were a pressure screen, a retinal scanner, and three video cameras covering the entire lift area. The Agent stepped forward, pressed his right palm against the screen, looked into the scanner, and said distinctly, "Agent Seven B." A clear chime sounded and he stepped away from the wall.

The two Operatives followed suit, then Caulston. He was impressed by the thoroughness of the security check, and more than a little curious, personally and professionally, about what would happen if any one of the lift's occupants failed to pass the test. Gas them all then sort them out? That would be the reasonable approach, but reasonableness was hardly a relevant standard for Fortuity, Bandura, or anything else associated with the last four days' events. *They might just lock the tube and let us rot,* he thought sourly. A moment later the chime sounded for him and the wall began to dissolve.

As the wall faded, Caulston heard a familiar voice. It was clear and yet sounded as if it were coming from the other side of the wall. It was the indefinably odd voice from the Chamber above, the voice of the Central Council member.

"Step forward, please." The wall had thinned to a transparent film. It was still there, but barely. The two Operatives pushed through, then Caulston, followed by the Agent. A faint hiss of air punctuated each person's passage, signifying higher pressure on the other side of the membrane.

Is the Council down here too? What more do they want? Caulston had taken about as much of their manipulation as he was going to. Operatives or not, he was going to try something if they didn't have a very good reason for this latest move.

The room they entered was circular and perhaps twice the

size of the lift tube compartment, with a faint medicinal smell in its air. Caulston barely had time to wonder about the odor before four large patches began to appear in the wall. Four new doorway membranes. The voice ordered Caulston and the others each to enter a separate doorway.

Again there was the pressure differential, but this time Caulston found himself in a small decontamination chamber. Following directions, he stripped and dropped his clothes into a disposal unit. He was then bathed alternately in ultrasonic vibrations, a fine chemical mist, and ultraviolet radiation, after which a clean set of clothes appeared, identical to the ones he'd disposed of.

The precautions annoyed Caulston, but they also intrigued him. *Whoever we're visiting, they're thorough and thoroughly neurotic.*

One more fading wall/doorway and he was in a larger room, a comfortably furnished office roughly ten meters wide by twenty meters long. The wall at the far end and the one to Caulston's right were floor-to-ceiling holograph screens creating the illusion of windows overlooking a seashore on some lush world. Waves rolled in, trees waved in the breeze, even faint sounds of water, wind and wildlife whispered into the room.

"Please be seated." It was the Councilor who'd spoken in the chamber far above, now gesturing Caulston to a pale blue plastifoam recliner the color of most planets' skies. He sat, and the red-haired Agent sat in a similar chair to Caulston's left. The two Operatives remained standing by the now solidified doorway.

As for the Councilor, he or she was seated behind a translucent white desk near the far end of the room, back to the illusory incoming waves. It bothered Caulston that he couldn't even tell this character's gender. The bland, homogenized features and the invariably calm expression made reading the Councilor nearly impossible. The distance between them didn't help, nor did the distracting panorama on the two walls.

"Having been sentenced to death, you may well be wondering what this is all about." The Councilor's statement invited a response, which Caulston would be damned if he'd give.

The Councilor continued after a brief pause. "You should know that the sentence can and may be carried out. Whether it is or not, you are now dead as far as the rest of the Union is concerned. Security Director John Caulston no longer exists for the general populace, his former colleagues, his superiors and subordinates. But you may continue to live an active, interesting and rewarding life for a very long time to come."

Again a pause. Again Caulston refused to respond, staring at the Councilor and giving away as little as possible. *What of Genesse, you bastard, and what do you want from me?*

The Councilor seemed to smile, ever so faintly. "You're wondering about the price. Put your mind at ease. By ceasing to exist, you have already paid the price. Simply stated, the Council is looking for a few very capable individuals to act as our, shall we say ... representatives ...? throughout the Union, and sometimes Beyond. You are one such person."

Caulston could contain himself no longer. "And my abduction? The trial? The charges against Officer Eurlis?" His voice was quiet but as intense as a megawatt laser. "Why the elaborate farce?"

"All quite necessary, I assure you." The Councilor leaned back in his/her chair and began ticking off the reasons. "First, we cannot know if you will accept our offer, and it would be unwise to leave you at liberty should you refuse. Second, you can only act effectively for us incognito, so the real John Caulston must be removed from the scene in a convincing manner. Execution serves that purpose quite nicely. Third, we believe that it is politically more effective to be seen as champions of the people rather than as their enemies. It tends to undercut the revolutionaries' base of support and mollify many potential malcontents. It also allows us to operate against the leaders of radical groups covertly without arousing much suspicion."

The Councilor leaned forward and looked at Caulston steadily. "Our goals are your goals; only the scope of our efforts and our strategies differ. If you don't believe me, ask Agent Seven B, whom you might have heard of as Planetary Overseer Djagd deMarnon."

DeMarnon! Caulston turned to look at the stocky Agent. Overseer deMarnon had had black hair and pale, nearly albino skin. The man's voice had not been so deep either, if Caulston's memory of their one meeting over twenty years ago could be trusted. Djagd deMarnon had been Overseer of Friedland, a troublesome planet, though one not in open rebellion. However, his methods of enforcing order had been more suited to war than to civil strife. Within a year of his meeting with Caulston, he had been tried and executed for abuse of his position and crimes against the citizenry. Or so it had seemed at the time.

DeMarnon grinned at Caulston. "It's true," he rumbled. "What I'm doing now is more discreet, of course, but within certain limits I have carte blanche. I can carry out my assignments as I see fit, and I have some very capable assistants." He rolled his eyes back toward the doorway. "As long as I don't implicate established Union authorities, I can use any means I choose to combat subversion, rebellion, and other threats to the Union, in areas specified by the Council. Exactly your goal, but without having to look over my shoulder all the time."

It made sense, Caulston had to admit, and it was an appealing idea. Especially considering the alternative. But there was one question neither the Councilor nor deMarnon had answered. He turned back to the figure at the far end of the room.

"What about Genesse? Where does she fit into all of this?"

"Ah, yes. We thought you would get back to her. As you probably suspected, she was indeed working for us, to monitor your activities and to assist with your capture should that prove to be the recommended course of action, which it did. What we had not planned on was her becoming genuinely involved with you. Her act shaped her real feelings, and we cannot dissuade her. You needn't bother denying that the feeling is mutual."

The Councilor spread his/her hands. "What can we do? She's too good an Agent to throw away, but she'll be useless now without you, as will you without her. The only solution we can suggest is that you become joint leaders of a team of Operatives. A less efficient use of resources than we'd like, but our only other option is to lose you both."

You mean, to kill us both, Caulston thought acidly. He hated the coercion, but he couldn't deny the joy beginning to grow inside him at the thought of reuniting with Genesse, of being able to work with her and be with her more fully than ever before. After all the doubts and fears of the past few days, it was almost more than he could handle. If he could have gotten away from prying eyes at that moment, he would even have allowed himself to cry.

"You already know my answer," he said in a controlled voice. "Of course I'll do it. When can I see Genesse?"

The Councilor again allowed a faint smile to appear. *Relief?* Caulston wondered. *Triumph?*

"You can see her shortly. We had in fact anticipated your acceptance of our proposal, and she is currently being briefed on the assignment you'll undertake. You'll both have to undergo a period of intensive training, and some slight cosmetic alterations will be necessary."

The Councilor's voice actually took on a suggestion of emotion, becoming more somber. "We're going to accelerate the process in the case of you and Officer Eurlis. You are both quite experienced in clandestine work, and she is familiar with the system under which our Agent-Operative teams operate. Moreover, we have a fairly pressing need to get teams out in the field as soon as possible, having lost two teams within the past year."

The Councilor paused, Caulston supposed to let the seriousness of the situation sink in. "We'll be sending you out to Wehring's Stopover as soon as you are ready. Do not take the assignment lightly. That is where we lost one of our teams." The Councilor pressed a panel on the desk and a wall began to form in the middle of the room.

"Not a very subtle way to end an interview," Caulston muttered.

"They're not much on tact," deMarnon agreed, "but they definitely know their business." He stood and pointed to a door forming in the wall to Caulston's left. "Come on, we might as well begin your orientation."

Caulston rose and followed the stocky ex-Overseer through the door. His thoughts were primarily focused on seeing Genesse again, talking to her, touching her. Mixed in with such pleasant anticipations were more practical questions about the orientation and the training to come. And then there was speculation about the assignment itself.

He'd never been to Wehring's Stopover, though he knew quite a bit about the place and had a deep admiration for its winemakers. It was a rather loose, quasi-anarchic Peripheral planet with little tolerance for the rules and regulations of the Union. No different from many others on the Periphery in that respect. Offensive as they were, the planet's anarchistic leanings didn't overly concern Caulston at the moment. What concerned him about this assignment to Wehring's Stopover was the question: Who or what could take on and eliminate a team of Special Operatives? And the Councilor had said *two* teams had been "lost." For "lost" Caulston read "killed," and twice seemed to rule out some freak accident as the cause.

His thoughts came full circle and he wondered just what he and Genesse were going up against.

(New Standard Year 891—Bekh-Nar)

6. A Woman's Gotta Do . . .

"Won't you reconsider, Overseer?" Alepha Conn-Lee kept her voice formal and correct, but it shook noticeably in the quiet of the large top-floor office.

Overseer Lanya Selius looked across her wide desk at the young woman who was both her capable personal assistant and her ward. "You know that is out of the question, Lieutenant Conn-Lee. The law and the facts are quite clear in this case. I have no choice in the matter." She was not lying, though her reasons were other than those stated. As Overseer of Bekh-Nar, she was given a great deal of discretion in maintaining order on the planet. However, she would have to answer to the Sector Council and the Triune. And she had an example to set.

Conn-Lee's dark blue eyes shone, on the verge of tears. "Those people are not criminals. They needed the food. They have children and elderly parents who depend on them."

And they are also your clan-kin, who ostracized you as a child, Alepha. What do you owe them? Aloud, Selius replied, "All their needs would have been provided for had they simply registered themselves and their dependents at their regional census office. Their failure to do so makes them by definition criminals, and their attempted burglary of a food warehouse merely adds to their offense."

"But—" the Lieutenant began, then paused. She was visibly upset, perhaps at her superior's/guardian's inflexibility, and perhaps at her own inability to produce a persuasive argument. A flush began to spread up her neck and across her face. It emphasized her pale skin.

Selius cared for Conn-Lee. She valued the girl's sharp mind and her courage, and she empathized with her social isolation. Alepha was a small, delicate flower shunned by most of her people, large rough weeds by comparison. Lanya Selius had likewise been an outcast in her youth, with the roles reversed. Among a people whose women were frail, subservient decorations, she had been bigger, stronger, and brighter than most men, and hadn't been shy about the fact. A tough childhood had made her a tougher adult, able and willing to do what needed to be done.

Now, she needed to show Alepha Conn-Lee that decisions aren't always pleasant and can't always be swayed by personal concerns.

"But nothing, Lieutenant. People are responsible for the consequences of their actions. Vieren Conn-Tir and the others chose not to become provisional citizens of the Interstellar Union. By their refusal, I can only assume that they are supporters of the rebels' cause and oppose full incorporation of Bekh-Nar into the Union. It is not my decision. They have put themselves beyond the protection of the Code."

Alepha Conn-Lee had averted her gaze, and was now looking down at her hands folded in her lap. She didn't say anything.

Overseer Selius resisted an urge to reach over and comfort her. This was not the time for softness. If Conn-Lee were to survive, let alone thrive, in the Union, she would have to learn to separate her feelings from her duty, and to make the latter her top priority. A hard lesson, but necessary.

Keeping her voice calm and businesslike, Selius continued, "Lieutenant Conn-Lee, I understand your concern in this matter, and I realize how difficult it is for you." She held up her hand to forestall a comment from her young aide. "But every case is exceptional to someone or other, and if we make allowances once, where do we draw the line? What is mercy or kindness to one is capricious justice to another, and the system begins to crumble. We cannot betray those who've sided with the Union. Vieren Conn-Tir and his four accomplices will face public chastisement in two days' time, and be sent off-planet when the next Security transport arrives. That is all."

"Very good, Overseer." Conn-Lee rose slowly. "I appreciate your hearing me out on this matter."

"Not at all, Lieutenant." Selius remained seated but gave her young ward an encouraging half-smile. "You were quite right to come to me with your concerns."

"Thank you, ma'am." The small woman saluted briskly, turned, and left the office.

Overseer Selius sat still for a time, her eyes not focused on anything in particular, replaying the conversation in her mind. It had gone fairly well, she thought. Alepha was obviously unhappy, but she seemed to have accepted the decision as necessary. That was all Selius had hoped for.

She pushed back her chair and stood up. Her neck, shoulders, and back were stiff and sore, partly from sitting all day and partly from the tension of her meeting with Alepha Conn-Lee. Now that it was over, it seemed as if all of her muscles had decided to tighten up in unison. She rotated her shoulders slowly several times, then reached up with both arms and pushed hard against one of the ceiling beams. Harder, harder. Almost, she could imagine it giving, bending upward however slightly. Although the beam was solid plastalloy, the imagined bending was not wholly inconceivable. At 190 centimeters and 80 kilos, without a gram of excess fat, Lanya Selius was strong by anybody's standards. She had been born that way and she worked to stay that way.

Her challenge to the ceiling was a daily ritual, a release she sought more frequently on especially bad days. Today had been so hectic that this was her first opportunity to attack it. Typical of her summers on Bekh-Nar, she thought.

For eight years she'd been on the planet, and for eight years her problems had been more numerous and more difficult during the summer. The heat and humidity seemed to bring out the worst in everyone, even the Narians. At times like this she longed for her own temperate home planet or fantasized about some cool snow-covered place with few people and fewer problems.

After a minute or so she relaxed, much of her nervous energy dissipated. She took ten deep, slow breaths, each breath moving her further than the last from the here and now, until she could almost forget the burdens of her office. She knew they would come back to her soon enough, but the momentary respite was invaluable.

Responsibilities and problems were always with her. The problems were the sole reason for her being on Bekh-Nar at all. Only planets with recalcitrant populations had Overseers running them, and an Overseer's job was to bring the people fully into the fold of the Interstellar Union. Fortunately, she was given power commensurate with her responsibilities. Unfortunately, she was given no more hours per day than anyone else had, and could delegate precious little of her job to others.

Her office suddenly felt too small, crammed with decisions already made and those yet to come. She walked across the room to gaze out its largest window. From there, she could see the sun just setting behind the Grayling Mountains some 200 kilometers to the west. The city below was already in shadow, as were the river next to which it huddled and the vast dense forest beyond. Out there, in the forest and the mountains, the rebels lurked. And perhaps in the city.

Selius's office was at the top of the Tower of Laws, in the center of the city of Tol-Nar. It was the largest building in the city, fully eight stories tall, and Tol-Nar was the largest city on the planet, with about 30,000 inhabitants. The Tower and the other buildings in the I.U. compound were made of shiny plastalloy and crystal and were surrounded by a powered security barrier. Tol-Nar's native buildings rose three stories or less, were made of stone and timber, and were surrounded by people, animals, and gardens.

The Overseer watched the darkening streets below gradually empty of traffic. Here and there islands of light appeared where groups of evening businesses gathered—inns, taverns, theaters. Otherwise the streets were given over to shadows and the nightly fog from the river, while the city's populace retreated to their cozy hearths and the comfort of their families.

A simple planetary capital for a simple people, Selius declared to herself, and withdrew the thought in the next instant. Far from simple, the Narians were intelligent and sophisticated and *chose* to live in a nonindustrial society. They'd had a few centuries to develop their pastoral culture, isolated from and ignored by the busier, more technological worlds. They had known about those other worlds through infrequent contacts with speculative traders, but had resisted any temptations they may have felt to modernize and urbanize. And even though the majority of the population had long since registered with the I.U. census offices, enough rebels remained at large and had enough covert support from somewhere to keep Bekh-Nar on provisional status, as it had been for the past eight standard years. The registered citizenry occasionally acted up too, going out on a general strike over some incident or Union policy.

Not simple—stubborn and resourceful, Selius reminded herself.

Eventually the planet would be assimilated into the Union, but it would take time. Time to wear down the rebels opposed to the Union, time to turn grudging acceptance of the Union into active support by the majority of the populace, time to develop pro-Union leadership from among the Narians themselves. When the off-planet troopers and regional directors would be withdrawn, then Overseer Selius could leave as well, and Bekh-Nar would be a part of the Union.

In the meantime, Selius saw herself as the Narians' stern parent, leading them in the proper direction despite their reluctance. It was her job to punish them when necessary and to reward them when she could, and to help them enter as soon as possible into full membership in the Interstellar Union.

Progress toward that goal had lately been at an impasse. It was as if she had gotten the number of rebel holdouts down to an irreducible minimum who could not be swayed. More puzzling was their ability to keep up the struggle despite being cut off from all significant predictable bases of support on the planet.

Just three days ago, in fact, they had ambushed a convoy carrying mining equipment north to the most recently discovered ore deposit. The rebels had had some advanced weapons and an apparently excellent communications capability. They had managed to damage heavily much of the machinery and many of the transport vehicles while causing only minor injuries to a few of the drivers and workers. The native Narian technology was not sufficiently sophisticated to support such an attack.

It was almost as if the rebels were being supplied from off-planet. Selius made a mental note to investigate the matter as soon as possible, and to tighten her skyward surveillance system.

She raised her eyes to look again at the distant mountains, but the sky had become completely black and all she saw was her own reflection in the window. Dull blond hair, intense eyes, thin lips, and a hooked nose. She wasn't pretty, but she was smart and strong, and rejuvenation treatments kept her physically young.

At the age of seventeen she had run away from home and enlisted in the Sector Security Force. It had been an impulsive act of rebellion, but she couldn't have done better with years of planning. In Security, she was judged solely on what she could do, and she'd done very well. Forty-five years later, here she was, a Planetary Overseer. One of her few occasional regrets was that she'd never had a child, someone to raise, to care for, to help along the road of life. Once she'd begun her rejuvenation treatments, she'd lost the ability to have children of her own. It was a price everyone paid, and she'd paid it willingly, but at times she wondered how things might have been.

And now, on the out-of-the-way resource-rich planet of

Bekh-Nar, she was getting her chance. Selius had taken it upon herself to raise Alepha Conn-Lee as the child she'd never had, and to train her into the life of a Sector Security officer. The girl had been rejected by her own people because of her light skin and small stature, which contrasted with the Narians' typically dark brown to black skin tone and large, big-boned physiques. Selius's anger at her own mistreatment as a child had long since faded, but the Narians' cruelty toward Alepha still made the Overseer want to strike out at somebody.

During her first year on the planet, Selius had come upon a melee in one of the back streets of Tol-Nar. Wading in, she had extricated the fourteen-year-old Alepha from beneath a pile of three older and much larger youths. Despite their advantage, the three had received almost as much as they had given. The girl's spunk impressed Selius, and when no family could be found to vouch for her and she herself claimed to be an orphan, Overseer Selius saw an opportunity to take a personal role in the assimilation of Bekh-Nar. She assumed complete custodial responsibility for Conn-Lee, and her sponsorship allowed the girl to gain full Union citizenship.

Eight years later, Alepha Conn-Lee was a Lieutenant in Sector Seven's Security Forces. She had gone to school with the children of the other Union personnel on Bekh-Nar and had received advanced military training along with the contingent of Security trainees sent to the planet. Over the years, Lanya Selius had given her what attention she could. Selius realized that learning from books, lesson tapes, lectures and simulators was necessary, but she felt that the most important learning was by actual experience and example. Until her adopted daughter was old enough to have acquired a sufficient store of experience, Selius was determined to show by example how to be a successful Security officer. *Work hard, stay tough, be fair.*

Selius turned off the lights in her office and took the lift tube down to the first floor. As she was walking over to the officers' living quarters she reminded herself to speak with Major Urtloew about increasing the coverage of the sky-scanning radar.

Urtloew was a good man. Too good to remain a Communications and Surveillance Specialist on Bekh-Nar for very long, even if he had volunteered for the post. If anything could be done to tighten planetary security, he'd be able to do it. Selius decided she'd better see him before he transferred away. Maybe she'd put in a call to Central Stores on Drinan IV too, to see if she could pry another surveillance satellite out of their miserly clutches.

7. ... What a Woman's Gotta Do

Three hours after midnight, the still, damp air of Tol-Nar was split by a rasping shriek. The sound rose and fell regularly and rapidly, until everyone in the I.U. compound was out of bed and at his/her duty station.

Overseer Selius personally shut off the alarm and demanded a status report from all units. In moments she learned that the two detention building guards were unconscious and that the five Narian prisoners were missing, along with a survey skimmer. Seated in her office, with all twenty monitor screens activated, Selius noted one other absence.

"Lieutenant Conn-Lee! Report to your station immediately!" The Overseer's voice boomed out over speakers in every room in the compound. She waited several minutes, then repeated the order. Still no response. The chair beside her remained empty.

She ordered a detail to search Conn-Lee's quarters, then sat back and waited impatiently for their report. Fingers drumming furiously on her desk top, she wondered what could have happened. Had Alepha been abducted? Had she been paying a visit to the prisoners and been forced to aid in the escape? Had she witnessed the escape and gone in pursuit of the criminals? It would be just like her to do something brave but foolhardy, Selius thought.

Let her be here, safe and sleeping through the alarm.

Selius pleaded to no one in particular. *Better a reprimand than death*.

Just then Major Urtloew called in from the comm center.

"Overseer, our radar has locked on to the missing skimmer. It is heading north-northwest at moderate speed. At its present rate, it will remain within range for two hours. Do you wish to send the deactivation sequence?"

Deactivation. Turn its power plant off. Watch it crash. *Is Alepha on board? Could she survive?*

"No, Major. Attempt to establish contact with the occupants and await further orders. If they respond, transfer the comm through to my office." She punched up the radar display on her main monitor and watched it for a few minutes. The skimmer was well beyond the river, flying over the densest, wildest part of the forest. Its blip paused for a moment, then proceeded. Had they stopped to let someone out or to pick someone up? Had they hovered momentarily just to confuse the trackers?

Her intercom came to life again. "Overseer, Sergeant Mahtzu reporting."

"Proceed."

"Yes ma'am. We found Lieutenant Conn-Lee's door locked. We issued several requests to open the door, utilized the door buzzer, and pounded on the door loudly. She did not respond in any way. Believing this to be a possible emergency situation, and considering the urgency of your orders, I had Corporal Goral burn through the door, being careful to limit the damage to the locking mechanism itself."

"Yes, yes. Go on." If the man didn't get to the point soon, he would drive Selius to drink or to murder. Maybe both.

"Inside, we found nothing. Lieutenant Conn-Lee was not there, nor was anyone else. There was no sign of a struggle or anything else untoward. It appeared that some of her clothing and personal effects were gone, as was her sidearm. A complete inventory is currently being made to determine exactly what is missing."

Gone. Nothing. "Thank you, Sergeant. Continue with the inventory and send me a copy when it is completed."

"Yes, ma'am."

Selius shut off the mike. No struggle. No message. No

note. *What is happening, Alepha? What are you involved in?* She could not believe, would not let herself believe, that Alepha was a willing accomplice to the rebels' escape.

She looked again at the radar trace. No change. It was still heading away from the city.

She called down to vehicle maintenance and ordered that Skimmer Number Two be readied for extended flight. Immediately. Then she contacted Major Urtloew again to arrange a scrambled comm link between the compound and Skimmer Two.

"And Major. Transmit continuously to the skimmer's screen a display of your radar image of both vehicles."

"Very well, Overseer. Do you want me to assign one of my people to the pursuit squad?"

"There will be no pursuit squad, Major. Not yet. I'm taking Skimmer Two by myself."

"But, ma'am—"

"No 'buts,' Major. I will contact you at least once every fifteen minutes. If twenty minutes goes by without a message from me, you are to send out a squad of your choosing. Understood?"

"Understood." The Major sounded glum, but was too professional a soldier, and had served under Selius too long, to argue further.

The last thing Selius wanted was a bunch of excited Security guards racing after the skimmer with Alepha on it. If she was on it. No sense spooking the escapees into doing something rash or risking a trigger-happy guard's response.

Selius was in the air ten minutes later, flying at a height of 100 meters. The fugitive skimmer had perhaps a one-hour head start, judging from the reports of the revived but groggy detention guards. They hadn't seen who'd attacked them, but they hadn't been out many minutes before one of their relief guards had discovered them and the open cell doors. They hadn't been hit—whoever had knocked them out had had a sophisticated gun capable of stunning without killing, such as a SecFor officer's sidearm. The cell doors had been opened by someone who knew how to use the guards' code keys. They must have somehow forced Alepha to help them.

Bekh-Nar's tiny moon had set over an hour ago, and the

night was very dark. Over two hours before any glimmerings of dawn would appear. By then, Selius would have to decide whether to deactivate the other skimmer or to risk letting it escape. If she knew that Alepha wasn't on it, the decision would be easy. If she knew that Alepha was on it, the decision would be hard, very hard, even if the girl's own carelessness was to blame for her predicament.

Selius flew on, keeping her skimmer at top speed, gaining steadily on the other vehicle. The escapees didn't seem to be in any hurry. They might not have realized they were being pursued, and the other pilot was almost certainly much less experienced than the Overseer, who had no qualms about pushing her skimmer to the limits at low altitude in the dead of night over a barely charted forest. She kept her cabin lights off to allow her eyes maximum dark-adaptation, but she could make out only vague contours of the forest roof below. The only guidance she needed was the topmost radar blip on her screen, coming closer by the minute.

The stolen skimmer paused again, briefly, then proceeded in a more westerly direction. Selius didn't speculate about the pilot's motives, but she did appreciate the opportunity to gain more ground on the other skimmer, and changed her course to intercept rather than follow its path. They *must* not know they were being so closely pursued, or they'd never have made such a maneuver. Straight-line flight was their best bet. They still hadn't responded to Urtloew's calls. Should she try contacting them herself? That might give away her position, but if Alepha were on board, Selius might be able to talk to her, get her to reason with the rebels. At least give her a little comfort.

"Attention, Skimmer One. This is Overseer Selius calling Skimmer One. Please respond."

Nothing. She waited thirty seconds and tried again.

"Skimmer One, this is Overseer Selius. If you do not land within the next ten minutes, I will be forced to deactivate your power plant. Reply if you have received my message."

Again, nothing. In twenty minutes at its current speed, the stolen skimmer would be just about at the limits of the compound's radar scanners, and consequently nearly beyond the range of the deactivation command. Selius didn't want to issue the order if it would jeopardize Alepha, but she would have little choice in the matter. A skimmer stolen by escaped prisoners could be cause for her recall or dismissal from Security, if her indecision or negligence were found responsible.

The deactivation relay was an integral part of the power plants of all Security vehicles assigned to unassimilated planets. It prevented hostile natives from stealing the machines and turning them against I.U. forces. A vehicle could be deactivated manually by its operator if it were in danger of being captured, or it could be deactivated by radio command from the vehicle's base of origin.

Under ordinary circumstances, no warning would be given. The signal would simply be sent and the vehicle would cease functioning. If it were in the air or travelling at high speed at the time, the result could well be the loss of the vehicle and its occupants. Regrettable, since not even skimmers and floaters were cheap or easy to replace. Getting a replacement from the bureaucrats on Drinan IV took time —there were forms to fill out, explanations to make.

But these were not ordinary circumstances. Alepha Conn-Lee was almost certainly aboard Skimmer One, and possibly piloting it. Lanya Selius wanted to give her adopted daughter every chance to survive. Maybe Alepha could persuade her captors to land the vehicle, and none of them would have to be hurt. She could explain how pointless it would be to try to run, how they couldn't escape with the skimmer.

The minutes dragged by, and Selius continued to gain steadily on the escapees. From the forest, an occasional branched giant reached three-quarters of the way up to her skimmer. Soon the green sea below would be rising with the land as the two vehicles approached the foothills of the Grayling Mountains. The mountains were as wet as the river valley, and as heavily forested up to the point where the air became too thin to support the larger vegetation. No clear landing spots in sight.

Selius was only twelve kilometers behind the other skimmer when the ten minutes were up. She tried raising its pilot one more time but again received no reply. She switched channels.

"Major Urtloew. Send the deactivation sequence, and fix

the last known reading from Skimmer One on my screen so I can home in on that location. Understood?"

"Understood, Overseer." The Major's voice came through sharply. In a moment the leading blip on Selius's screen stopped moving and began to flash rapidly.

"Shall I send out the pursuit squad now?"

"Yes. Have them first drop a small search party at each of the two locations where Skimmer One paused. Then the rest can come out and meet me where the skimmer went down." She swallowed dryly. "There shouldn't be much to deal with on this end."

"Very well, Overseer." He paused, then added, "And good luck."

"Thanks, Major." Selius cut the connection and sped forward into the night. Her sense of duty and her desire to see an end to the night's troubling events drove her on, even as a part of her was shying away from what she might find. If only Alepha weren't on the skimmer. Maybe she'd been taken off at one of the earlier stops. She could neither keep herself from hoping for the best nor make herself believe it.

All too soon she reached the spot where Skimmer One had dropped out of sight on the compound's radar screens. At that point she donned her night-sight helmet and began to search visually, looking through the skimmer's wide, curving front window. Almost immediately she spotted the long tear in the forest canopy where trees had been brushed aside or knocked over by the plummeting skimmer.

Thank the Powers there's no fire, thought the Overseer. In the next instant she was circling the crash site and wondering whether anybody could have survived, even without a fire.

It was a slanting 150-meter trench carved out of the living fabric of the forest, and at its deep end lay an inert mass of gleaming white metal, partly covered by fallen branches. *Please don't let her be in there.*

Selius guided her skimmer cautiously, at minimum speed, down through the torn vegetation. She brought it to rest on a clear patch of ground some ten meters from the wreck. Skimmer One was still in one piece, but obviously beyond repair, bent into a U around the base of an immense tree it had partially uprooted. From this close Selius could still see no sign of fire. She also saw no sign of the skimmer's occupants, alive or dead.

Go look, Lanya. You can't wait forever, she chided herself. She removed her light-intensifying helmet and switched on her skimmer's floodlights. She always relied on her own natural senses when she could, rather than artificially enhanced ones. Under the present circumstances, she wanted to be sure no one would creep up on her from the shadowed undergrowth, and she was convinced that the night-sight helmet restricted her peripheral vision and her hearing.

She slipped out of the rear hatchway into an eerie scene. The forest was completely silent. All of the wildlife must have been frightened away by the crash, the second skimmer's arrival, and the bright lights. The lights bore down on the ruined skimmer and its immediate surroundings, casting intense shadows everywhere. No wind stirred the foliage. Nothing moved.

Selius edged around the outskirts of the lighted area, looking for evidence that anyone had left the deactivated skimmer, listening for sounds of any sort, but especially the kind that don't belong in a forest. Moving as quietly as she could, she made her way cautiously toward the wreck, her gun in her hand.

The going was difficult. Unlike most dense forests, this one had heavy undergrowth. The trees' lowest branches were several meters above head height, but a tangle of plantlike growth rose from the forest floor to a height of two meters and more. Bereft of sunlight, it was parasitic, drawing its sustenance out of the trunks of the large trees.

In the skimmer's harsh floodlights, the thick, twisted vines looked deep purple, and the knobby protuberances sticking out of them were a pale bluish gray. The plants were soft and slightly sticky. As careful as she was, Selius nevertheless snapped through several of the vines as she walked. Where they were broken, they leaked a sap that looked and smelled like red wine gone sour.

Selius made slow progress, but felt certain that nobody else was nearby, stalking her.

She had just reached the shadow cast by the nose of the stolen vehicle, where the large black "1" had been nearly obliterated by smashing against the trees in its descent, when she heard a sound coming from the open forward hatch. It was a low moan that faded away almost as soon as she noticed it. Selius waited, and it came again. The sound made her shiver. It was too familiar and too full of pain.

Staying in a crouch, Selius ran around to the lighted side of the skimmer and leaped through the hatchway. Inside, the skimmer was a shambles. The far wall bulged inward where it had slammed into the tree. Shattered equipment lay in a heap against the base of that wall. The rear storage lockers had exploded outward from the force of the impact. The four passengers' seats were twisted sideways and forward, though they had not come loose from the floor. The wide front window was shot through with cracks but remained intact. And in front of that window, in the pilot's chair, was the sole occupant of the skimmer.

Why is she here alone? How did the others get away? The suspicion that she had been hiding even from herself since she had discovered Alepha's absence suddenly came to the fore. There had been no others.

The Overseer rushed over to her young aide. The girl's safety straps had been half-torn by the crash, and three of the chair's six anchoring bolts had been snapped, but somehow Alepha was still alive. She was breathing in sharp, painful gasps and her face was a rigid mask of agony. Blood was soaking through her uniform in a line from her left shoulder to her right hip. A large stain was spreading across her abdomen, and twin patches of blood flowed down from each knee, where she'd jammed against the control panel. Alepha's skin was chalky white. Her forehead was one large bruise and her eyelids fluttered weakly, half-open.

Selius gave the girl a quick examination, touching her as lightly as she could, then fumbled frantically through the mess from the storage lockers until she found the emergency medkit, still intact. The only thing in it of any use was the airjector of anesthetic. Selius wasn't even sure that would help, but she knew nothing else would. Alepha was dying. A major rejuv center might be able to save her, but nothing on Bekh-Nar could.

She set the airjector for maximum dosage, pressed it

against Alepha's neck, and watched as the girl's face relaxed and her breathing eased. Then Selius pushed the pilot's chair back into the reclining position, using all her strength to force the balky mechanism, stripping its twisted gears when they resisted. With Alepha now lying back and in no danger of falling over, Selius unfastened the safety harness and knelt down beside her.

"Why, Alepha, why?" Selius whispered, her face next to her dying daughter's.

Alepha's eyes shifted slightly to focus directly on Selius. Her lips twitched as she struggled to get the words out. "I . . . I couldn't betray my people, Lanya. My planet."

The older woman's jaw clenched in anger, but she spoke softly. "They rejected you. You didn't owe them anything." *Least of all your life.* "You could have gone far in the Union."

"Not for me, Lanya." The girl paused for several shallow breaths. "Don't be angry. I love this place and the Union will destroy it." She swallowed hard and her whole body shook with the effort. Her eyes began to close.

"Oh, Alepha," Selius began, but could think of nothing more to say.

Alepha's eyes opened again and she looked intently at Selius. She could barely speak, but she strained to continue, each word taking a lifetime. "Just as I love you, Mother, and . . ." The words trailed away into silence. Her eyes stayed open, but the light faded and died.

Selius gently closed Alepha's eyes, but the expression on the girl's face was etched in her mind. It was an expression of love, and of sorrow. *For me, after I've killed you, Daughter?* She wanted to rage, to shout, to beat her fists on the metal floor, but she remained kneeling instead, cradling Alepha's head in her arms. She stared at the buckled wall of the skimmer. In its crumpled, shadowed landscape she saw a plucky pale-skinned girl, small for her age, standing up to bullies nearly twice her size. She saw Alepha laughing, crying, learning, arguing, and growing into a strong, proud young woman with a bigger heart than Selius had ever imagined. She saw the caring, independent, outstanding officer Alepha could have become, a woman whom Selius would have been proud to call "friend."

"No it won't, Alepha. Not your planet, not your people," she whispered, kneeling in the ruined skimmer in the midst of the silent green forest, "and not me."

By the time the sun came up, casting its rays through the shattered branches and splintered trunks, Overseer Selius had done what was necessary. Her fabrication was as thorough as she could make it in the time she'd had.

When one of the pursuit squads arrived shortly thereafter, it was clear to all what had happened, even without the Overseer's corroboration. The rebels had taken Lieutenant Conn-Lee hostage and fled. All but one had been dropped off along the way. That one had forced Conn-Lee to keep flying despite Selius's warnings. Perhaps he'd thought it was a bluff, or perhaps the transmissions hadn't been received.

When Skimmer One eventually crashed, Conn-Lee was fatally injured. The rebel suffered only minor injuries. He and Selius exchanged fire and she was severely wounded in the right leg. She must have passed out from shock and loss of blood, and when she came to, her wound had been treated and the rebel had fled. She didn't know how much of a head start he had, for she'd revived just before the pursuit squad had arrived.

There was a clear track for a short distance into the forest, but it quickly faded out. Everyone agreed it would be useless to try to pursue him, and that the Overseer had to be taken back to Tol-Nar for professional medical treatment. They hoped the leg could be saved.

Six months later, after the official reports had all been filed, the events surrounding the escape of the rebel Vieren Conn-Tir had still not been forgotten. The actual escapees were never recaptured, and some Union personnel were inclined to leave things that way, considering the humane gesture the last man had made in aiding Overseer Selius.

Rebel activity on Bekh-Nar remained significant, as did Union efforts to control the rebels. But the level of violence decreased noticeably, and more lines of communication opened up between the two sides.

The Overseer survived her ordeal, and the doctors didn't

have to remove her leg, although she did end up with a permanent limp.

Lieutenant Conn-Lee was posthumously awarded the Medal of Distinction, the second-highest honor granted Security personnel by the Union. Selius displayed the medal proudly on her office wall.

The Lieutenant did not, contrary to custom, receive a formal military burial. Some members of her clan petitioned the Overseer to allow a traditional, civilian burial for their blood sister, and the Overseer saw fit to grant their request.

The entire incident went unnoticed by the Central Council of the Interstellar Union, and even the Triune and Security Director of Sector Seven paid it little attention.

On another planet far beyond the Periphery, however, the events were noted with interest. An order went out to watch Overseer Selius more carefully, and to approach her with certain offers should the circumstances seem appropriate.

(New Standard Year 892—Wehring's Stopover)

INTERLUDE

"We're not going to get any further staying here, John."

"And where we've gotten so far is practically nowhere. Do you think we ought to recommend dropping the case?"

"And then what? We'd get stuck trying to deflate that incipient insurrection on Easystreet or chasing rumors about Reversionist conspiracies. This is far more interesting. Besides, there *is* something out here—there must be. Phantoms don't kill Special Operatives."

"I think you underestimate the Reversionist threat, Gen, but I see your point. We have a unique opportunity with this case. Still, where can we go with it now, and what excuse can we give for continuing the investigation?"

"Granted, the woman is out. No name, no identifying information of any kind, and she's disappeared without a trace. Phillips, of course, we can always locate and investigate, but if there were anything significant in his background, it would have been flagged years ago."

"That leaves Kirowa. He's disappeared too, but at least he had a name and a traceable background. Do we recommend backtracking on him—checking out his activities, his contacts?"

"That's what I'd favor, John. It keeps us on the case and lets us cover a lot of interesting territory. He stayed mostly on the Periphery, so if there is something Beyond, he'd be a logical contact."

"Let's do it, then. You send the message and I'll start packing our bags."

PART II

Thickening
Strands

(New Standard Years 890–907)

8. The Dream

Dead man's hands reaching for his throat.

Rizlov's laughter ringing in his ears.

"I didn't mean it!"

Phillips woke with a start. His heart was racing, panicked. *Calm down.* It was all right. He was in his own bed, safe, alone. *Quiet. Relax.* The shout that had awakened him had been his own, the dream the same one that had haunted his sleep off and on for the past ten years.

"It wasn't my fault," he muttered, staring toward the night-hidden ceiling. "I couldn't have known."

Then why the dream? Some part of him asked, taunting.

"I don't know. I don't know."

It came most often and most vividly during and immediately following his rejuvenation treatments. He hadn't told anybody, hadn't dared confide in the rejuv experts for fear of what they might conclude about his psychological state.

Phillips's eyes began to close, his breathing slowed.

"Not my fault," he mumbled into his pillow.

INTERLUDE

"You know, Gen, the only reason they haven't pulled us back in is because of our ancillary accomplishments."

"Ancillary nothing. They're our *only* accomplishments. A few smuggling rings broken up, some corrupt planetary administrators uncovered, an illegal settlements program disbanded. Hardly the stuff of legends, John. Still, there have been hints."

"Maybe that's what's bought us all this time. But we have to stop kidding ourselves. As questionable as Kirowa's activities and contacts were, and as tantalizing as his unexplained disappearances between stops are, we can't go anywhere with them. They just add up to a large question mark."

"So, do you want to drop it? We could always get our hands good and dirty on Easystreet or Gnilkpyk without even leaving the Sector. Sooner or later *somebody's* going to have to settle those places down. And, of course, there's still the black hole of Reversionist rumors to get sucked down into."

"Now be fair, Gen. I agreed with you on that years ago. And I'd rather leave Easystreet and Gnilkpyk for later, if you don't mind. We have one more thread to follow, and I think we should take it."

"Phillips? It's a thin thread, John."

"But our only one, and not so unlikely if you think about it. He had several contacts with Kirowa, and then there's his peculiar behavior during the Stellar Cellar incident—reporting the contact, then meeting with Kirowa and the woman anyway. Furthermore, he's said nothing about it since then. If those two had forced him, he would have talked to Security later."

"Conclusion: either he was duped or he became a willing accomplice?"

"Those are the two most reasonable options."

"So we do a background on Phillips?"

"A background, a foreground, a surveillance on him and on anyone who contacts him. Anything at all suspicious, we follow up on."

"Maybe they'll balk at giving the treatment to a Triune Adjudicator."

"You can be very persuasive when you want to be, Gen. I'm sure you'll come up with just the right way to phrase our recommendation."

"Thanks a lot, dear."

(New Standard Year 906—Bekh-Nar)

9. When Push . . .

"The situation is intolerable, Overseer!" Councilor Uhlat Breglum's round face was far from jolly, and the soft mass of his body fairly shook with indignation. Even seated in Selius's air-conditioned office, he was flushed and sweating. His garish black-and-gold striped suit was stained under the arms and around the collar.

Lanya Selius attempted to remain calm. It was late and she was tired, but she would gain nothing by antagonizing the pompous Sector Council member. "Sir, believe me, I understand your concern. But we've had general strikes before, and they always peter out in a few days. Too many of the Narians depend on our credits and our goods to sustain a strike for long."

"And in the meantime the mines stay shut down, while you and your troops just sit by and watch?" He seemed about ready to burst.

Selius looked sternly at the man overflowing the chair across the desk from her. "Councilor Breglum, we are here to maintain order and to further the influence of the Union. If we were to attempt to squelch every strike by force, we would soon have no order at all, and the Union would be universally despised by the Narians." *And if you and your assistants would keep your fat asses back on Drinan IV and out of my way, we'd all be a lot better off.*

The Overseer knew Breglum and his fellow Councilors weren't stupid. They were all just too impatient, too eager to trample the Narians into the ground. Negotiation and compromise seemed to be alien concepts to them. Selius forced herself to tune in to Breglum's continuing list of grievances.

". . . Longer than any planet on record. Some members of the Council wonder if you're really interested in bringing Bekh-Nar into the Union at all." He rested his pudgy hands on Selius's desk and leaned forward ever so slightly. "You would be well advised to take your official mission here more seriously." His fat-sunken eyes glinted at her like two malevolent black opals. "It would be unfortunate if the Council were to decide that your extended stay on this backward planet had caused your allegiances to become confused." He sank back into his chair, a slight smirk on his face.

"*My* allegiances?" Selius began, her muscles tensing, then chose a less confrontative tack. "It is my understanding that the Union's interests will be best served by a lasting assimilation of Bekh-Nar and guaranteed access to its natural resources. I could have brought the Narians under Union control by now if I had quadrupled my troop deployment and used battle skimmers and airdrops to sweep the forests and foothills. But that would have achieved only a sullen acquiescence, always threatening to break out again in armed rebellion. You need look no further than Gnilkpyk and

Easystreet in this sector for examples of quick victories gone sour."

She looked Breglum square in the eye and saw him wince. It was common knowledge that he owned, indirectly, a large portion of the mining interests on Easystreet. "They each have over twice as many troops as we do here, and yet the mines have become less productive over the past two years due to increasing rebel attacks and sabotage."

Breglum started to say something, but Selius continued, talking over his words. "I sympathize with the Council's desire for speedy assimilation of newly relocated planets. But the native populations have had centuries to develop their own cultures. They often see assimilation as a threat to their freedom and their identity. The use of military force only heightens such fears."

She lowered her voice and a distant look came over her face. "There is a way to guarantee pacification of a planet by force, but the cost is very high. Golconda is a prime example. Nearly sixty years later and still no one can live there or even begin to extract its mineral resources. Biological resources no longer exist."

Breglum cleared his throat noisily. "Harrumph! I'm familiar with Golconda. You know as well as I that that was a special case—a lost settlement that retained interstellar military capability. Their rebellion might have spread to other systems. The situation was unique."

Don't tell me—I was there, thought Selius. She smiled thinly at the rotund Councilor. "Every situation is unique, Councilor. But I have yet to see a planet brought satisfactorily into the Union when force was the principal method of dealing with the inhabitants."

"Oh?" Breglum raised his eyebrows in an exaggerated expression of surprise. "Then why is the military in charge of our assimilation efforts?"

The Overseer sat straighter, taller, barely containing her resentment at this soft, pale civilian who was telling her how to do her job.

"My approach may not be as quick as some people would like, Councilor Breglum, but the result will be a lasting friendly bond between the Union and the Narians. The bulk of the current generation will recognize that the tangible benefits of assimilation outweigh the costs, as they see them. The next generation will be full-fledged citizens of the Union, no different from you or me."

"Really, Overseer?" A predatory smile slowly appeared on Breglum's face. "And I suppose the current general strike is the Narians' way of expressing their loyalty to the Union?"

The smile vanished. "I am not a mental deficient, Selius. I can see what's going on and I don't like it. And I don't think the rest of the Council will like it either."

The man's genetically unreasonable! With his high-pitched, penetrating voice and his bright clothes, he reminded Selius of one of the large local insects that became quite vicious when its nest was disturbed.

"But Councilor Breglum, this is not typical of the Narians' attitude toward assimilation! If the truth were known," —and here she paused momentarily, recognizing the two-edged nature of her argument—"the current strike only began when word got out of your tour of inspection of Bekh-Nar. The Narians who have grievances saw it as a good opportunity to draw attention to their cause and to themselves. Only a small proportion of the strikers are actually instigating the protest. The rest are merely going along out of loyalty to their friends or to avoid being ostracized by their fellow workers. Perhaps a lower profile . . ."

The Councilor raised his bulky form as quickly as he could. "Now you're trying to blame *me* for the unrest!" He pointed a shaking finger at Selius. "Let me make this clear, Overseer. My investigation will continue as planned. You can believe that the Sector Council is going to receive a full report on the lack of progress here and on your peculiar attitude." With that, he turned and left the office, moving slowly and with all the stiff-backed dignity he could muster.

Selius watched him go, realizing the futility of further argument. After the door had slid shut behind him, she leaned back in her chair and sighed. Why did the officious fool have to come now, she wondered, with the sun at its peak and everyone sweltering? The city lay in a wide, humid, densely forested river valley not far south of the equator. In contrast with its idyllic winters, summers in Tol-Nar were always hard, physically and otherwise.

The valley was hot and sticky and uncomfortably still, so different from the wind-tossed grain fields surrounding Yurograd, the home town of her youth on Vashnoya. In her silent, empty office, she closed her eyes and drifted back to those yellow-brown fields under a sparkling blue sky. She saw a tall, rough-edged girl running through the head-high grain, dodging the harvesting machines and playing hide-and-seek with the other children. Until she grew older and was expected to "act like a lady." Be quiet. Be pretty. Stay home. Such subservience was foreign to her nature, so she did what she had to—she rebelled.

The Vashnoyans were a conservative people who valued their traditions. Going her own way against them was not easy. Her friends left her—she made them feel insecure; she didn't fit in. Her teachers admonished her—she challenged their assertions; she was too outspoken. Her parents worried, argued, and pleaded, but never understood. She wasn't one of them. So she walked through the fields by herself, communing with the wind as it blew through her long blond hair.

On her seventeenth birthday, she had found a way out, enlisting in Sector Security. It cost her her home, but gave her the opportunity to be herself.

It was, she reflected, the best decision she'd ever made. Still, there were times when she thought of those clean azure skies and longed to wander through the rolling fields in a cool breeze.

Times such as now, for instance.

Ever since she'd arrived on Bekh-Nar over twenty-three years ago as Planetary Overseer, she'd had trouble with summers. From the start, they had put her on edge, and they seemed to make even the Narians more restless, more irritable, less predictable. And then, in her eighth summer on the planet, came the escape of the five Narian rebels. The incident had culminated in the tragic death of her daughter/protégée Alepha Conn-Lee and her own nearly fatal leg wound.

Through her death, Alepha had taught Selius something of loyalty and of love. It had marked a turning point in Selius's relations with the Narians, from which she'd made gradual but steady progress toward assimilating the planet into the Interstellar Union. It had also left scars. Every summer her leg ached dully and constantly, even in her air-conditioned office. And every summer Alepha's Medal of Distinction, framed on Selius's office wall, was an especially painful reminder of what might have been, as well as an inspiration to continue on her chosen course.

The Overseer stood up, wincing as she put weight on her right leg. It had been a long day. The general strike was bad enough, but having to cope with Councilor Breglum's hostility, suspicions, and insinuations had nearly pushed her over the edge. Why couldn't the man just keep a low profile until the protest wore itself out? Summers did tend to raise the level of unrest among the Narians, especially in the city, with its concentration of Union facilities. But summer's heat also tended to sap the energy of the protesters, so their actions didn't last too long, and caused no real harm.

Oh, but Breglum knew better, having been on Bekh-Nar a whole two days! Selius would gladly have strangled the fat Councilor with her bare hands. She could have, too, despite being nearly eighty years old with a bad leg. But how would that have looked on her service record? It might even have cost her her retirement benefits.

"Almost worth it," she muttered as she turned out the lights in her office and locked the door. She limped over to the lift tube. Outwardly, she was a sturdy thirty-year-old woman with a game leg. Inside, she was feeling her full age. Selius knew she could bring Alepha's people into membership in the Union while still preserving much of their culture and protecting them from the worst exploitative tendencies of people like Breglum. All she needed was more time. She'd come far, but she wasn't there yet. The Narians weren't quite ready.

Selius took the lift tube down to the first floor of the Tower of Laws. The lobby was empty except for the lone night guard. Despite the general strike and Breglum's visit, she'd kept to the normal duty roster, which meant a skeleton crew at night. She acknowledged the guard's salute at the front entrance and stepped out into the heavy summer night. It was silent except for the muted hum of the Compound's condensers and the furtive scritchings of small nocturnal creatures. The Narian protesters outside the main gate had long since gone home for the day.

She walked across the Compound to her quarters, savoring the quiet. *A few more years is all I need*, she thought hopefully. *Just a few more years*.

10. ... Comes to Shove

Dawn in Tol-Nar in the summer was a misty affair. The nighttime fog lay heavy and gray in the streets and forest, often deep enough to cover the Tower of Laws and even the tallest trees. The coming of a new day was presaged by a gradual brightening from the east, turning the dark mists by imperceptible steps into a glowing white. It was a magical moment for Selius, no matter how many times she saw the transformation.

All too soon the sun rose above the treetops and burned away the translucent vapors, ushering in another stifling day. But in those few minutes between night and day, Selius felt as if she stood in the midst of an unformed universe, alive with an infinitude of possibilities. It waited to reveal its latest self to her or to be shaped by her desires—she was never quite sure which. Then the sun came up, destroying the illusion.

Still, illusion or not, Selius kept rising early and wandering through the Union Compound or the nearby city streets in the morning mists. For one thing, she believed in leadership by example, and getting a quick start on the day's work was something she wanted to impress on those under her command. For another, it was the coolest, most comfortable time of day to be outside in the summer. Finally, there was a small part of her that actually believed her fantasy, or at least pretended to, and didn't want to miss out if something really interesting were created or revealed by the melting fog.

On the day after her confrontation with Councilor Breglum, Selius rose as usual, showered, and dressed, then stepped out into the cool grayness. The mists had not yet begun to lighten. Favoring her right leg, she walked slowly, carefully, toward the Compound's main gate, to have a word with the guards there before the Narian protesters arrived. She wanted to be sure her people did nothing to provoke the Narians and did not overreact to whatever provocation might be offered them. Her boots clicked on the smooth stone, a measured muffled tapping.

The fog was unusually thick this morning, and Selius navigated by intuition and memory more than by sight. She was about twenty meters from the main gate before she saw the floodlights atop it, reduced to a pair of dim yellow blobs even at such a short distance. As she came closer, she could hear voices which resolved into those of the two guards and Councilor Breglum. Selius had practically bumped into the three before their words were decipherable.

". . . Are our orders, sir. I'm sorry, but for their own safety, we can allow no one to leave without the Overseer's permission." It was Sergeant Mwambe, senior of the two guards this morning. The Sergeant was doing an admirable job of restraining herself. Her fellow guard, Corporal Elten, looked as though he wanted to burn Breglum on the spot.

"My own safety!" Breglum snorted derisively. "Listen, girl, I've gotten out of tighter scrapes than you'll ever see. You can't confine me here. As Sector Councilor, I demand . . ."

Selius stepped in at that moment. "That will be all, Sergeant, Corporal. Return to your posts. I'll deal with this."

"Yes, ma'am," the guards replied in unison, looking relieved as they saluted and turned away. A few steps and they had blended into the fog.

"Now then, Councilor, what can I do for you?"

"What can you do for me?" Breglum rounded immediately on this new opponent. "I'll tell you what you can do for me," he said in a quiet, oily voice. "You can stop getting in my way. You can let me do the job I came here to do."

His voice was rising quickly in volume and pitch. "You can open those gates immediately or explain to the Sector Council, and maybe the Triune, too, why you feel it necessary to interfere with an official Council investigation of conditions here on Bekh-Nar!" he concluded in a near-screech.

Selius noticed that the fog was beginning to brighten, but the moment was ruined by the human toad posturing in front of her. "Please, Councilor, there's no need to shout. There's also no point in going out until the fog has dissipated. It's hard to investigate what you can't see, but all too easy to crash into it. My responsibility is not only to cooperate with your investigation. It is also to ensure your safety to the best of my abilities."

The mists had started to thin out by now, and Selius could make out the vague bulk of Breglum's floater some distance away. "In another half hour, the visibility will be good enough. I will order the *back* gates opened then."

"Overseer Selius, I will not be . . ."

"You will be free to travel anywhere you wish, although I advise some discretion, considering yesterday's incident." Breglum had attempted to drive directly through a street rally instead of going around it. A lot of shouting and pushing and some stone-throwing had resulted from a previously low-keyed demonstration.

Breglum puffed himself up for another sally. "Again you blame me for the illegal violence of these Narians?"

"No, Councilor, I'm merely advising caution." *I'd like to advise you to take a hyperjump without a ship.* "And I will be assigning a guard to ride with your party today, for your own protection. And before you object," she continued quickly, "I will order him, in your presence, not to interfere with your investigation. He will be there to provide any information you may need and to act only if there is clear and imminent danger to yourself."

The Councilor considered this for a moment, then reluctantly agreed.

Selius still didn't trust the man to behave reasonably, but she'd done the best she could. "I'm going to have a maintenance tech give your vehicle a quick once-over, to make sure all the systems are functioning." *Especially the locator unit.*

"I'll meet you at the back gate in twenty-seven minutes and you can be on your way." She turned and headed toward the dining commons, where the off-duty personnel would be in the midst of breakfast by now. She'd check the roster to see who was available. Whoever she chose was going to be in for a long day, she suspected.

The fog cleared, and Breglum's small party left without further incident. A few of the Narian protesters had arrived at the Compound's front gate, but the back entrance was deserted when the four-person floater left. One of Breglum's aides was driving, with Breglum next to him in front, and in the rear seats were the Councilor's secretary/recorder and Sergeant Churg. The Sergeant was a large, dark-skinned, gregarious fellow who seemed to have a good rapport with the Narians. Unlike most of the personnel under Selius's command, he had established several social connections amongst the natives. If anybody would know where Breglum should and should not go, it would be he.

Selius watched the group speed directly away from the Compound for several blocks, until they turned a corner and disappeared. Breglum had the floater's bubble fully retracted, against Selius's advice, so he could "get closer to the situation."

The Overseer shrugged and turned away, ordering the gates closed. The floater was fully stocked with food and water and emergency supplies, and Breglum had expressed his intention to be gone most of the day. *Just as well,* Selius thought, *as long as Churg can keep him out of trouble.* She had enough to do without having to placate the bombastic Councilor every five minutes. Mentally reviewing her morning schedule, she decided she just had time to drop in to the cafeteria for a delayed breakfast.

Despite its unpleasant beginning, the rest of the day went as Selius had planned. Better, without Breglum grumbling around. She did check in occasionally with the communication and surveillance unit to see where Breglum was doing his "investigating." As she'd expected, he seemed to be spending his time near various hot spots of protest activity, no doubt confirming for himself how far out of control the situation was. Clearly, the man's report to the full Sector

Council was going to be anything but favorable. Selius wondered how the rest of the Councilors would interpret Breglum's findings.

She could understand why Breglum reacted as he did to her policy on Bekh-Nar. For one thing, he had a very personal financial interest in a quick and complete pacification of the populace. A large portion of the mining interests on the planet belonged to him and other members of his family. At a more basic level, though, his entire life must have pushed him toward the position he was now taking. Eldest child of a wealthy, powerful family, he had surely been raised to believe in the Union as a necessary social, economic, and governmental entity.

Breglum's own experience would only have confirmed such teachings—without the Union, who would have protected his family's status, and how would he have been able to rise to a position of such power and prestige? He'd never experienced the downside, never known what it was like to be an outsider, someone who doesn't fit in. The Narians' reluctance to submerge themselves in the Union's system was something he would probably never understand.

So the man had his reasons, but Selius didn't agree with any of them. Still, she would have to make the best of his presence here and hope she could blunt the effects of his inevitable official condemnation of her program of gradual, peaceful, negotiated assimilation.

A buzz from her intercom interrupted Selius's musings.

"Yes?"

"Overseer, Major Urtloew here. Sergeant Churg has just reported in. It seems that they ran into some trouble at Mine Number Three." The Major's voice was steady, calm. Despite working with the man for over twenty years, Selius still could not read him. Beneath his professional exterior might be anything. She was thankful that he'd turned down promotions and opportunities for assignments to much more attractive commands, but she couldn't figure out why he stayed. Did he like Bekh-Nar that much? Did he feel some extravagant unexpressed loyalty to herself? Was he hiding from something? Selius had no idea.

Her curiosity did not keep her from following the rest of

Urtloew's message. "Churg requested that the back gates be cleared and open and that the medical team be ready. Then he signed off."

Medical team? What in the name of the Void had happened out there? Selius wondered. Whatever it was, she was willing to bet her commission that that fool Breglum had been responsible.

Mine Number Three was over fifty kilometers north of Tol-Nar and a few kilometers east of the river. Churg made it back in record time. A squad had barely managed to move the protesters away from the Compound's back gate before the Sergeant arrived with the Councilor's party. The floater's bubble was closed, its warning siren was on, and it hardly slowed down as it went through the gate. It came to a sliding stop two-thirds of the way across the compound, trailing clouds of dust behind it. By the time its bubble slid open, the medical team had surrounded it with four portaunits.

All four of the floater's occupants looked as though they could use life-support units. Sergeant Churg was able to climb out by himself, though his left arm hung limp at his side and his forehead was gashed. The Councilor's secretary/recorder was conscious but moaning in pain. She had numerous cuts and bruises on her face and her jaw appeared to be broken. Breglum's driver had a huge bruise on his right temple. He was slumped in the front passenger's seat, silent and motionless. Breglum himself was in the back, next to his secretary. His right eye was swollen shut, there was a trickle of blood coming from the corner of his mouth, and his left ear was partially torn. He was breathing in quick, shallow gasps.

Selius reached the floater just as the medics began lifting the Councilor and his people out and onto the portaunits. Churg was forcefully resisting the efforts of two medics to make him lie down.

"Sergeant!" He looked up at the sound of her voice. "Will you let these people do their job!"

"Your pardon, Overseer, but I'm not that badly hurt, and my report can't wait." His taut features belied his self-diagnosis, which made Selius believe the rest of his statement all the more.

"Very well, Sergeant. But make it fast, then you go to the infirmary." She motioned for him to follow as she walked a short distance away from the others. "Now then, what happened?"

Churg stood stiffly at attention, wincing slightly. He began his report. "Well, ma'am, the morning was uneventful. We left here and made stops at several Union installations where protests were going on. The Councilor seemed interested initially in simply recording the time, location and size of the protests, but as we proceeded, he became increasingly upset. He began making disparaging remarks about the Narians and . . ." The Sergeant paused, looking uncomfortable.

"And about my handling of the situation?" Selius filled in with a thin smile.

"Your pardon, yes, ma'am. Then he began asking me questions about how often these strikes occur, how long they last, how extensive they are, who the leaders are. I told him what I know to be the case, but that didn't seem to satisfy him. I think he wanted me to express some opinions on the subject." Selius could practically feel the distaste Churg put into that last sentence.

"And then what, Sergeant? That hardly explains your injuries and hasty return."

Churg took a deep breath and continued. "No, ma'am. I think the trouble began when we stopped for lunch early in the afternoon. It was in a clearing just off the main road heading north out of the city. The Councilor took his aide aside for a private discussion which became quite animated. They came back to the floater, the Councilor declaring that we would go visit *his* mine, by which he meant Mine Number Three."

Churg looked pleadingly at Selius. "I warned him, ma'am. That's a particularly sensitive place where a lot of Narians have lost their land and others are strongly opposed to the destruction of the forest. Even those who work there and accept the mine are constantly speaking out against the working conditions. I tried to explain, but he wouldn't listen."

"That's all you could do, Sergeant," Selius reassured. "So he ignored your advice and went there anyway?"

"Yes, ma'am. When we arrived, we found a group of protesters blocking the entrance. A few of the mine's local guards were on duty, but the strikers were not attempting to enter the facility and did not seem disposed to violence. Everything was peaceful and well controlled."

The Sergeant's voice became grimmer as he continued. "The Councilor had his aide drive right up to the line of protesters. We'd been driving all day with the bubble down, so the Councilor stood up and ordered the crowd to let us pass. When they refused, he identified himself and again ordered them to part. That drew some derisive shouts from the strikers. The Councilor became irate and started yelling at the strikers, which led to an escalation of abuse and profanity on both sides.

"One of the local guards approached us and requested that the Councilor return at a more propitious time. The Councilor accused him of being a 'Narian rebel' and pushed the man away. At that point someone in the crowd threw a rock that struck the Councilor's secretary on the jaw. The Councilor turned to me and demanded that I fire on 'those murderous thugs.' I refused, making it clear that the appropriate course under your orders would be for us to leave the area at once. Another rock was thrown, bouncing off the side of our floater. The Councilor then ordered his aide to drive forward toward the gate, which the man promptly did."

Churg paused again in his report. He swallowed, then continued. "I couldn't stop him. It happened too fast. He ran right over the protesters and rammed the gate, which buckled but didn't break. Then they were all over us, swinging sticks, throwing rocks. The guards couldn't stop them. I managed to shove the driver aside and get at the controls to lower the floater's bubble, but not before the Councilor and his aides were all badly hurt. I'm afraid that several of the Narians were seriously injured. Some may have been killed."

It was evident to Selius that Churg's pain was much more than physical.

"Overseer, I could have done nothing to help them. They

would have murdered the Councilor's party if we'd left the floater. I did request that Major Urtloew dispatch the local Narian emergency squads. It seemed like a situation they would have a better chance of handling."

Sergeant Churg looked as if he was about to collapse. Selius put her hand on his shoulder and walked him back to the waiting medics. "You did all you could, Sergeant. Now let the medics do their job. When you've had a chance to rest there will be time enough to get a formal recorded statement."

As the medics helped Churg onto the portaunit, Selius ordered them firmly, "Don't release him until he's fully recuperated. No matter how much he argues." This last with a stern glance at the Sergeant.

The sun was low in the sky by the time the medical team wheeled Sergeant Churg away. Selius walked slowly around the now abandoned floater. Inside, there were several large rocks, some broken sticks, and a few bloodstains. Outside it was dusty and marked by dozens of small nicks. On the front was a larger dent, presumably where it had rammed the gate. Also on the front were two large, dust-covered stains, a deep rust-red in color. She stood for long minutes, staring at those stains, her shadow mingled with that of the floater.

You bastard, she thought, feeling her rage grow. *You pompous, narrow-minded, self-serving* . . . Selius turned away and limped back toward her office, her body rigid with anger. She was already phrasing her formal protest to the Sector Council.

Having just gone off duty, Major Urtloew was lounging in a shadowed doorway, watching the Overseer's inspection. His usually bland youthful features were marked by a thoughtful, somewhat worried expression. He knew his superior officer quite well, and was certain that she would not let this matter rest. From his brief encounters with Councilor Breglum, he also had some idea of that worthy's likely course of action. They would both undoubtedly be sending high-level communiqués in the next day or two. How the Sector's top authorities would respond was less predictable. To be on the safe side, Urtloew decided he would have to confide in Selius soon.

A Security squad had come out to the Councilor's floater

as soon as Selius left and was now busily taking holopics from all angles and gathering every conceivable type of physical evidence. They worked under a ring of bright lights, the sun having set behind the Grayling Mountains by this time. Like Selius bfore them, they too were oblivious to the slight, black-haired Major in his gray uniform. He was a shade of the twilight, observing them but himself unseen. Had they been able to read minds, however, his tumultuous thoughts would have been impossible to ignore.

Urtloew's stomach rumbled a reminder of how long ago he had eaten lunch. He stepped out of the doorway and began walking toward the cafeteria. When he'd volunteered for this assignment over twenty-three years ago, it had been highly speculative. Now, it seemed a much better bet. He was not pleased with the tragic events that had pushed Selius toward him. If he could have done anything to prevent the death of Alepha Conn-Lee years ago and this incident with Breglum today, he would have. But he would be letting his own people down not to take advantage of the situation. Unless he was drastically misreading her, Overseer Selius would be quite willing to side with them against the Union. And she might be able to use some help herself, depending on how much influence Breglum had on the Sector Council and the Triune.

The next afternoon, Selius paid a visit to the Councilor the moment the doctors gave the go-ahead. It would be unpleasant, she knew, but it was her duty. Besides, a part of her was eager to confront Breglum, to tell him just what she thought of him. She found him propped up in bed, bandages covering one ear and his right eye still closed. He looked awful, which suited her perfectly.

"Councilor, the doctors tell me that you'll suffer no permanent injury." Her tone was reserved.

He glared at her with his left eye. "Indeed. And what is that to my aide who was murdered? And the agony and inconvenience my secretary and myself are suffering?"

Selius was mildly surprised that the man could take the offensive so fast and so intensely, given his weakened condition. However, she was not going to be bullied.

"I sincerely regret the human tragedy that occurred yesterday, including the three Narians killed and five injured when you ran over them. And I intend to express my opinion in the strongest possible terms to the Sector Council. Do not misunderstand me, Councilor. I have already spoken with your secretary, and she has my deepest sympathy. I am going to send a message of condolence to the family of your aide, and try to see that they receive special compensation for his death."

She leaned over the bed, staring down at the Councilor with repugnance. "But as for you, I'm going to ask for your removal from office. I would expect more responsible behavior than yours from even the rawest Security enlistee. You're a disgrace to yourself. You're a disgrace to the Council. You're a disgrace to the Union."

Breglum spluttered, "You overstep yourself! Remember who I am! I will not be talked to like this!"

"You are *being* talked to like this. Your thickheadedness has gotten four people killed and eight more injured, including one of my best men." She straightened up and assumed a more businesslike tone. "You will be leaving Bekh-Nar in three days, when the latest supply transport departs. Until that time, you will remain inside this compound. Any attempt to leave will result in confinement to your room until the ship's departure."

The Councilor started to reply, then caught himself. After staring at Selius coldly for a moment, he said quietly, "Very well, Overseer. Here I must follow your orders. But you have made a serious mistake in siding with the Narian rebels against me."

She shook her head. "I haven't sided with rebels. I've sided with sanity." With that, she turned and left the room.

We'll see, he thought in the now silent room. *Fantel and Olias on the Council will side with me, and Rizlov on the Triune. Let's see how haughty you are when you're facing a court-martial on Drinan IV.* Muttering imprecations against the military and radicals alike, he fell back into an uneasy sleep.

That evening, Councilor Breglum sent messages to Councilors Fantel and Olias, and Adjudicator Rizlov. The mes-

sages were designated Private-Privileged, so all Major Urtloew knew for sure about them was when they were sent,
and to whom. Their general substance he could guess.

It wasn't until two days after the incident at the mine that
Selius transmitted her preliminary report to SecFor Headquarters on Drinan IV. She also sent a personal message to
SecFor Director Malvasian, advising him of her intention to
protest formally to the Sector Council regarding Breglum's
actions. Her protest to the Council went out the moment
Breglum boarded the outbound transport, four days after the
incident. By then, she felt she had as much corroboration for
her charges as she was likely to get or to need. Her only
regret was that his position made Breglum immune to direct
punishment on Bekh-Nar itself. Had he been a Security officer under her command, he would have been a good candi-
date for court-martial and a long term of corrective
incarceration.

Major Urtloew watched the messages flowing from Bekh-
Nar to Drinan IV. Given the personalities and positions involved, he knew that matters would come to a head quickly.
The day following Breglum's departure, Urtloew managed
to be passing the Tower of Laws as Selius was leaving to go
to lunch.

"Good day, Overseer." His manner was at once casual and
respectful. "I was wondering if I might have a word with
you."

"Of course, Major." Selius was glad of anything to take
her mind off her conflict with Breglum. "Join me for lunch
and tell me what I can do for you."

"If you don't mind, ma'am, I'd prefer somewhere more
private," he replied diffidently. "This is a very sensitive subject, and it concerns what I may be able to do for you."

Selius was puzzled. For all their long years of association,
she and Major Urtloew had never actually confided in each
other. At times she had even suspected that he had some
highly classified position outside normal SecFor channels.
No ordinary Major would have refused promotions for over
twenty years, as Urtloew had. No ordinary Major qualified
for rejuvenation status, but Urtloew had not aged noticeably
during his years on Bekh-Nar. And finally, no ordinary

Major could seriously offer her assistance under the current circumstances, but Urtloew had just done that. Maybe now she would find out who he really was.

"Very well, Major," she said with only the slightest hesitation. "Meet me at Vehicles in thirty minutes. With things beginning to calm down around here, I'd like to inspect some of our outlying facilities. You can be my driver and technical adviser."

"Thank you, ma'am." It was perfect. Their conversation would be eavesdrop-proof and yet their being together would have a simple explanation and not call attention to itself.

Exactly thirty minutes later, Urtloew and Selius left the Compound's rear gate in a floater with its bubble closed. They were headed for an automated communications relay station nearly eighty kilometers to the east. They drove in silence for a few minutes.

"So, Major. What can you do for me?" Selius tried to keep her tone light but not mocking. She was genuinely curious, but the burden was on Urtloew to produce.

"May I ask you one question first, Overseer?"

She nodded. "No harm in asking."

Let's hope not, he thought. Aloud, he said, "Thank you, ma'am. I've been with you on Bekh-Nar from the beginning, and it seems to me that you've taken great risks with your policies here. You've done a lot to accommodate the Narians and to slow the imposition of full Union rule." He swallowed and continued, "My question is, if you were reassigned as Overseer to another planet and had to leave Bekh-Nar, would you follow similar policies on that planet?"

Selius frowned. "An odd question, Major."

"Yes, ma'am. But I assure you it is quite sincere." He thought he knew already what her answer would be, but he had to hear it from her.

"You want to know whether my policy here reflects some affection for the Narians in particular, or is based on a more general disaffection with the Union's process of assimilation." She smiled conspiratorially. "I'll bet Breglum would love to know the answer to that one. Do I have Reversionist sympathies or have I been unduly influenced by this specific backward culture?"

"Overseer Selius, I did not wish to offend you."

"You haven't." If he were really working for the Sector Council or the Triune, he would have been much more subtle in his approach. "I've asked myself the same question for some years now. Ever since..." She hesitated. "Well, for quite a long time. And I've decided that I'm just doing on Bekh-Nar what I think ought to be done in every case. There is value in the Interstellar Union, but its authority has long since exceeded that value. Does that answer your question?"

"Indeed it does," Urtloew said with relief, "and it frees me to confide in you in return. You might think it presumptuous for a mere Major specializing in communications to offer assistance to a Planetary Overseer, especially when her opponents may be members of the Sector Council and Triune."

Might I? Selius thought. "Shouldn't I?"

"You certainly should, if that's all that I were. But there are a few inaccuracies in my personnel file, such as name, age, parents and planet of origin." He looked at Selius appraisingly. "You don't seem surprised. Well, I knew the ruse would only work so long before you developed suspicions of some sort or other. I won't bore you with all the details, especially since this inspection trip we're on can't last all day. The essential fact you need to know is that I'm from a planet called Seelzar that is as yet undiscovered by the Interstellar Union, and whose inhabitants would like to avoid the fates of Golconda, Easystreet, or even Bekh-Nar. Moreover, although we aren't nearly as powerful as the Union, we do have our resources."

The floater slowed to a stop as it reached Comm Relay Station Four. Urtloew shut down the power plant and turned toward Selius. "I believe you will be sympathetic with our cause once you learn more about it, and that you may be able to help us. I know we can offer you some valuable assistance should Councilor Breglum convince his colleagues to take action against you. Interested?"

Selius tried to see behind Urtloew's eyes, but was as unsuccessful as ever. "An interesting story, so far. How can I know it's true?"

Urtloew smiled. "You can't. Oh, I can give you some physical corroboration, but you could explain away my proofs if you wanted to. I propose to tell you as much about our situation as I can, and to give you the name of a person on Drinan IV to contact should the Council bring charges against you. You'll have little to lose if I'm lying and much to gain if I'm not."

The Major preempted Selius's next question. "And why should I trust you? Primarily because I trust myself in such matters, and secondarily because you have to take some risks if you expect any gains. Also," he added matter-of-factly, "given your current relations with the Sector Council, we could destroy your credibility rather easily if you were to attempt to denounce us."

Selius had to admit the Major's answers made sense. Especially, she noted wryly, his third point. "So, Major Urtloew or whoever you are, let's get out and inspect this relay station, and you can tell me your story while we're at it. No promises, understand, but I'm willing to listen."

The Major retracted the floater's bubble and stepped out. "I'm not asking for any promises, just an open mind."

By the time Urtloew and Selius returned to the Compound, the Overseer knew the basics about Seelzar and its intentions regarding the Union. She also had the name of a Seelzaran on Drinan IV, whom she was seriously considering contacting should the need arise.

He's right, she thought as they parted company after dropping off the floater. *What do I have to lose?*

Two days later, an official message arrived from Drinan IV, co-signed by Chairman Olias of the Sector Council and Senior Adjudicator Rizlov of the Sector Triune. Selius was surprised only by the number and variety of charges it contained. She hadn't thought Breglum's influence was so strong. She had one week to appoint a temporary Overseer and to report to the Hall of Justice in Drinan City to answer charges of insubordination, incompetence and treason, to name just a few.

Five days after receiving the summons from the Council

and the Triune, Lanya Selius was at the outer portal of a ship bound for Drinan IV, leaving Acting Overseer Urtloew in charge on Bekh-Nar. She carried in her mind the name and address of Urtloew's alleged compatriot. In her travel case she carried her daughter's Medal of Distinction.

Let Urtloew or my successor find their own memories, she thought, standing on the boarding ramp of her ship and looking back on Tol-Nar and the forest and the Grayling Mountains, perhaps for the last time.

During the trip back to Drinan IV, she spent most of her time reviewing the facts of the case, planning her defense and constructing countercharges against Breglum. If her judges would only listen to the facts, she knew that she would be exonerated. She also knew how large an "if" that could be.

(New Standard Year 907—Rejuvenation Center Seven)

11. All the King's Men

Kirowa was standing there, a charred hole in the middle of his blue-uniformed chest. "I trusted you," he said hollowly, then began to reach across the table.

Phillips cringed back from those grasping hands, those accusing eyes. "It was a mistake! I didn't mean to!"

The Pilot's hands closed on his throat and he began to lose consciousness. Dimly, he thought he heard Rizlov's sardonic laughter ringing in his ears.

And then Kirowa and the nightclub vanished, and Phillips was lying in absolute darkness with a soft *pinging* in his ears. He slowed his breathing, his heart gradually stopped pounding, and he remembered where he was. Rejuvenation Center Seven, final stage diagnostics cocoon.

Even as he became fully awake, the dream clung to him, as it always did. So much of it had actually happened—the nightclub, the Pilot, the conversation. Only the ending was imaginary, a product of his fears at the time and his guilt later.

Seelzar. Beyond the Periphery. An entirely unknown world, among probably many more, out of the reach of the Interplanetary Union. If only he had trusted Kirowa, instead of suspecting a plot by Rizlov. He might have visited there, and the Pilot might still be alive.

The cocoon's upper half shifted gradually from opaque to translucent, allowing his eyes to adjust to the dim light of the recovery room beyond. Finally the top half hinged open and Phillips began tensing and relaxing one muscle at a time in his own methodical revival ritual.

Sometimes he wondered if there really was a Seelzar. Kirowa's mother had said he would be contacted again when the time was right, but it had been twenty years without a word. Had Niala not trusted him after all? Despite her words of forgiveness, did she in fact blame him for her son's death?

The room's dim ceiling and walls gradually brightened to reach normal levels by the time Phillips was ready to rise. He sat up, carefully swung his legs over the side of the cocoon, then stood. A wave of dizziness staggered him momentarily, but passed quickly.

He swallowed; his throat felt raw. He tried to wet his lips but his mouth and tongue were too dry. Even his skin felt strangely dry and tight. He had a sudden fear that the treatment had not taken at all this time. *Easy,* he thought. *Calm down. Relax.* He knew that hysteria was an occasional side effect.

He walked across the soft warm floor to the omnimirror and studied his images. They reassured him. Front, back, right and left, he saw a slightly muscular thirty-year-old man a bit over 180 centimeters tall, with dark brown shoulder-length hair and bluish gray eyes. He looked fit and healthy, his posture erect, his skin smooth and glowing with youth. Everything seemed to be fine. Everything except . . .

Except the eyes. Phillips examined his eyes closely. Yes, the dullness, the weariness, the age still lurked there. Three weeks of treatment had erased it only superficially. Deep down, in his marrow and his sheathed nerves, the weight of a lifetime lay heavy on his soul. He sighed and turned to get dressed.

Inside the small closet, as he had known it would be, was his black-and-silver uniform.

The small, thin Director of Rejuvenation Center Seven rose from behind her desk. "Please be seated, Adjudicator Phillips."

"Thank you." Phillips looked around the office. It had changed little in the three years since he'd last been there. Three walls were bare white, the fourth covered with view-screens showing critical sections of the Center. The small desk had a built-in data terminal with screen and printer, and an intercom. A single beige folder lay on its shiny black surface. There were two utilitarian though comfortable chairs, one behind the desk, one in front.

"I trust you are feeling well?" The Director's voice sounded flat in the sound-dampened office. She had not changed much either. She still seemed the embodiment of cool detachment. Her light brown hair was even pulled back from her face in the same severe style Phillips remembered from three years ago.

"No worse than I expected," he replied. "Did your staff discover anything this time?"

A look of professional sympathy appeared on her ageless face. It did not include her pale brown eyes. "I'm afraid not, Adjudicator. Our tests have found nothing that could explain your post-treatment regression rate." She handed him the folder. "Here are our results. All of your measurable parameters are well within the normal range."

"Measurable?" Phillips asked, pondering the word's implications. His throat felt suddenly dry again.

"Of course," the Director replied, "there may be toxin accumulations too minuscule to detect but sufficient to accelerate your aging. I do think that possibility is unlikely. Perhaps an interaction among several individually insignificant factors." She shrugged. "We've had the computers working on it, but so far they've come up with nothing."

Phillips breathed easier, thankful that psychological explanations were still out of favor with the rejuvenation specialists, as they had been for some time. "Not measurable" meant "too small" or "too few" rather than "emotional" or "attitudinal."

"So you have no recommendations for me?" Phillips asked, masking his relief.

"Not officially," Albing said, then paused to pat a stray strand of hair back into place. She pursed her thin lips and seemed reluctant to continue. "Adjudicator Phillips, I hope you will not take offense, but . . ." She glanced down at her blank desk top.

"Yes?" he prompted, afraid of what she might say but needing to know.

"Please understand. This is not even a conjecture, merely a suggestion, another avenue to explore." Albing looked directly at him, her pale eyes unreadable. "Have you thought about consulting the psychtechs?"

Phillips blinked. "Psychtechs?" The word hung ominously in the air.

The Director essayed a small smile. "Just as a precaution, Adjudicator. Nothing more. But given your accelerating response trend,"—she spread her hands, palms up, and the smile disappeared—"we felt it would be wise not to ignore any of the possibilities, however remote."

"Indeed." Phillips nodded. He felt cold inside.

"Forgive me, sir," Albing added quickly. "I'm sure they would find nothing. We will continue to study your case and inform you if we determine the cause of your deterioration rate."

"Thank you, Director Albing." Phillips rose. "I appreciate your time. And your honesty." The door membrane attenuated to let him pass into the corridor, then thickened behind him.

Gloom followed Phillips out of the Director's office. If his problems really were psychological rather than physical, his career might be over. And Albing had seemed to have no other answer, no more appealing, simpler diagnosis.

Lost in thought, Phillips wandered toward the bank of lift tubes on the Center's Administration level. He met no one in the gleaming corridors, and the only sound he heard was the faint hum of machinery circulating aseptic air at constant temperature throughout Center Seven.

The Center was just like the other seven throughout the Union, Phillips knew. It was a spherical station a few hundred meters in diameter, circling a relatively minor planet near the center of Sector Seven. It was equipped with the most advanced life-extension technology, efficiently managed, expertly staffed, and extremely exclusive. Not many people ever saw a rejuvenation center in person, and of the countless billions living in each sector, fewer than a thousand qualified for rejuvenation.

As Phillips rode a magnetic disc down four levels from Administration to Transportation and Storage, he'd have sworn that the Center was deserted, but he knew that on levels three and four there were probably between six and ten people in various stages of rejuvenation, and perhaps three times as many staff members working in shifts to monitor their progress.

Rejuvenation, he reflected, was a mixed blessing, and some people even declined the honor of receiving the treatments. For three weeks every eight to twelve years, depending on individual physiological factors, each rejuvenant was analyzed intensely and treated as necessary. Defective or deteriorating organs and tissues were replaced or repaired, and the toxins of age were flushed from the body's systems. The treatments did not grant immortality, but they could give the average rejuvenant a healthy, youthful body for well over 150 standard years.

The price was sterility. For everyone, males and females, without exception. Despite intensive study, the experts had yet to find a way around that particular consequence of the treatments. There were other prices, not physical, most rejuvenants found after their second or third treatment. Some became increasingly lonely, some became increasingly jaded. A few didn't change at all.

The lift tube's disc reached the Transportation level, and Phillips stepped off. Most people, himself included, were willing to pay the price for rejuvenation. After all, it was a simple, regular, guaranteed way to extend one's physical youth well beyond the normal life expectancy.

But no longer for me, Phillips thought, walking slowly along the corridor. *Not anymore.* Ever since his last trip to the Periphery, twenty years ago, the interval between treatments had been shrinking. Initially it had been nine years; now it was down to three. Moreover, the treatments no longer revitalized him as they should—he was left with a residue of fatigue that would not dissipate.

Why this deterioration? Phillips asked himself as he approached his assigned docking port. *The cause,* he thought wryly, *is not "measurable."* He fingered the smooth rich fabric of his uniform and nodded at Captain Inyuko, the Pilot assigned him by Sector Security.

The Captain saluted crisply, a smile on his face. "Good to see you again, sir." The smile wavered as the Captain noticed Phillips's expression. "Anything wrong, sir?"

"What? Oh, no. Just thinking." Over the three years that Inyuko had been his Pilot, the two had developed a relationship bordering on friendship. They were generally quite open and honest with each other, but Phillips didn't feel he could talk about his current problem with the Captain. It was too personal, too serious.

"Very well, sir." Inyuko slid open the security gate and followed Phillips to the ship.

They walked through the ship's airlock to the central lift tube, Inyuko sealing the ship's outer and inner hatches behind them.

"You're looking well, sir," the Captain said in a half-comforting, half-inquiring tone.

Phillips turned toward him. "Thank you, Captain. I . . ." He paused, then decided against sharing his burden. "Thank you."

They rode silently up the lift tube to the control room, where the Captain slid into the pilot's chair and asked, "Back to the capital, sir?"

In ten days the next Session of Sector Seven's Triune would begin. Not much time for a vacation, but Phillips had no desire to spend all of the intervening time in the Sector's capital city on Drinan IV. Besides, there was somebody he wanted very much to talk with on his home world. One of the few people he could trust. One of the few people he could open up to completely.

Phillips shook his head. "Not directly, Captain. Set a course for Norhaven," he said, already eager to be gone. "Vilmar City."

(New Standard Year 907—Norhaven)

12. Homecoming

Phillips sat in the ship's small passenger lounge, gazing dully at the viewport. He saw the kaleidoscopic images of hyperspace flashing through its large ovoid aperture, their number and configuration shifting with each slight movement he made. He had once found the flowing, flickering patterns intriguing, until he'd realized that each minute image element was simply a view of whatever ship he was traveling. Here an extreme close-up, there a black spot with the ship lost in infinite distance, in one corner a spread out, all-points view like a Mercator projection.

Nonspacers seldom tired of the inconstant scenes, looking for the most amusing or unusual image or seeking some overall pattern amidst the randomness. For Phillips, however, the novelty had waned after his first few space flights. Besides, he knew just enough of the mathematics of hyperspace to realize that there was no meaning in the multitude of reflections, and that there was no escape from that visual closed loop—nothing new to be seen.

With a sigh, he opaqued the port's clear crystal and returned to his cabin.

He'd been trying for the better part of a day to put Director Albing's words out of his mind. They clung tenaciously. No matter how tentatively she'd mentioned it, Albing had clearly suggested that Phillips's problems were psychological rather than physical. It was a possibility that he himself had first considered several years ago.

Even before his final meeting with Shardon Kirowa, he had begun feeling the stress of opposing Aldon Rizlov, and that was when Kaswan Bakhtaswani was carrying the majority of the fight. Then Kirowa was killed because of Phillips's suspicions and shortly thereafter Bakhtaswani was assassinated by Rizlov's Security Director, Caulston. Those two deaths had magnified the pressures on Phillips immensely, both from within and from without. Maybe he couldn't handle the strain. Maybe his mind was looking for a way to quit without seeming to give up.

Phillips lay on the bed in his cabin, staring at the ceiling. Its color—a pink so pale it was nearly white—was supposed to be soothing, but he wanted an answer, a solution to a problem he didn't even fully understand.

What he did understand was that "psychological incapacity" was a diagnosis that would have no good consequences. At best he would be removed from the Triune and given a figurehead position somewhere in the Sector's bureaucracy, possibly losing his rejuvenation status in the process. At worst, he would be required, "for his own good," to undergo reconditioning, a program of drug-aided psychobehavioral indoctrination that would essentially wipe out the personality of Umberto Phillips and replace it with someone who was not burdened by cares and worries. Reconditioned people tended to forget much of their pasts and to be as bland and pleasant as the ceiling of Phillips's cabin.

He closed his eyes and tried to conjure up a competing image. Something peaceful but strong. Something individual. Something from his own life. The pink turned to pure white and began swirling. Slowly it settled into a rough snow-covered plain. A cold wind blew steadily, shifting the snow over and around rocky outcroppings. In the distance, icy mountains glittered silver and blue in the light of a heatless sun. Nearer, so close he could almost touch it, was a blurred something. A long blue-white mound, it was neither ice nor snow, but of them. He stepped toward it for a better look. More distinct, it was still not quite recognizable. *I know what that is,* he thought. *Just one more step.* But the wind came up and swept him away in a frozen white cloud. . . .

Several hours later, Phillips was awakened by the reemergence alarm. He rose, took a quick shower, and was standing before the viewport, now clear, when his ship dropped back into normal space a few thousand kilometers above Norhaven.

The planet hung motionless in his view, its rotation cancelled by his ship's orbital speed. Two continents sprawled along the equator, nearly touching at both ends, separating the circumglobal northern and southern oceans. The continents were predominantly the dark green of hardy perennial forests, and both reached toward the large polar ice caps with frostbitten peninsular fingers.

With virtually no axial tilt and nearly circular orbit, Norhaven had only one season, which nonnatives, as they were optimists or pessimists, characterized as late fall or early spring. Norhaven's small orange-yellow sun, approximately three-fourths A.U. distant, could not warm the planet up to what would be summer on most settled worlds.

Phillips could not see Vilmar City from this far up, but he knew where to look for it. It was located near the southern edge of the continent below him, at the base of a large peninsula. By turning up the magnification of the lower right-hand quarter of the viewport, he could make out the grayish circular area where the forest had been cleared to make room for the city. It was not large, but then Norhaven wasn't a heavily populated planet. The people living there didn't go in for large families, and there was very little immigration —Norhaven was not one of the Union's garden spots, nor was it endowed with the surface mineral wealth that could inspire a rush of prospectors and miners with promise of quick riches.

From the ship, Phillips scanned the area east of Vilmar City, but he knew the magnification was too low to spot the family home, even if it weren't sheltered among the tall trees. Looking down at that dark green sea, he could almost smell the brisk forest-scented air of his home. He thought of the hunting trips he'd taken as a youth with his father.

Gregor Phillips had been an outdoorsman of renowned skill. Married late in life, he'd not been a buddy to his sons, but he had seemed determined to pass on to Umberto, his eldest, all the knowledge he had, along with his love for the wilderness. Under his guidance, Umberto had begun to feel less threatened by the dense trackless forest and to appreciate the austere splendor of the frigid arctic wastes.

As much as his father had been a part of Norhaven, Umberto reflected, his mother had seemed out of place there.

Mariella Steurdant-Phillips had been the only daughter of a representative for a multisector trading company. A confirmed urbanite, she had nevertheless fallen in love with rough-hewn Gregor and forsaken the city for him. The petite, graceful, cultured woman had brought a measure of social sophistication to her sons' upbringing. Unlike her husband, she had never ventured beyond the oases of civilization on Norhaven, and had been in a constant state of anxiety whenever Gregor was gone on one of his outings.

White, dark green and blue, Norhaven shone against the blackness of space, framed by the viewport's silver edging. It was a beautiful world, but rugged, where even a hunter as experienced as Gregor Phillips could become prey.

Umberto had been thirteen years old, and his brother Frederick seven, when their father had gone on his last hunt. Alone, as he so often was, he had been missing for twenty-nine days before being found, frozen beneath the body of the ice cat that had killed him in its own death throes.

Even now, so many years later, Phillips could feel the chill that had run through him when his father's body had been returned home for burial. Never again could he be complacent about death. If it could happen to his father . . .

With that death, Mariella had withdrawn as completely as possible from other people and from Norhaven itself. She secluded herself in the house that Gregor had built, and died there of a stroke five years later.

Umberto was eighteen when his mother died. He became Frederick's legal guardian and remained on Norhaven for six years in that capacity. He pursued his schooling diligently, eventually graduating with honors from Vilmar University. As time allowed, he still went camping and hunting, trying to pass on to Frederick the skills he had learned from their father. But wherever he went, he felt the tall silver-haired figure of Gregor Phillips watching him, reminding he of what this world could do and of whose wilderness it was.

Umberto left Norhaven as soon as Frederick himself reached eighteen and became a legal adult. Having excelled in languages and law at the University, Phillips had enlisted in the Military Advocates Corps, where his brilliance and dedication to duty had led to a rapid succession of promotions from Clerk to Interpreter to Investigative Officer to Advocate General.

"You've come a long way, Umberto," he whispered to himself, looking down at the small gray circle surrounded by green. He smiled wistfully, wondering how his rugged, practical, self-sufficient father would have felt about his son becoming a Triune Adjudicator. Would he have been proud, surprised, satisfied, ashamed? Probably a little of each, and more, Phillips thought, turning away from the viewport as the ship began to descend toward Vilmar City's spaceport.

"Here we are, sir. How does it feel?"

Phillips and Inyuko stood at the top of the ship's ramp, looking across a kilometer of thermalloy to the spaceport terminal.

"Good, Captain. It feels good." Five years since he'd been here last, and the place looked exactly as he'd remembered it. Simple, functional, uncrowded.

The Captain breathed in deeply. "Certainly beats shipboard air. What's that tangy scent?"

A cool breeze puffed across the field, ruffling Phillips's hair and bringing him the aroma from the nearby forest. "Those are niktals—a flowering vine. Their berries are used for food and for making brandy."

"If they taste anything like they smell, they must be delicious."

Phillips smiled. "They taste even better."

Inyuko turned to him in mock reproach. "And Norhaven's been keeping these all for itself, sir?"

"Ah well, Captain. You know how it is," Phillips replied smugly. "The best way to keep a good thing is to keep it secret. You won't tell, will you?"

"Me?" Inyuko asked, eyes wide in innocence. "I wouldn't dream of it. Of course, to really keep the secret, I ought to know what it's all about. Will you be requiring me to stay with the ship while we're here, sir?"

Phillips laughed. "Blackmail, is it, Captain? Very well, you're free until midday tomorrow. Just don't get arrested for anything. Norhaven jails are colder than most."

"I'll be careful, sir," Inyuko assured him.

"I'm sure you will, Captain. Try to enjoy your visit too."

"You too, sir," he replied as Phillips started down the ship's ramp. "And good luck," he added, so quietly that Phillips barely heard him.

At the base of the ramp, Phillips hefted his travel bag. *I could use a younger body,* he thought as he stared across the wide expanse of landing field to the small terminal.

Vilmar City was the largest population center on Norhaven, and received the bulk of off-planet visitors. Even so, the inhabitants had no desire to impress or cater to travelers accustomed to the luxuries of most major spaceports. Here there were no flowing walkways or luggage carriers. Assistance was available only for the physically incapacitated.

Phillips's mouth twisted in a wry grin as he trudged toward the terminal. The simplicity he'd once taken pride in (and still did, in principle) now weighed heavily on his legs and arm. He shifted the travel bag to his other hand.

I've let myself grow soft, he thought. Step by slow step, feeling his chronological rather than his physiological age, he walked on. By the time he reached the terminal, his black-and-silver uniform was darkened in patches by sweat, despite the cool breeze.

There was no reception committee awaiting him and he had expected none, though a Triune Adjudicator's visit was newsworthy on more prominent planets than Norhaven. It was enough to know he was expected, and his brief pre-shift communication from his ship had assured him of that.

He walked through the nearly deserted terminal building to the public transit island, where three ancient but shiny autocabs waited. He stepped into the first in line, set his bag on the passenger seat, dropped his identicard into the fare slot, and typed in his destination.

As the cab rose quietly on its cushion of air, then accelerated onto the main roadway, Phillips lay back and closed his eyes. He tried to reestablish his connection to this place, this rugged world where he'd grown up and which he'd left so many decades ago. Somewhere in his cells and in his psyche he had always felt a resonance with Norhaven, with its scents, colors, texture. He was having trouble finding the sympathetic vibration this time, as if he had become something other. His trips back had been infrequent and too brief, he knew, his career responsibilities always pulling him away before he was ready to leave. The ties between himself and his home had gradually weakened, and now he was left with distant memories and one living link—his brother.

After perhaps an hour of smooth high-speed flight, Phillips felt the cab slowing down and he opened his eyes. Yes, he was nearly there. The district had undergone some development, but it was still recognizable, and still sparsely inhabited.

An address marker came into view by the side of the road —a boulder with inset metal letters spelling PHILLIPS. The family house itself was out of sight, built a few hundred meters back into the trees, unreachable by the autocab. The cab stopped next to the boulder, at the beginning of a narrow, winding path. Phillips retrieved his identicard, lifted his travel bag, and began walking toward the house.

Gregor Phillips had laid down the square white stones of the path three years before the birth of his first son, Umberto. Now the stones were worn from over a century of coming and going. Each step Phillips took felt like a step backward in time. Here he and his brother had played at hunting and tracking one another, Umberto stalking slowly and leaving obvious signs so as not to lose the younger Frederick. Here, too, he had begun studying wilderness and survival skills under the firm but loving tutelage of his father.

As he walked, the massive black-barked Oagrun trees closed in behind him, hiding the roadway.

The hum of the autocab faded and was gone. Following

the cool white stones through the shadowed trees, he began to hear a murmuring, a voice. Deep, familiar, it came from all around him, too faint to understand.

Phillips stopped for a moment and ran his hand along the rough bark of a tree whose trunk nearly touched the stone on which he stood. The trees seemed as large, as overwhelming, as when he'd been a child, the fissures in the bark just as cryptic. He'd once thought that there were messages in those cracks and bumps, and that he could decipher each tree's story if only he studied them hard and long enough.

When he'd mentioned his theory to his mother, she had taken him into her refuge—a small library/study filled with books, art reproductions, and a computer. "Meaning requires mind, Umberto," she had said, "and intention." She had proceeded to explain representationalism and symbolism, metaphor and literalism, and the arbitrary nature of languages. The explanations continued until her death, and beyond, when he went to the University.

His father's response had been to clap him on the shoulder and laugh. "Very good, son. But it's not just the trees." He had pointed to footprints in the soft ground, a telltale pattern of animal droppings near a thicket, the color of the sky that presaged a blizzard. "Everything has a meaning," he'd said, "if you know how to read it."

The bark was cool and dry under Phillips's fingers. Faint scurrying sounds of small animals came to him from high in the trees and from beneath the ground cover of scattered thick bushes and dead leaves. He closed his eyes and breathed in deeply of the forest's pungent aroma.

In his mind's eye, he could see Gregor Phillips's tall, strong figure before him, questioning with his sharp, gray eyes.

His father's son began to stir within the Adjudicator. He opened his eyes and let his hand fall to his side. The stones felt softer under his boots, his travel bag lighter.

He walked more briskly the rest of the way to the house. A one-story octagon of dense black logs and light brown stone, it sat in a small clearing, hemmed in on all sides by the forest. Phillips paused momentarily just inside the edge of the trees and looked around. Seeing no sign of his brother outside, he crossed to the front door and lifted the ornate knocker. Once, twice, he raised the heavy iron weight and let it fall against the door.

The sharp *thunk* of metal on wood had barely stopped echoing through the trees when the door swung open and Frederick stood before him.

"Umberto! Welcome!" The old man smiled warmly. "Come in, come in." He stepped aside and motioned Phillips inside with one gnarled hand, the other gripping the head of a carved black cane.

"Thanks."

Phillips entered. He thought Frederick had changed little in the past five years, though the cane was new. He set his bag down as his brother turned from closing the door. "It's good to see you again," he said, clasping Frederick's right hand in both of his. "How have you been?"

The old man's gray eyes sparkled. "Well, Umberto, well." He tapped the floor once with his cane. "A little slower, perhaps, but I'm as quick as I need to be." Frederick fixed his brother with a steady gaze. "And how have things been with you?"

How, indeed? thought Phillips. "It's a long story, Frederick," he said, trying to sound casual.

Frederick raised one bushy white eyebrow, but didn't press for details. "If it's all that long, let's eat first. There's a haunch of shade deer roasting in the oven as we speak. I'll see what I can find to accompany it for dinner while you get yourself settled in."

With that, the old man turned back toward the central chamber of the house, to which all the rooms were connected.

Phillips remained in the entrance hallway, letting his gaze linger on the shiny paneling, the handwoven rugs, his mother's sunny pastoral watercolor. It was all so old, yet it seemed so new.

Frederick stood at the end of the hallway. "Have you forgotten the way, or do you expect me to carry your luggage for you?" he asked wryly, shaking Phillips out of his reverie.

"What?" He looked up, an embarrassed grin on his face. "No, I'll carry it. I didn't bring enough for a tip."

"Cheapskate," Frederick grumbled as he headed for the kitchen.

Phillips bent down to pick up his bag and his grin widened. He was home again.

A hearthfire crackled in the main room, filling the space with a warm glow. The two brothers sat in heavy chairs, half-facing the fire. A low carved Oagrunwood table stood between them.

Phillips swirled the amber niktal brandy in his goblet and looked around casually at the room's black-paneled walls.

Frederick chuckled dryly, the lines on his face creasing more deeply with his grin. "You won't find any new additions to the collection. I'm a little too old for that anymore."

Phillips gave a guilty start. He'd never gotten used to his brother's apparent ability to read his mind. When they were growing up, it had occasioned some sibling strife but on the whole had brought them closer together. Then, the insights into Umberto's thoughts and feelings had made the younger Frederick seem at times an old man in a child's body. Now, Phillips reflected sadly, it was Frederick's body that was aged and his mind that seemed young.

"Besides," Frederick continued, "where would I find room?" With an abbreviated sweep of his age-spotted hand, he invited Phillips to continue his survey.

"Was I that obvious?" Phillips asked ruefully. "But since you insist . . ."

He set his goblet down and rose from his deep leather armchair. Turning slowly, he studied the room's four main walls. Frederick was right, he realized. The mountings, heads of large carnivores and herbivores, took up virtually all of the available space. Or rather, Phillips thought, they took up the space so well that additions would have upset the room's balance, would have been awkward interlopers among the bared fangs, twisting horns, and bright glass eyes.

Even the small inner wall, its doorway leading to the house's central vestibule, was occupied. On the panel to the left of the door, a small bloodred raptor was mounted, its wings outspread as if it were about to take flight. On the right panel, a white-furred arctic predator, thin and elongated, rose up on its hind legs and stared directly toward the hearth.

"I know people who'd call this barbaric," Phillips said, easing himself back down into his chair and reaching for his drink.

"You were never much of a Devil's advocate, Umberto. Don't start now."

Phillips took a sip of his brandy, savoring its heavy mint-like aroma and the smooth burning in his throat. He shook his head deliberately.

"That's not it. It's just that every time I come back here, it takes me longer to feel completely a part of the place. It's as if . . . as if I had learned a new language and were gradually forgetting my native tongue." He paused and looked into the flames dancing in the fireplace. "I'm afraid that one day, one year, I'll lose it completely."

One of the burning logs shifted and slid to the bottom of the pile with an ash-muted *thump*. A flight of sparks whirled up the smoke-blackened stone chimney.

Frederick leaned forward, wrinkled elbows resting on thin knees, cupping his goblet in both veined hands. "How long has it been since you left, Umberto—almost ninety years? What does it matter if it takes you a few hours, even a day, to feel at home again? Norhaven will always be a part of you," he insisted. "You couldn't get rid of it if you wanted to."

He sounded so confident of himself, so certain. And Phillips wanted to believe him. "You may be right, Frederick, but I'm not sure I could make the transition without you. You're the only human link I have, except for my memories."

"Don't underestimate your memories, Umberto." Frederick leaned back in his chair with a sigh. He lifted his goblet to his lips and drank slowly of the amber liquor, all the while keeping his eyes on his brother. "Is that what you've really come to talk about?"

He's done it again, Phillips thought wryly. He downed the rest of his brandy in a quick swallow, then refilled his glass from a decanter on the low table between his chair and Frederick's. He glanced over at his brother and away again.

"I've come to talk about dying."

Frederick raised his eyebrows but said nothing. A sharp *crack* came from the fire, now burning low. The sounds of the forest came faintly through the room's two large windows: the whistles and cries of night creatures, the sighing of the wind in the treetops far overhead, the groan of branches rubbing against each other.

"Anybody's death in particular?" Frederick's tone was light, but Phillips recognized the brotherly concern in his voice.

"Mine."

Frederick remained silent, waiting him out.

"The treatments aren't effective anymore." Phillips raised his hand to forestall any interruption. "I know, I know. I look as young as ever. But the effect doesn't last long—a few years at the most. And inside," his voice dropped to a whisper, "inside, I feel old, Frederick. A thousand years old."

"I see." Frederick swirled the brandy around in his goblet, looking down thoughtfully at the circling liquid. "What do the rejuvenation experts say?"

"Nothing. As far as they can tell, everything's normal and the treatments should be working." Phillips rose abruptly and walked over to one of the windows. It was a clear, moonless night. The cold wind had become stronger, reaching deeper into the forest. The trees were restless, brooding shadows against the starry sky.

"And what about you, Umberto? Do you have any idea why this is happening?" Frederick prodded.

Tell him, a voice whispered mockingly. Phillips thought he saw a pale blue figure among the trees. *Tell him about betrayal and death.*

Kirowa? Phillips wondered in panic. He looked more closely and the figure disappeared.

"I . . . don't really know. It just seems that I'm tired of everything—the regulations, the ceremony, the privileges. The routine." His reflection stared back at him palely from the window's smooth, cool glass. He grimaced briefly and turned toward Frederick, still seated near the fireplace.

Looking down at his brother sunk deep into the large dark leather chair, Phillips suddenly noticed how thin Frederick's hair was.

"I'm sorry, Frederick," he said with chagrin. "I have no business burdening you with my troubles."

"You'd rather burden someone else, Umberto?" The corners of his eyes crinkled with amusement. "Isn't that what brothers are for? What friends are for?"

"No!" Phillips half-shouted, wanting to smash his goblet against the black wooden wall. "No," he said more quietly. "I have no right."

Phillips paced back and forth by the window, chewing his lip. "Just look at us, Frederick." He walked over to his chair and gripped its back with both hands. The hands were young, smooth, strong.

Frederick looked up at him, sharp gray eyes in a wizened face.

Phillips wanted to cry. "Even if I never had another treatment, I'd have years to live." *And you, little brother*, he thought, *how long?* "Already I've had a better, longer life than all but a few people in the entire Sector. Shouldn't that be enough?"

"Why should it?" Frederick set his goblet down heavily on the polished wooden table. "You've earned your rejuvenation status, and you have every right to expect the benefits to continue."

Philips gave a short harsh laugh. "I'd say my genes earned it." he turned toward the window again, toward the accusing darkness.

"Listen, Umberto," Frederick said sternly. "You may not admit it, but I've always been smarter than you, and my memory was always better. Probably still is. You succeeded because you studied and sacrificed and worked harder than anybody else. You trained yourself to make difficult decisions well. I could've done what you did, but I didn't want to. Maybe I just didn't have the mental toughness." His eyes glinted in the firelight. "Don't talk to me about genes."

"Toughness?" Phillips asked thoughtfully as he walked

back to the warmth of the fire and sat across from Frederick once more. "Maybe that was part of it. Hell, maybe that was all of it at one time. But I don't feel that way anymore. I feel..." He paused and gestured vaguely. "I feel empty somehow, and not at all sure of myself."

Phillips took another drink of his brandy, rolling it on his tongue before swallowing it. "I've begun second-guessing my decisions as an Adjudicator. Not just some of them, but all of them. No matter what the Triune decides on any case, there are good arguments for the other side. The problems with obvious answers never reach us." He glanced over at his brother's wizened face. "I used to be comfortable with that, confident that I could balance competing interests, interpret accurately the relevant laws and precedents, make the best decision."

Another log shifted in the fireplace, and the entire stack collapsed. Phillips stared into the flames as he continued. "Now all I see are the errors, the ambiguities, the costs inherent in every decision. And Rizlov is always pointing them out. It's becoming harder and harder to fight him." He sighed. "I've lost my faith, Frederick. I'm bright, well-trained, and experienced, but I'm also human. And fallible."

"And that comes as a surprise to you, Umberto?" Frederick asked, chiding him gently.

"You needn't be so smug," Phillips snapped, angry at himself, at his weakness, and at Rizlov. "Of course I knew I could make mistakes, but that remained hypothetical—a possibility. I never knew whether or not a given decision was actually a mistake." His voice was thin, strained. "And I never fully realized how terrible the consequences could be. Everything was abstract, governed by logic, rules of order and procedure. Nothing was personal or immediate, until..." Phillips's words trailed off and he sat still, following his thoughts to another place and time.

Frederick watched him, waiting for his tension to ease. "Until what?"

"Hmm?" Phillips turned slowly, gradually refocusing his attention on the room, the fire, and Frederick.

"None of your decisions were personal until what?" Frederick's voice was soft but insistent.

Phillips took a deep breath and let it out slowly. "It was twenty Standard Years ago, on a planet called Wehring's Stopover, on the Periphery. I knew a man there named Shardon Kirowa. He was a Pilot and a man of great personal integrity and little respect for arbitrary rules and regulations."

He paused to empty his goblet, finding some comfort in the burning that spread down his throat and into his stomach. "I had met Shardon on a trip to the Periphery during the previous year, and had made a point of looking him up on this visit. He seemed to know everyone and everything of interest out there, which made him the ideal guide."

Phillips related the story as if under a spell, in an expressionless monotone but totally absorbed in the telling, omitting no detail, no event, no reaction. When he finished, he slumped in his chair and smiled weakly at Frederick.

"How's that for fallibility?"

Frederick studied his older brother through age-dimmed eyes. "So self-assurance becomes self-doubt, and you no longer want to go on living because you're imperfect. What am I supposed to say?"

Phillips shook his head impatiently. "Umberto Phillips, the man, can make mistakes and deal with them in his own way. Triune Adjudicator Phillips cannot afford to make mistakes. Too much hangs in the balance, too many lives can be affected. How can I deal with that?" There was anguish in his voice as he appealed to his brother.

Frederick rose slowly, leaning on his cane, and shuffled across to stand by Phillips's chair. "Only you know your options, Umberto, and what's best for you. All I can tell you is that there is always a place for you here, and whatever help I can give." His gnarled hand squeezed his brother's shoulder briefly, firmly. "Now you must excuse me. It is late and I am tired."

Frederick left the room, closing the door quietly behind him.

Phillips remained in his chair, staring at nothing. After a long while, he wiped his eyes and reached for the decanter of brandy. Outside, the wind blew lost and mournful through the trees. Inside, the fire was a dim, red glow of embers, fading. Above the mantel, in splendid isolation, commanding the room and looking down at Phillips, was the proud snarling head of a blue-white ice cat.

The next morning, after breakfast and some casual conversation with Frederick, Phillips went on a brief pilgrimage of sorts.

They stood side by side: two white stone slabs one meter high and one-half meter wide. A lifelong friend of Gregor Phillips's had carved each of them without being asked and without asking anything in return. That was the way of things on Norhaven.

GREGOR	MARIELLA
KARL	ANNA
PHILLIPS	LOUISA
746–809	STEURDANT-PHILLIPS
	769–814

The graves were in a clearing behind the house, just a short walk away. Gregor had made the clearing by cutting down four large trees, removing their roots, and burning off the thick undergrowth. He had then planted a hardy off-planet grasslike ground cover that kept the native plants from moving back in. The project had been an anniversary present for Mariella, to give her a green, sunny place of escape from the shadowed forest.

Phillips stood looking down at the two graves. The stones sparkled in the late-morning sun. *Such different lives*, he reflected. *Such different deaths*.

As unexpected and violent as his father's death had been, Phillips did not feel sad for him. Gregor Phillips had chosen his way of life and had died living that life to its fullest.

His mother was another matter. Phillips had watched her die, suffering, over the last five years of her life. Now, looking at her stone next to Gregor's, Phillips felt both pity and anger. Pity because she had sacrificed much to be with Gregor, anger because she had not tried to fight back and salvage her life. She had simply given up.

The soft ground-cover plants waved back and forth in a

light breeze, washing up against the gravestones like a gentle green surf.

One day all too soon, he thought, he would have to find someone to carve a stone for Frederick. The thought should have made him sad, but he recalled the sparkle in his brother's eyes and knew that Frederick's grave would be filled with few regrets and doubts.

"So, Umberto," he whispered to himself, "whose example do you follow?"

The small sun felt almost warm when he finally turned and headed back toward the house.

Later that afternoon, Frederick walked down to the highway with him. Frederick's parting words stayed with Phillips long after his brother's waving figure had disappeared in the distance. "You know you've made your choice, Umberto. Now you have to decide to live with it."

With the crisp air of Norhaven filling his lungs and its pale sky cloudless above, Phillips found it not so difficult to agree.

(New Standard Year 907—Drinan IV)

13. Back in the Saddle

Captain Inyuko turned halfway around in his pilot's seat. "They've given us a slot, sir." His round face clearly showed his relief.

"Finally!" Phillips's mouth twisted in a wry grin. "I thought they were going to keep us up here till the Session was over."

"Not likely." Inyuko laughed. "I don't know what the holdup was, but it disappeared when I offered to find an alternate landing site in the Botanical Gardens."

"Very resourceful, Captain. I'll recommend you for promotion." Phillips rose from the passenger's seat. "How long before we land?"

"Still about an hour." The Pilot sounded apologetic.

"That'll be fine," Phillips said cheerfully. "Gives me time to finish packing." He turned toward the door at the rear of the control cabin. He let his smile drop. The pleasant facade had been for Inyuko's benefit. He'd been packed for hours, but this further delay was hardly his Pilot's fault.

Landing at Drinan City's spaceport was an event for many travelers. The port was an immense multispoked wheel dotted with hundreds of launching/landing pads to accommodate small-to-medium-sized ships and the shuttles of those too large to land themselves. A steady stream of rising and falling sparks marked the departures and arrivals. It was a magnificent sight, one that most visitors eagerly awaited.

Phillips stayed in his suite and kept his viewports opaqued. He was here on business, and the business would not be pleasant.

For years, each Triune Session had been more of a strain than the last, more acrimonious, more divisive. Rizlov on one side, Phillips on the other, Doriani in the middle.

Lying on his bed, eyes closed, he tried to relax. *No use*, he thought wryly. *I'd rather be hunting ice cats barehanded, but nobody's giving me the choice.*

A soft chime sounded, followed by his Pilot's voice over the intercom. "Landing clearance received, sir. We'll be down in ten minutes."

"Thank you, Captain." Phillips sat up slowly. Another Session. He'd get through it, as he had the previous one and all the ones before that. It might take a few more stimtabs, and he might have to let some cases slide to focus on the more important ones. Still, he *would* get through it. He wasn't going to resign with Rizlov still in charge. Whatever his doubts, that much he did know. They'd have to carry him away. He couldn't live if he abandoned the struggle against Rizlov's tyranny. He'd never be able to face Frederick, and he'd never be able to face himself.

He stood and went into the bathroom. He splashed some cold water on his face and ran a comb through his hair. As ready as he was going to be, he left his suite and stepped across a short corridor to the central lift tube. The tube dropped him two levels to the ship's airlock just as the ship settled into one of the spaceport's sunken landing pads. Six days before the Triune Session was to begin.

In contrast to Norhaven, Drinan IV was overrun with rules and regulations and officials to enforce them. Also in contrast to Norhaven, Phillips's status counted for something on the Sector's capital planet. As a consequence, he always wore his Adjudicator's uniform there, especially when he was in Drinan City Spaceport, either coming or going. Once he was OK'd by the automated identity verifier blocking the exit gate from his landing pad, Phillips went through the rest of the spaceport with little hindrance. Better, even. While the throngs of ordinary travelers on business or pleasure were standing in lines waiting to be quizzed, checked, scrutinized and generally bothered, the Spaceport's guards and inspectors were stumbling over themselves to clear Phillips's way.

He felt a little guilty, seeing the tired and irritated men, women and children being grudgingly allowed to leave the terminal. But he also enjoyed the respectful, almost obsequious treatment he received. It gave his ego a boost and saved him considerable time. Despite his twinge of guilt, it seemed fitting that here, on Drinan IV, he should receive his due as a Triune Adjudicator. So he walked briskly past the other travelers, head high, uniform shining, looking as little to left or right as possible.

He'd been through the routine so much, it had become second nature to him. He nodded casually to the Chief Customs Agent and had a few brief words with the Spaceport's Assistant Security Officer as they smiled and sped him on his way. He paid no attention at all to the anonymous brown-suited laborer who loaded his luggage into a commercial floater. The laborer stared after Phillips's vehicle for a while before heading for another, private floater parked near the Spaceport entrance.

Phillips arrived home in the late afternoon. No one greeted him. He lived alone, as did many who had rejuvenation status. It was too painful for most to become attached to someone who would age at the normal rate, slowing down, tiring, dying before their eyes. Some rejuvenants jumped from one temporary liaison to another, but the mental and emotional immaturity of their companions usually began to wear on them. The ideal solution was to find another, compatible rejuvenant, but it was difficult—their numbers were relatively small and they were almost by definition unusual, individualistic, not well-suited to the give-and-take of a committed relationship. A few managed it, but most chose Phillips's route.

He did not even have human servants, though they would have been cheaper than the elaborate housekeeping systems he had installed in his home. One could become too fond of servants, who would all too quickly age and die. His mother, his father, his few childhood friends, one day Frederick. Why add more to the list?

So he entered his empty house, unpacked as quickly as possible, and ordered up a light dinner from his kitchen unit. A soothing cool shower before dinner, a small glass of wine after, and he was ready for bed. He put his household comm unit on "record," his door monitor system on "he's not home at the present time," darkened his windows, shut off his lights, and slept.

He didn't awaken until the sun was well up in the sky the next morning. Sunlight channeled through optical fibers shone on the wall several meters to the left of his bed. The floor-to-ceiling bank of plants covering that wall glowed brilliant green, with scattered yellows, reds and blues from the morning-bloomers.

Phillips opened his eyes reluctantly and tried to make them focus. *What? Where?* Eventually he remembered where he was, the view made sense and the time of day impressed itself upon his brain. With a groan he rolled out of bed, barely getting his feet under him in time.

He shuffled into the bathroom and endured a nerve-jolting cold shower that left him gasping but on the road back to life. To complete the journey, he returned to his bedroom and had the kitchen unit produce a large cup of his emergency tea—very strong, very dark, very appropriate for limited use and then only when necessary. The tea slid out of a wall dispenser near his bed, and Phillips grabbed it gratefully.

After the tea, his body was more or less ready to face the rest of the day. He knew he should spend it studying the briefs for the first few cases of the Session. He knew that, but his mind shied away from the prospect. He wasn't yet ready to argue with Rizlov over people's lives. Thoughts of death and human fallibility were still too much with him.

He reached over to his bedside comm unit to summon an autocab. The shower and the tea were for his body, but they did little for his psyche. There was one more ritual he had to perform, his usual way of clearing and relaxing his mind for the rigors of a Triune Session. When the cab arrived, he ordered it to take him to the Drinan Botanical Gardens.

Why, why, why? I shouldn't have to do this, Phillips thought angrily. His anger was fueled by worry. His visit to Norhaven had given him a renewed sense of purpose, but not the confidence to match. What could he expect from this artificial substitute?

Even so, the Gardens were marvelous, by themselves worth the trip to Drinan IV according to most travelers, whether novice tourists or blasé veterans of hundreds of the Union's vacation spots. They covered nearly two square kilometers of land in the southwest section of the city, surrounded by an imposing gray wall but open to the public, for a fee.

Of the thousands of domed and open-air displays in the Gardens, many visitors seemed to find the genetic experiments the most fascinating, especially the ones that were so bizarre that they could not survive except in laboratory conditions simulating human-hostile environments. Plants designed to live in methane clouds or on airless moons were always surrounded by wide-eyed crowds. Phillips was not drawn to such.

When he had first come to Drinan City over eighty years ago, he had visited the Gardens and taken in everything. It was new, it was huge, and much of it was flashy and exotic, so different from the dark solid forest of Norhaven. But over the decades, as his trips back home became less and less frequent, he'd found himself drawn more to the quiet, mundane, less traveled parts of the Gardens—the stand of brooding conifers, the woodland meadow, the patches of prairie grasses and wildflowers. They weren't from Norhaven, but they let him connect with the planet of his birth or, rather, the essence of it that he'd carried away with him when he'd left there a lifetime ago.

The autocab deposited him at the Gardens' main entrance. He went through the gate without being charged—a minor perquisite of office he was fairly sure Rizlov had never used. Humanity *seemed* too little in control of much of the Gardens for Rizlov's taste, Phillips guessed. And the parts where control was definitely present were filled with botanical mutations and genetic manipulations that might be uncomfortable reminders of the Senior Adjudicator's own unfortunate physical condition.

It was late morning of a normal working day, so the Gardens were not at all crowded when Phillips arrived. He passed the more spectacular introductory displays without more than a glance. He found no attraction in the prismatic Gemleaf vines from Narrakus, the motile three-ton Rovellan slug bush, the fish-catching Netweaver weeds from Coelinth. He sometimes wondered if they were even real, or just fabrications for the tourists.

Under a clear blue sky, Phillips wandered toward the nether reaches of the Gardens. By the time he reached his favorite spot—the temperate coniferous forest—he was beginning to feel a little tired. The air seemed heavier and warmer than usual, harder to breathe. Worse, he could not put aside thoughts about the impending Triune session. He gazed at the straight, rough tree trunks, followed them up until they were lost in the branches over head. *Dozens of worlds*, he thought, *Billions of people. How long can I do the job? How well am I doing it now?* The green needles and black bark had no answers.

He walked on, but found no solace in the stream-bordered woodland meadow, nor in the waving green-yellow grasses of the sample prairie. The worries and doubts wouldn't go away. If anything, they became worse as he tried to avoid them. Phillips was so distracted that a person could easily have followed him around the Gardens from late morning to late afternoon without his taking any notice of the fact. By the time he caught an autocab to take him home, his mind was no clearer or more settled than when he'd stepped out of an identical autocab that morning. He was just more tired.

Later, twilight turned to evening as Phillips sat slumped in his dim study, lighted only by Drinan's afterglow coming through the large west-facing window. Case briefs lay unopened on the desk before him. He'd glanced over them quickly on his flight from Norhaven, but he knew he would have to study them carefully to be prepared for the various Advocates' oral arguments. The first case was scheduled to begin in less than five days.

Why so lethargic? he asked himself, staring dully at the closed beige folders. *Is it physical or mental?* Had Rejuvenation Director Albing told him all she knew? Had she withheld some facts or surmises out of professional caution or to protect him? He wondered whether some physical flaw in his rejuvenations was affecting his mind, or if his mental state was interfering with his rejuvenation treatments, as Albing had seemed to suggest.

Phillips reached for the glass of wine sitting next to the pile of case briefs, but set it down again without taking a drink. As drowsy as he felt now, the last thing he needed was alcohol. His attention was wandering and his concentration fuzzy enough without any help. Instead, he reached into the bottom left-hand drawer of his desk and pulled out a small red medispenser. He pressed it twice and swallowed the two tiny stimtabs without water. Almost immediately he began to perk up, and within minutes he was alert and eager to start working.

He regretted having to use stimulants—one more sign of weakness. Years ago it had been unnecessary. Last year, before his rejuvenation, he'd relied on them during the tougher cases and when the work piled up near the end of the Session. Now he was using them before the Session even began, and immediately after his treatment when he should have been at his peak. He feared that eventually even the stimtabs wouldn't be enough, forcing him to resort to stronger drugs until nothing worked. And then retirement, voluntary or otherwise. And then Rizlov would have won.

This Session could be his last. His last chance to counter Rizlov's unreasonably conservative and authoritarian ideology. His last chance to engender in Kia Doriani the will to oppose Rizlov more often and more openly.

Phillips thought the junior member of the Triune was at heart more sympathetic with his own moderate stance than with Rizlov's reactionary one, but she seemed to be holding back, more an observer than a participant in most of the Triune's difficult cases. Perhaps she was still trying to determine her own course; perhaps she was waiting to see where the power lay before committing herself to one side or the other. Phillips didn't know. But if he didn't sway her this Session, he might not get another chance.

With the stimulants rushing through his system, he began thinking over the cases so far scheduled. Some were ideologically neutral, but some were bound to put him at odds with Rizlov. He decided to concentrate on those cases most likely to divide him from the Senior Adjudicator, where they would both be fighting for Doriani's support.

Sometimes Phillips wondered whether or not it was worth the physical and emotional strain. Sometimes, in his darker moods, he felt as if he were one puny man trying to shift the enormous social and political momentum of the Interstellar Union, personified by Aldon Rizlov. Sometimes, but not now, not with the stimtabs still working. They would wear off within a few hours, however, so he knew he had to start on the cases without further delay. He didn't want to have to take a second dose of stimulants in one night.

He sat up straighter and turned on the light panel directly over his desk. Shadows ran away to the corners of the study, leaving the desk and folders atop it brightly illuminated. He shuffled through the folders until he came to the one he knew would be the most difficult, most divisive case of this Session, and perhaps of any Session. *Sector Councilor Breglum vs. Planetary Overseer Selius*. Phillips opened it and began to read.

By the time Phillips started working, night had long since fallen. The streets of Green Hills, Phillips's exclusive residential district, were largely deserted. Most of the people living there drew inward to their own private amusements after dark. Why walk around trying to see through others' hedges and fences when so many entertainments were available behind one's own hedge or fence?

There was one apparently casual late-evening stroller. He looked to be a moderately well-off businessman or an upper-level bureaucrat no different from the majority of the Green Hills residents. The stroller noticed the light go on in Phillips's otherwise darkened house, checked his watch, then walked briskly to his floater parked two blocks away.

14. Not to Question Why

"Sorry, sir, but it's our duty," the guard apologized as he checked Malvasian's identicard. The guard operating the retinal scanner seemed equally ill at ease.

The retinal scanner beeped its confirmation of Security Director Malvasian's identity, and the General smiled encouragingly at the two SecFor sergeants guarding Rizlov's house.

"That's quite all right, gentlemen. If you hadn't checked me I might have had to reassign you to Brinktown or the Records Office." His tone was light, but he meant every word of it. His people either did their duty or found themselves in places where they were driven to think of the errors of their ways.

"Thank you, sir," the guards said in unison. One of them pressed a sequence of control buttons and the heavy gate in Adjudicator Rizlov's security barrier slid open.

Malvasian returned the guards' salutes and stepped through the gate. His first impression was one of massive contradiction. Rizlov's grounds were surrounded by an imposing security barrier—a slick silvery gray wall four meters high. Its detectors could locate a fly crawling on its outer surface, and it had sufficient weaponry to hold off a small army. The two guards Rizlov had requested, both heavily armed, completed the picture of a man at odds with his fellows and perhaps with the world in general.

But inside that barrier, Malvasian saw a rambling, airy house in the midst of several acres of beautifully landscaped lawn. The house blended easily into the contours of the land. The house and grounds suggested that Rizlov was a man at peace with himself and possessed of a true appreciation for the natural order of things.

I wonder which is closer to the truth? Malvasian had his suspicions, but he would wait for more information before calling them conclusions. He moved away from the gate, keeping his eyes and mind open.

General Grestahk Malvasian was a large block of a man, with a naturally erect posture and graying black hair cut militarily short. He carried his seventy-three years very well indeed. For forty-seven of those years he had been a member of the I.U. Security Forces, the last eighteen as Director of Security for Sector Seven. His career had taken him throughout the Inner Systems, around much of the Periphery, and occasionally Beyond. He was used to commanding and being commanded, and rank received from him only its due, nothing more.

Malvasian was one of those rare persons who qualified for rejuvenation and refused the honor. In his case, it was due to his conviction that one life lived well on its own terms is better than several lived in anticipation of the next. He was not a smug nor an overly proud man, but he had tested himself in the fires of life and was satisfied with the results.

The General was not a man easily impressed. Even so, there was a certain tension behind his sharp blue eyes as he walked the shredded-wood path to Rizlov's house. As Senior Triune Adjudicator for Sector Seven, Rizlov was one step away from membership on the Central Council, which was the highest position possible in the Interstellar Union. A personal summons to such a man's home on a "confidential matter" was hardly an everyday occurrence.

Malvasian had had occasional dealings with Rizlov during

the past eighteen years, but their meetings had been brief and official. No personal closeness had developed between the two men, and the General doubted that Rizlov went beyond formality with anyone. The General probably knew him as well as anybody did, and that was very little. Which made the current meeting especially perplexing and, Malvasian admitted to himself, especially worrisome.

The path led in a precise sine curve from the barrier gate to the central unit of the house. Malvasian noticed that the wood chips under foot were not loosely strewn, as they at first appeared. Instead, they were connected to each other or to an underlying surface in such a way that they could shift slightly but could not be dislodged. The appearance of natural disorder without the attendant mess.

It was Malvasian's nature to be curious and his profession not to be fooled. He scrutinized the surrounding greenery more carefully, searching for further evidence of Rizlov's mentality.

The grass was a healthy greenish yellow, trimmed neatly at about two centimeters, but it had none of the irregularities that even the best kept lawns have. Malvasian guessed that it required no cutting or watering, just as the perfect globes of dark green and purple shrubbery would never have to be trimmed or fertilized. None of their pale blue flowers were wilted, and there were no twigs or dead leaves on the ground beneath them. From a distance or casually, the place would look attractive and well tended. Up close, it was dead. Malvasian sniffed the air and it too was clean and sterile, tainted by none of the interesting but unpredictable pungencies of life.

A shame he can't unbend a little, the General thought with a trace of apprehension. Throughout his years in SecFor, from Enforcement Trainee to Director, he had seen the value of flexibility, and the price to the individual or the group of too strict adherence to one pattern of behavior or one point of view. Worry deepened the lines in his forehead as he wondered more than ever what would cause a man like Rizlov to go outside the normal channels in consulting him.

As he approached the house, the pseudo-wood chip path broadened and formed a two-meter semicircle with its base against a blank stone wall. As the old soldier stepped into that half-circle, a chime sounded pure and bell-like from within. He straightened the collar of his pale gray uniform, squared his shoulders, and steeled himself for his meeting with the Senior Adjudicator.

After a moment, a rectangular section of the wall began to blur and fade. A figure became visible standing on the other side. Even before the door segment disappeared completely, Malvasian recognized the man facing him.

No one who met Aldon Rizlov ever forgot him. Less than one and a half meters tall, with the body of a child and head larger than most adults', he was a grotesque monument to his parents' ideology and his own defiant self-sufficiency.

His parents' Radical Purism had condemned him to birth with his deformity uncorrected. It had also ultimately condemned them to a penal colony on Karnheim. They had died there long ago.

With the doorway now transparent, Malvasian studied Rizlov's ascetic gray eyes, thin lips, and high forehead with two faint vertical frown lines over the nose. It was a young, stern face, framed by shoulder-length pale blonde hair, and it hid a soul nearly 140 years old.

Rizlov had access to all the medical resources in the Union, yet he had not sought corrective treatment for his condition. Every rejuvenation reemphasized his deformity and his past. He looked now much as he must have looked at the age of ten.

"Come in, General." The merest beginning of a polite smile poised on Rizlov's mouth, then he turned and led the way into the house, with no gesture and without looking back.

Malvasian followed Rizlov through a narrow archway and found himself at one end of a long rectangular room. One side of the room was a single enormous window overlooking a gradually sloping lawn and a small lake. The other three walls were charcoal gray at the base, brightening to pure white where they curved into the high ceiling. The floor was shiny black shot through with streaks of silver. At first glance an extravagantly exposed room for one as security-minded as Rizlov. But Malvasian's practiced eye recognized the inconspicuous nodes spaced regularly along the window's circumference. Shielding reinforcers. The room's openness was illusory. No one could see in and nothing could get in as long as the power was on.

Rizlov walked briskly over to a low table and two chairs midway along the room's length and near the window. There was no other furniture in the room.

"Please be seated." The adjudicator's sharp voice made it more a command than an invitation.

Malvasian sat opposite Rizlov and noted that the steel and synmesh chair had an almost military stiffness to it, adjusting but minimally to the user's form. Quite a contrast, he thought, to the soft luxury he usually found among the powerful and the wealthy. *It's personality, not principle*, he reminded himself uneasily. The only thing predictable about Rizlov was his hardness.

"There is a problem, General," Rizlov began without preamble, looking directly into Malvasian's eyes. "What is your assessment of the Reversionist threat in this Sector?"

"Reversionists?" Malvasian paused to consider. "Threat" was not a word he would have applied to that movement. Why had Rizlov chosen it?

"Their support has been growing for the past several years in this Sector and throughout the Union," he replied, "but they are no more than a small minority of any planet." *What does he want from me?* "We've been able to neutralize the bulk of their propaganda. As for direct action, we can attribute very little to them. A few acts of sabotage by their more extreme members, but certainly nothing major. The movement as a whole seems to have neither the inclination nor the ability to oppose Union authority with force."

"So you discount them as a concern for SecFor Security?"

Malvasian wondered if Rizlov was trying to trick him into saying something he would regret. He chose his next words carefully. "We keep a watch on them, of course. However, they do not rate a high priority at this time. A much more serious problem is the independence movements that continue to arise on rediscovered planets. Another is the smuggling and other illegal activities on the Peripheral planets.

Compared to such concerns, the practical influence of the Reversionists is negligible."

Rizlov's eyes were as intense and unwavering as a snake's, and less readable. His staring seemed not so much rude as vastly impersonal, and caused hard-bitten Grestahk Malvasian to shiver ever so slightly.

"And if I were to tell you that a member of the Triune is a Reversionist?" The corner of Rizlov's thin mouth twitched minutely, perhaps in amusement at the General's discomfiture.

"I would ask how certain you were, and on what evidence you based that conclusion," Malvasian replied cautiously. He felt the claim was extremely unlikely, but realized that the Senior Adjudicator was deadly serious.

"Of course you would. Reasonable questions." Rizlov waved his hand over a corner of the table and a section of the table top faded, revealing a small compartment containing a single beige folder. "Most of the 'evidence' is in there. Read it over and tell me what you think."

"Right now?"

Rizlov nodded.

The General leaned forward and picked up the folder. It wasn't very thick. He glanced up at Rizlov, who was still gazing at him without expression. He disliked making decisions faster than necessary, and determined not to commit himself to any more than these materials actually warranted, despite the Senior Adjudicator's obvious position.

The folder, unlabeled, contained a hodgepodge of items relating to Umberto Phillips, second in seniority to Rizlov on the Triune for Sector Seven. There was a brief biographical sketch of Phillips's early years on Norhaven, with special emphasis on his father and on Norhaven's social and political climate. An eight-page list described trips Phillips had taken to the Periphery dating back over forty years. Another list going back equally far analyzed major Triune decisions where Phillips had been the dissenter. Following that was an official report, suspiciously vague to Malvasian's eyes, of an incident involving Phillips with some "disapproved" individuals twenty years ago.

A second official report, from the Director of Rejuvenation Center Seven, described the decreasing efficacy of Phillips's rejuvenation treatments over the past eighteen years. It was in great detail but inconclusive, concluding with the suggestion of possible undetermined psychological problems. Finally, there was a list of persons who had had some connection (remote in most cases) with Phillips over the past forty years and who were known or suspected Reversionists, or who were thought to be Reversionist sympathizers.

Dull reading was Malvasian's first thought as he finished the last page of the file. He saw the possible relevance of most of the material, but Rizlov's conclusion still seemed highly speculative.

"You said this was most of the evidence. Where's the rest?"

"In here," Rizlov said, touching his head with one small finger.

In response to Malvasian's quizzical look, Rizlov added, "Forty-five years of working with Phillips and observing him. I know this man, General."

The General sensed a rising intensity in Rizlov's manner. Uneasily, he proceeded, "I take it that answers my first question too?"

"Definitely," the Adjudicator replied, "from *my* point of view."

Malvasian handed the folder back to Rizlov. "I don't believe I can take any action based on this information alone." He braced himself for a sharp rejoinder.

"Of course you can't. Not even with my supporting impressions." Rizlov gave another microscopic twitch of a smile. "It's risky to challenge someone as influential as a Triune Adjudicator."

Especially a Senior Adjudicator? Malvasian wondered. Aloud, he said, "What are you asking me to do, then?"

"I want you to find the necessary evidence. I have neither the time nor the resources to go beyond this." He tapped the folder. "You do."

"And if I can't find such evidence?"

This time Rizlov actually did smile, which made the General think of a snake eyeing its prey. "A man can find anything if he looks hard enough."

Malvasian glanced once more at the thin folder, then looked at the Adjudicator's coldly smiling face. "Very well. There's little else that demands my personal involvement right now. I'll do the best I can."

"That is, of course, all one can expect." Rizlov put his smile away and rose. The General followed suit, frowning slightly at the odd emphasis Rizlov had given to "of course."

The two walked silently back to the building's entrance. The door segment dissolved, and Malvasian was about to step through it when Rizlov stopped him. "General." His voice was as close to a confiding tone as it was likely to get. "This is a more important task than you perhaps realize. I and certain other parties would look very favorably on its discreet and successful conclusion."

"Indeed?" Malvasian asked mildly.

Rizlov continued, "There will be an opening soon on the Sector Council. It would be an excellent opportunity for a dedicated public servant."

"It certainly would," the General replied, fuming inside. *Bribing me to carry out my responsibilities, and with a desk job!*

"You will keep me informed." Rizlov flattened the question into a statement.

Malvasian stepped through the doorway and turned. "As soon as I have anything to report."

Rizlov nodded once and the doorway began to solidify between them.

The stocky General walked back to the security barrier hardly noticing his surroundings. His attention was focused inward, reviewing his session with the Senior Adjudicator. Malvasian knew he could have made a better case against himself as a dangerous Reversionist than Rizlov had against Phillips. His refusal of rejuvenation alone was more damning than anything in that beige folder, not to mention the scores of politically and socially unorthodox individuals he had associated with over the years, some in the line of duty but many because they were interesting people who could think for themselves.

He kicked at the path's bogus wood chips, his heavy black boot rebounding from them as if from a rubber mat. He realized that Rizlov was an exceptionally shrewd man, despite his obvious peculiarities. The Senior Adjudicator couldn't possibly be basing his charges solely on the information he'd just shown the General. Either he was holding back some evidence or Reversionism was just a pretext, hiding his real reasons for wanting Phillips eliminated.

At the gate, the two guards repeated the identity verification process before allowing Malvasian to leave. He breathed easier as the gate closed behind him, although he knew the security barrier didn't really separate him from Rizlov and his machinations.

A small cloud of questions followed the General the short distance to his private floater. *Does he really think I'll falsify evidence for him?* The floater was ostensibly a standard two-passenger civilian model, dull gray with a translucent bubble and no insignia. *He's bribed me to succeed—what's the price if I fail or refuse?* Inside, there were a few nonstandard features: a defensive shield generator, long-range detectors, a weapons control unit. *Why is he so obsessed with Phillips and the Reversionists?* The floater also had a military-grade power plant filling what ought to have been storage space.

Malvasian filed the questions for future reference and accelerated back toward the main traffic routes at a speed that left the two guards gaping after him. He wondered about that too—why Rizlov insisted on such stringent security measures, including armed guards, on a planet as stable and secure as Drinan IV. The Director of Security for Sector Seven decided that Umberto Phillips was not the only Triune Adjudicator he would investigate, personally and discreetly.

Back in his long black-floored room, Aldon Rizlov sat facing the vast expanse of glass, his eyes focused light-years beyond it. The beige folder lay on his thin lap. He was tapping on it with the fingers of one small hand and saying to no one, to himself, to the universe at large, "Purist, Reversionist, whatever you call yourself, I'm going to put a stop to your meddling once and for all." He dropped the folder into its compartment and solidified the table over it again. "If Malvasian won't do it, I'll find somebody else who will."

INTERLUDE

"Not much so far, John."

"No, but there are signs."

"Please don't be mystical, love. It doesn't suit you. Besides, we'll have to show deMarnon and the Council more than signs."

"Give me *some* credit, Gen. Even you will agree things are heating up in the higher levels of Sector government. If our theory about Phillips is right, this would be an opportune time for them to approach him, have him exert some leverage, maybe engineer Rizlov's ouster."

"To what end?"

"We won't know that until we talk with one of them. How aggressive are they? How powerful are they? How many systems do they control?"

"Do they even exist?"

"Hey, you were the one who recruited me, remember!"

"Any regrets, John?"

"You know better. Mmmm . . . Enough of that! Back to work!"

"Doing what?"

"I have an idea, Gen. The Triune has an interesting case before it this Session."

"You mean the Bekh-Nar situation?"

"Uh-huh. Why don't we focus in on the participants there, along with Phillips? We'll see if anything meshes with our own plentiful suppositions and meager evidence."

"And if not?"

"I'm afraid, dearest, the Council may finally send us to the rock piles."

"Suspicions intact, case unsolved, opportunity lost."

"Exactly."

"In that case, John, I suggest the utmost diligence. There's not a moment to lose!"

"Perhaps just a moment to . . ."

"Really! . . . I mean, perhaps . . ."

"It might clear our minds for the task ahead."

"What does this have to do with our minds?"

"Enough. Trust me."

"Ahhh. Of course. Just a little lower. Yesss. Much clearer."

(New Standard Year 907—Rejuvenation Center Seven)

15. A Loose Thread

"Grestahk, you anachronistic marvel, you've done it again," Malvasian crowed, waving a small strip of printout in one hand. Alone in his spaceship, he could afford to let himself go a little—no subordinates around to see the chink in the old man's impassive armor. He was professionally satisfied and personally pleased that his hunch had been correct and that his ploy had produced confirmation of it.

Rizlov and Albing. Hah!

He sobered quickly as he tried to estimate the odds of Rizlov discovering what he'd done. Minuscule and nonexistent, he thought. The tracers were set to reprogram as soon as they'd tracked Albing's call, and the comm tech who'd set up the initial programming didn't know enough to give Malvasian's plan away. Rizlov might have his suspicions, but he probably couldn't find out for sure. The General would settle for that.

Malvasian swiveled around to the ship's computer console and typed in the commands to activate the autopilot and to return home, to Drinan City. No sense floating around out here in the Hospeth system next to Rejuvenation Center Seven when there was serious work to be done back in the capital. He still had no actual legal proof of conspiracy.

With the computer fully in charge of launch preparations, he leaned back in his chair and wondered if Rizlov would appreciate the irony of the situation. If the Senior Adjudicator had not called attention to Phillips's rejuvenation problems, Malvasian probably would have assumed they were solely a matter for the medical people. But when Rizlov had implied that Phillips's ineffective treatments made him unfit to be on the Triune, that had seemed a little too convenient for the General.

So he went out to the Hospeth system and talked with Director Albing.

Albing had been cordial and concerned. "Adjudicator Phillips? Yes, a sad case. Very puzzling. No, no idea what the cause could be. Yes, we're still working on it, but we've just about run out of avenues to explore. Maybe the psych-techs..."

Beneath Albing's smooth professional manner Malvasian had sensed some tension. He asked her whether anyone could be tampering with Phillips's treatments in some way, one of the Center's employees, perhaps.

"No! That is inconceivable. I or my assistant would have noticed such an attempt almost immediately. There are too many safeguards built into the system."

The General had thanked her and left. Back in his own ship, he'd patched in to his link with SecFor's comm traffic monitors. A single line of data was sent his way via a secure hyperwave channel, and his shipboard comm unit printed it out for his perusal.

Albing had made a call only a few minutes after Malvasian had left her office. Scrambled, so he didn't know what was said. But the destination told him all he needed to know. She'd called a private residence on the outskirts of Drinan

City. Rizlov's house. He didn't think they'd been talking about the Senior Adjudicator's next rejuvenation treatment, which wasn't due for four more years.

Malvasian looked at the strip of paper one more time to make sure he'd read it right, then he crumpled it up and tossed it into a disposal chute. *I've got to stop Rizlov,* he told himself as his ship dropped into hyperspace. *The man's too devious and too dangerous to be on the loose.*

PART III

Breaking Point

(New Standard Year 907)

16. The Trial

There were only four people in the large, dim hearing room
—Sector Seven's three Adjudicators and the Advocate for
Overseer Selius.

Rizlov sat in the middle, on a seat raised to compensate
for his small size. Phillips sat on his right, Doriani on his
left. The Junior Adjudicator was slim and nearly as tall as
Phillips, with thin reddish blond hair that hung straight to
her shoulders. Her face was all angles and lines, and her
pale green eyes—at times sparkling and childlike, at others
as cold as space—were an enigma to Phillips. Despite the
years they had served together on the Triune, he still found it
impossible to predict what she would do or say.

Standing, Phillips reflected, the three Adjudicators would
look like two capital *L*s bracketing a lower-case *i*. Even so,
he realized, no one would mistake that middle member for
the weakest of the three.

They sat behind a tall curved desk on a lighted dais at the
far end of a long, dark, high-ceilinged room. Before them,
in the Presentation Circle's small pool of light, stood Advocate Jarnice Chou, well into the final arguments of her case.
Phillips looked down at her, puzzled.

Over the decades, he had seen thousands of Advocates,
and he had long since stopped thinking of each new one as a
unique individual. Face after face, year after year, they had
blurred together to form a composite, from which each suc-
ceeding Advocate was merely a slight deviation. The composite was more male than female, a little above average
height, slender, around sixty years old, with grayish brown

hair. Chou didn't match the composite at all. She was female, short, heavyset, around thirty-five years old, with thick black hair and light brown skin.

Beyond appearances, Chou didn't behave as Phillips had expected either. Even veteran Advocates showed some signs of tension or nerves at the start of a case, and with good reason. The Triune was for most the court of last resort, and getting there wasn't easy.

The Triune Hearing Chamber was located in the heart of the Justice Building, in the middle of the Government Complex that was the hub of Drinan City. No one appeared in the Chamber who was not supposed to, and those who reached it did so only after running a gauntlet of secretaries, clerks, guards, and automatic security devices. The gauntlet did not look threatening, being composed mostly of smiling faces and calmly efficient voices spread throughout the Government Complex, but it was quite effective. It was also wearing. Inexperienced Advocates especially showed the strain of the delays, the monotonously repeated questions, and the worry that one would be late for one's presentation or refused admittance altogether on some technicality.

But Jarnice Chou had not shown any signs of nervousness, even though it was her first case before the Triune. She had been calm and composed from the outset, walking unhurriedly along the darkened Chamber to the bright Presentation Circle, waiting there for Rizlov's invitation to proceed. No irregular breathing, no perspiring brow, no anxious glances around the shadowed room. Very unusual.

The other thing that puzzled Phillips about Chou, even more than her calmness, was that she was there at all. Why would a novice Advocate be undertaking a case as important as the defense of Overseer Lanya Selius? Sector Councilor Uhlat Breglum was an influential man, and the charges he had leveled at Selius were extremely serious. Her career, even her life hung in the balance. If the Triune found against her, she could end up in a penal colony mine or in a reconditioning facility. Hardly a suitable case for a beginning Advocate.

And yet Chou had handled the case very competently. She had been thoroughly prepared, made a clear opening presentation, and responded well in the cross-examination period between herself and Breglum's chief Advocate. Now she was making the final statement for the defense, to be followed by questions from the Triune. After that, the Triune would deliberate at some length and render its decision.

Phillips squinted, trying to study Chou as she concluded her remarks. His vision had been blurring in and out of focus all afternoon.

"Your Honors, Overseer Selius has proved her loyalty and worth to the Union through her brilliant military career and years of distinguished administrative service. Her bravery during the rebellion of Golconda even led to a commendation from the Central Council itself." Chou seemed to be looking primarily at Rizlov, her dark eyes calm and confident.

Phillips glanced to his left and saw that Rizlov had stiffened at mention of the Central Council. He wondered if the Senior Adjudicator was offended by the name-dropping, or if his reaction was based on his not-so-secret ambition to become a member of that all-powerful body. He turned his attention back to the Advocate.

"As Planetary Overseer, Lanya Selius has made Bekh-Nar one of the most peaceful of the provisional planets. This is not the record of a traitor or an incompetent. To the contrary, the Union would profit immeasurably if everyone had her dedication and abilities."

Chou set her notes on the small stand next to the Presentation Circle, just inside the patch of light, and took a step forward. "Though Councilor Breglum may be sincere in his accusations, the accusations themselves are groundless. Your Honors, I plead with you to set aside the charges and preserve the reputation of this exemplary citizen and servant of the Union."

Her summation ended, Jarnice Chou stepped back and dropped her gaze from the three Adjudicators as she waited for their questions or comments.

With her leaf green suit and her dark complexion, she was a bit of the natural world, insinuating itself into this bastion of human mechanism and laws.

Phillips shook his head to clear it of the fanciful illusion.

He had been having some difficulty following the intricacies of the case. Throughout the four days of arguments he'd been suffering from a splitting headache, perhaps a reaction to the stimulants he'd been taking. But even in his befogged state, it seemed to him that Selius's position was much the stronger. He already knew Rizlov's decision. Which side would Doriani support?

Phillips turned slightly toward Rizlov. He noticed that Doriani, on Rizlov's other side, had done likewise, an expression of mild inquiry on her face. As senior member of the Triune, it was Rizlov's prerogative to begin the questioning.

In clipped, flat tones, Rizlov asked, "Are you saying that we should accept the word of Overseer Selius over the word of Councilor Breglum?"

Not very subtle, Phillips thought. *Is that the best he can do?*

Chou refused to rise to the bait. "No, your Honor. I ask only that you consider the evidence I have presented."

Rizlov pressed the point a step further. "And that evidence includes statements from the Councilor and Overseer contradicting each other."

"Indeed it does, your Honor," Chou replied, "but . . ."

"Well then, whom do we believe?"

Phillips had seen Advocates pushed off their ground before by such tactics, especially as used by the Senior Adjudicator. Rizlov's manner could be quite intimidating. From his own point of view, Phillips saw it as a superficial and irrelevant line of questioning, but *he* was not appearing before the Triune for the first time, staring up at three black-robed figures, hearing his responses fade and die in the shadows of the sound-dampened Chamber.

Chou's answer was firm, but not offensively so. "Your Honor, I am not asking you to take either party's unsupported word." Her posture was at once relaxed and unyielding. "Individuals differ in their perceptions and interpretations of events. I am saying that the evidence, taken as a whole, supports Overseer Selius's position in this case."

Phillips found himself more inclined at this point to observe his fellow Adjudicators' reactions than Advocate Chou's. She seemed quite capable of handling herself. Rizlov looked more irritated than when he'd begun. Doriani looked slightly amused.

"Advocate Chou," Rizlov began, steepling his fingers and looking over her head toward the rear wall, "is it not a Planetary Overseer's first duty, according to the Revised Assimilations Code, to bring a rediscovered planet into full Union membership with all due expedition?"

"That is the duty listed first in the Code, your Honor," Chou replied. She sounded as if she wanted to continue, but Rizlov cut her off.

"And Bekh-Nar has been provisional under Selius for how many years?"

Phillips winced at Rizlov's omission of Selius's title. The Senior Adjudicator was a stickler for the forms of respect. The omission was either an intentional slight or an indication of just how upset Rizlov was.

How can the man be so damned petty? Phillips wondered. *Doesn't he care that this is Selius's life he's playing with?* Phillips made a note to pursue the point Rizlov had raised about the Code, to give Chou a chance to elaborate.

Chou looked directly at Rizlov, not rudely, but clearly with no intention of backing down. "*Overseer* Selius has been in charge of Bekh-Nar for twenty-nine years, your Honor."

Phillips was certain he'd heard the emphasis on "Overseer." He saw Doriani nod ever so slightly.

Rizlov's face reddened. "Provisional longer than any other planet. And we are to believe that the *Overseer's* loyalty is entirely with the Union, and not diluted by personal affections?"

"Your Honor," Chou replied, her voice quietly intense in the echoless Chamber, "If you are referring to Overseer Selius's adoption of the Narian Alepha Conn-Lee, I am prepared to submit several statements in evidence related to that matter. The relationship neither weakened nor signified a weakening of the Overseer's primary loyalty."

"Those statements are the holotape recordings of interviews with various Narians and with Security personnel under the Overseer's command?"

"Yes, your Honor. They are listed under 'Supplemental Evidentiary Materials' in my written brief."

Was that in the pre-trial brief? Phillips couldn't remember whether or not he'd read something like that while preparing for this case.

"Subordinates and subjects make such objective witnesses," Rizlov commented, the sarcasm so thick it was almost visible. "And the Overseer's explanation of her failure to protect Councilor Breglum and his aides from a Narian mob? That is corroborated by similarly reliable evidence?"

For just a moment, Phillips thought Chou was going to give in to the anger and frustration she must be feeling. He would have spoken up himself to challenge Rizlov except that it seemed unnecessary. In Phillips's mind, Rizlov had raised no substantive objections, and had only revealed his own bias. If anything, the longer he went on as he had, the more likely Doriani would be to side with Phillips. However, Chou couldn't know that Rizlov spoke more and more for himself alone.

"Your Honor, in addition to the statements examined already in presentations and cross-examination, I do have several eyewitness accounts included in 'Supplemental Evidentiary Materials' that testify to the Overseer's conscientious attempts to protect the Councilor." Her calm, reasonable manner contrasted markedly with Rizlov's own.

"Undoubtedly better sources than the Councilor, who was in the middle of the riot," Rizlov remarked to the room in general. It swallowed his skepticism as it had Chou's earnestness—without a trace. "Are there any other questions for this Advocate?" he asked in a tone that clearly implied an interest in ending the inquiry quickly.

The privilege passed to Phillips, as second-most senior Adjudicator. He wished his head could stop hurting. Why had he forgotten his pain pills this morning? He took a slow breath and said sharply, looking directly at Rizlov, "Yes, I believe there are a few items that should be clarified." Past Rizlov, he saw Doriani studying a list she'd written on her notepad. Her expression was bland, giving nothing away. He turned toward Chou.

"Advocate Chou, you've prepared your case quite thoroughly. I assume your evidence was all gathered according to approved procedures?"

"Yes, your Honor. Each statement was taken twice, by different interviewers, and stress analyzers were employed."

Phillips nodded approvingly. "So the statements in evidence have been verified as being true?"

Chou paused for a moment, as if caught off-guard. "Not precisely, your Honor. They have been verified as being sincere. The witnesses have not lied in the interviews. Statements where dissembling was indicated have been excluded."

Of course, you dolt! Phillips berated himself. *How do I salvage this line of inquiry?* "Umm, of course, of course. And the same applies to the contrary eyewitness evidence?"

"Yes, your Honor." Chou's tone and tentative smile seemed to invite him to go on, but his mind was blank. He couldn't think of where to go with his questions. He had something else to bring up, but he couldn't remember what it was. He glanced down at his notes, but they were indecipherable. *Say something!*

"Thank you very much, Advocate Chou," Phillips said hurriedly. "You have explained your position quite well. I, for one, look forward to examining these corroborative evidentiary statements."

Next to him, Rizlov snorted contemptuously. "Is that it, Adjudicator Phillips?"

He looked at Rizlov and nodded, feeling miserable. Selius's life was on the line, and he'd just weakened her case. "I have no further questions, Senior Adjudicator." *I've slipped worse than I thought.*

Rizlov held his gaze for a moment, then turned toward Kia Doriani. "And you, Adjudicator Doriani?" he asked slowly, each syllable distinct, a challenge.

Phillips watched the junior member of the Triune anxiously. He tried to affect an attitude of calm indifference, all the while hoping fervently that she would assert herself against Rizlov, and make up for his own blunder.

As Phillips watched her, her eyes seemed to shift past Rizlov and focus on him for a moment. A flash of spring green. It was a glance so fleeting, he wasn't sure it had actually happened. But her next words convinced him that it had.

"Yes, indeed, Senior Adjudicator. I too would like very much to examine the Advocate's supplemental evidence." Her face gave nothing away, and her voice expressed only sincere interest, but Phillips felt a small bubble of hopeful laughter rising inside of him.

"No, no," Rizlov said in a pained, patient tone. "Do you have any questions for Advocate Chou?"

"Oh!" Doriani's face broke into an apologetic half-grin. "I'm sorry. Yes, I do have a few questions for the Advocate." Then turning to look down at Chou still standing in the Presentation Circle, its pool of light surrounded by darkness, she asked, "Advocate Chou, we have established that everybody's eyewitnesses believe they are telling the truth. How many witnesses' statements do you have?"

"Twenty-eight, your Honor."

"And how many has your opponent Advocate filed?"

"Five, your Honor," the short, dark Advocate replied.

Rizlov shifted forward as if to speak, but said nothing. Doriani continued.

"All of your witnesses have spent considerable time on Bekh-Nar?"

"Yes, your Honor. Each is either a native or has served there for three years or more."

"And the opposing witnesses?"

"Really, it is not the Advocate's position to evaluate her opponent's evidence!" Rizlov admonished sternly. He sounded as if he just added Doriani to his list of enemies.

"Your pardon, Senior Adjudicator," Doriani replied, red highlights glinting in her hair. "I was just trying to follow up on some questions you have raised earlier. But let us move to another matter," she continued, giving Rizlov no chance to respond. "The question was raised earlier of Overseer's duties under the Revised Assimilations Code. Advocate Chou, is 'expeditious assimilation' an Overseer's only duty?"

Chou shook her head. "No, your Honor. An Overseer is also required to secure the resources of a rediscovered planet for the benefit of all the Union."

That was it! Phillips recognized the argument he'd intended to pursue but had forgotten. His head actually began to feel a little better.

"And those resources include the native inhabitants?"

"That is the standard interpretation, your Honor."

"Would assimilation by destruction of the resources be considered within the framework of the Code?"

Again Chou shook her head, her black hair waving slightly. "Your Honor, such a course has been found acceptable in the past only to prevent a threat to the Union itself."

Phillips was impressed with how clearly and cleanly Doriani brought out her points. At one time, he reflected, he could do so too.

Doriani was pressing on. "And 'secure' in this context has been taken to imply permanence, stability?"

Chou nodded. "Indeed it has, your Honor. Overseer Selius's policy on Bekh-Nar has been to gain reliable, permanent assimilation on the planet without endangering its resources in the process."

Doriani glanced at Rizlov, who was staring at Chou, his brows drawn together in an angry frown. "That is certainly consistent with my interpretation of the Code, Advocate Chou. One final point."

What could this be? Phillips wondered. At this point, it was clear that Doriani had taken Selius's side. The case was over, for all practical purposes. Was she just rubbing it in for his benefit? For Rizlov's? Did she realize that he was on her side?

"There have been some implications during this hearing that outside elements may have been influencing events on Bekh-Nar. Who was in charge of securing Bekh-Nar from extraplanetary interference?"

"Major Urtloew, your Honor. He has served in that capacity throughout Overseer Selius's assignment."

"And the Major's credentials?" Doriani asked mildly.

Where's she going now? Phillips wondered. He saw Rizlov shifting irritably.

"Your Honor, Major Urtloew has the highest recommendations for his position. His previous assignment was as Chief Security Officer for Morin's World."

Morin's World! Phillips gave a start. That had been Kirowa's reference point for locating Seelzar, revealed in their furtive conversation some twenty years ago. As Doriani drew out more information about Urtloew's qualifications, Phillips's mind wandered back to that last night on Wehring's Stopover.

It was as hard now as it had been then for Phillips to fight off his sense of guilt and shame over Kirowa's death. Maybe harder. If only he'd trusted Kirowa, he told himself, and not been so blinded by his suspicion of Rizlov's intrigues!

Phillips's dark study was interrupted by an exclamation from Rizlov.

"Nonsense!" The word was more a loud hiss than a shout. It hung suspended in the still, dark air of the Chamber, drawing everyone's attention.

Rizlov was turned slightly toward Doriani, his right hand clenched tightly and pressing down on the desk top. Doriani was glaring at Rizlov with a cold spark in her eyes. Her lips were pressed together in a thin line. Jarnice Chou stood quite still, her mouth slightly open, her eyes wide with surprise. She seemed to be looking at a spot midway between Doriani and Rizlov.

What have I missed? Phillips wondered frantically.

"A harsh word, Senior Adjudicator," Doriani said in a voice that was almost a whisper but not at all submissive.

Blast my wandering mind! Phillips raged.

"For a harsh fact," Rizlov answered heatedly. "These arguments about surveillance patterns and infiltration by Reversionists are beside the point. And going into this Major Urtloew's experience and training is a waste of time!"

"I was only trying to clear up a claim suggested by Councilor Breglum's Advocate yesterday, Senior Adjudicator." Doriani's tone was icy, barely civil. "If Major Urtloew could be trusted to secure Morin's World from intrusion, he could certainly be trusted to detect any attempts at infiltration of Bekh-Nar by Reversionists."

Rizlov looked in exasperation from Doriani to Chou and

back again. "The situations are different. Morin's World is isolated, and has no indigenous population. This is all irrelevant, anyway. Let's decide this case on the facts, not implied hints of possible accusations!" He pounded his fist on the desk for emphasis, but made a barely audible *thud* on the thick plastalloy.

Phillips almost smiled. The outburst was uncharacteristically blunt even for Rizlov, who was not noted for his tact. He seemed surprised by the junior Adjudicator's opposition, and was not handling the situation well at all. One look at Doriani's knotted jaw muscle and her laser-straight posture told Phillips that only a miracle would get her to side with Rizlov now. Overseer Selius was not going to become one of the deformed fanatic's victims.

Before Chou or Doriani could say anything, Phillips spoke up. "It seems to me, Senior Adjudicator, that we should withhold judgment on this case until we've studied the evidence more thoroughly." Rizlov twisted around as if he'd been struck from behind. "Now sir," Phillips continued in his most reasonable, practical manner, "We owe it to the entire Union to deliberate carefully on these charges. Overseer Selius's career, indeed, her life are at stake here. And Councilor Breglum's accusations deserve serious consideration."

In the prolonged silence that followed, some of the tension in the chamber seemed to dissipate. Phillips could see Doriani's back and shoulders slump into more relaxed lines. Rizlov looked at Phillips steadily, but the anger faded from his face by degrees. *At least I did something right today.* Phillips could hear Chou shift her weight from one foot to the other. She must have been getting quite tired, he realized, having been standing in the Presentation Circle for several hours under circumstances that were difficult at best.

"Very well, Adjudicator Phillips," Rizlov said at last. "We shall 'study the evidence,' although it seems pretty clear that you and Adjudicator Doriani have made up your minds already. Does either of you have further questions for Advocate Chou?" he asked, turning to Doriani, who shook her head slowly, then back to Phillips, who replied with an abrupt "No."

"So." Rizlov gave Phillips a fleeting, humorless smile. He looked down at Jarnice Chou, standing perfectly still now in the lighted Presentation Circle. She returned his gaze bravely. "Advocate Chou, you will please file your 'Supplemental Evidentiary Materials' with the Chief Clerk as you leave. The Triune will consider your arguments and your information and render a decision within twenty days. Please remain in Drinan City and available to answer additional questions until you have been notified of our decision."

"Thank you, your Honor," Chou replied solemnly. "My client and I appreciate the Triune's consideration of our appeal." She bowed formally, then calmly gathered up her evidence and other materials and headed down the long dark aisle toward the Chamber's exit.

Phillips watched the stocky Advocate's orderly departure, wondering how she was able to handle such a heavily charged case so well, her first time before the Triune. Inexperienced or not, her performance had been exemplary.

Not until the door at the far end of the Chamber had closed silently behind Chou did Phillips turn toward his two colleagues. Doriani was slipping the notes she'd made during the days' arguments into the pre-Session brief on Selius's case, a faint smile on her lips. Rizlov was sitting motionless, staring toward the exit doorway with a piece of notepaper crumpled in his left hand.

"Adjudicator Rizlov?" Phillips prodded, his words swallowed quickly by the still air of the Chamber. It was a matter of protocol for the Senior Adjudicator to leave first at the end of a day's hearings.

"Go," Rizlov said without looking left or right. "Don't wait for me."

"As you wish." Phillips rose, followed by Doriani.

"As I wish? Hah!" Rizlov began to laugh quietly. Phillips and Doriani walked slowly down the Chamber's long aisle, neither of them saying a word. "As *I* wish?" The sour laughter followed them all the way to the exit.

Outside the Chamber's door, Doriani turned to Phillips, giving his upper arm a friendly squeeze. "We're going to have to do something about that man," she said, then walked away, leaving Phillips staring openmouthed behind her.

The remembered pressure of Kia's fingers and the image of her warm smile kept Phillips up very late that night. He wasn't sure he understood her any better now than he had at the beginning of the trial, but his confusion was of a much more pleasant sort.

INTERLUDE

"Finally!"

"Yes, this looks good."

"Exactly like Kirowa. The records disappear just over twenty years back."

"And those trips to the Periphery. Nobody vacations out there *that* much, John."

"Even at that, I might have my doubts, but that microcommunicator we found is certainly not Union technology."

"I wondered about that. Awfully careless. Could it be a bit of misdirection?"

"More likely overconfidence, Gen. Didn't think anyone would look. And up until now no one has had any reason to. If we weren't as tenacious as Narrakan sand trackers, no one ever would have."

"Now that we've tracked one down, when do we pounce?"

"This may sound stupid . . ."

"Never!"

". . . But I'd like to continue with tight but *very* discreet surveillance until the Phillips-Rizlov matter finally comes to a head."

"Just to satisfy your curiosity? I've always thought you were more practical than that, John Caulston."

"It's partly curiosity, but practical too. Everyone's very tense right now, very wary. After the explosion, whoever wins, people are likely to relax if they've won and get reckless if they've lost. Whichever side our friend is on, it should be easier for us to make a clean snatch then."

"Aren't you tempted to help out Rizlov?"

"Once I might have been, Gen. Not anymore. Anyway, we're onto something much bigger than Rizlov and Sector politics. Maybe bigger than even deMarnon realizes."

"What do you mean, John?"

"Haven't you wondered why the Council is being so cautious about this search for Seelzar? Why not send a fleet out to do a full-scale sweep for the planet?"

"Well, that could take years."

"Which we've taken anyway."

"*And* a lot more manpower."

"Come on, Gen. The Union has more ships and soldiers than it could possibly need for internal security alone. You know that."

"You're suggesting what, then?"

"I don't know. It's as if the Council is stalling for some reason."

"Hmm. Maybe they want to locate Seelzar without establishing contact with it?"

"And why do you think they'd want to do that? They couldn't be afraid of one planet, could they?"

"Maybe they know something they haven't told us?"

"I'm sure they do."

17. Rude Awakening

The music cube had just played through the first of its six sides, and Phillips was debating the merits of a partial replay and another glass of wine versus going to bed. Bed was winning out. He'd been up since before sunrise dictating opinions on several of the current session's cases, proofing and revising the transcriptions as they came out of his desk unit.

For the last hour or so he had just sat in his softly lighted living room, letting the problems of the day drain away, replacing them with the music and the deep red wine. His thoughts drifted toward Kia Doriani. The reddish highlights in her hair. Her cool green eyes.

The chair's massage system gently eased his tense muscles. He felt he could have stayed that way forever, but he had another day's worth of work still waiting in his office. He knew that if he didn't get enough sleep, tomorrow would be even longer than today. Besides, he suddenly realized in the aftermath of the music how late it really was. The faint background sounds that even his secluded residential area normally produced had ceased—everyone else had retired for the night.

He could remember a time when he was able to work forty hours or more at a stretch without tiring. Not any more. His most recent rejuvenation had been a mere thirty days ago, and already his stamina had dropped to near pretreatment levels.

With an effort, he turned to look at the pale blue light-sculpture clock floating in the corner to his right. He willed his tired eyes to focus on the dimly glowing projection until its configuration became clear. One-thirty. "One-thirty?" he mumbled. "How did it get to be so late?" he asked the clock accusingly, but it didn't answer. It just kept pulsing the seconds away, shifting its minutes element every sixty pulses, its hours element every 3600.

Phillips watched the clock's regular, subtle movements for a while. He started drifting into the borderlands of sleep, marveling fuzzily that the seconds, minutes, and hours of Old Earth had followed humankind to the stars. The days, months and years might differ from one planet to the next, but the little, immediate pieces of time stayed comfortably the same. He smiled and began to nod off.

"Adjudicator Phillips, a visitor calls." The voice was sharp and penetrating but not overly loud.

"Adjudicator Phillips, a visitor calls." The voice was individually synthesized to awaken Phillips or to attract his attention without startling him. He awoke at its third announcement and quickly stumbled over to a metal-framed hologram of a snowy forest scene, recessed partway into the wall to the right of the blue light-clock.

"Entrance monitor, visual and audio receive," he said distinctly, and the forest was replaced by a face-on view of a woman wearing the plain silver-gray uniform of the Sector Security Forces, a colonel's insignia on the tight collar. Her hair was cut short, as prescribed for SecFor personnel regardless of gender. Its deep blue-black hue contrasted sharply with her pale skin. Her eyes were nearly as dark as her hair. She looked vaguely familiar to Phillips.

The colonel was standing with a stiffly erect posture, looking directly at the front door camera. Her expression was at once official and relaxed. *Professional but pleasant*, Phillips thought, all the while wondering where he'd seen her before. It disturbed him that he could not remember clearly someone of such a high rank and with such a striking appearance.

"Audio transmit," he said, then continued, "Who are you and what do you want?" He hoped he sounded more alert than he felt.

"Adjudicator Phillips?" Her voice was pitched quite low for a woman. "I am Deputy Security Director Echeverria. I apologize for disturbing you at such an hour, but Director Malvasian insisted that time was of the essence." The woman cast a quick glance to either side, as if expecting to see someone lurking in the darkness. "May I come in, please? I assure you this is an urgent matter."

Phillips nodded to himself. Of course he'd seen her before. This was Felice Echeverria, General Malvasian's very able second-in-command. She was around fifty years old, but looked more like thirty. Like Malvasian, she had been granted rejuvenation status for outstanding service to the Interstellar Union. Unlike him, she had accepted it as an honor.

"Yes, certainly. Come in." Phillips pressed the lower right-hand corner of the monitor's metal frame, causing the front doorway to desolidify momentarily.

Echeverria stepped forward, leaving the camera's field of

view. The moment she passed through the door, it reformed behind her. She was in a small foyer with four doorless walls on which hung several paintings in shades of white, blue and gray—a stormy seascape, a range of white-capped mountains, and a flat, sun-drenched snow field among others.

One of the paintings on the wall to her left slid aside to reveal a small scanning screen and, underneath it, a narrow metal-rimmed slot. Phillips spoke to her through a concealed speaker. "I hope you will forgive my caution, Colonel Echeverria, but this is, as you observed, an unusual hour for a visit. Please press your right palm against the screen and place your identicard into the slot. Merely a formality, you understand."

Triune Adjudicator or not, he saw no reason to be rude to SecFor's second-in-command, if that's who she was. But he also didn't see any reason to simply take her word for it. No harm in checking. Besides, if she found the security measures a little bothersome, that might balance the inconvenience to himself of her call this late, unannounced.

In less than a second, the palm print and identicard number were transmitted to the Sector's personnel computers, where they were checked independently and together. The computers sent a signal back to Phillips's residential unit, and a green light blinked on and off in the center of his living-room monitor.

The computer check confirmed the Colonel's identity. Phillips realized that a clever person could fool the system, given access to Security's files, but he could think of no reason for anyone to go to the trouble. Any unwanted visitors, from assassins to those seeking personal favors, would find countless better times and places to approach him. He knew his home's security was minimal compared to the fortress Rizlov lived in, but the only place where he was safer from intrusion or attack was the Government Center itself. So he wasn't particularly worried that the Colonel could be a sinister impostor.

Beside, the foyer's hidden scanners had detected no weapons on her person.

There might well be people who would like to see Phillips

dead, but it didn't seem as if his current visitor was one of them.

Two seconds after Echeverria had inserted her card, it popped back out and she pocketed it.

"Thank you, Colonel," Phillips said, and pressed twice on the lower right-hand corner of the monitor's frame. The wall of the foyer opposite the outside entrance faded away, pictures and all, revealing a short hallway, at the end of which was a fragile-looking spiral staircase leading upward and two open archways, one to either side.

With a verbal command, Phillips transformed the monitor back into the forest hologram. He brought up the room's lighting and called out, "Come, come, Colonel. The night isn't getting any younger."

And neither am I, he thought irritably, squinting slightly in the brighter light. Echeverria stepped briskly through the archway on her right, into the living room. The foyer's inner wall solidified behind her. She stood there for a moment, as if sizing up the room and its occupant.

Phillips gestured to a chair next to the one he'd been relaxing in. "Have a seat, Colonel, and tell me what's so urgent that it couldn't wait for the sun to rise."

"Thank you, sir." Though her voice was low, the words came out crisply, with little borders around each one. It sounded to Phillips not so much harsh as very military, very controlled. Her movements were precise and economical as she walked over to the chair and sat down.

Phillips returned to his own chair. He sat, then gave a sudden start. Embarrassed, he switched off the chair's massage system and turned an inquiring glance toward Echeverria, now seated straight-backed in the chair facing his on the left.

"Wouldn't a call have been quicker?" he asked bluntly, still a bit unsettled.

"It would, sir, but General Malvasian insisted that I contact you in person. Even the secure communications channels can be intercepted. Without coding and scrambling, it's too risky." She paused for a moment. "The General has uncovered a threat to the stability of the Union in this Sector,

Adjudicator Phillips. The plot originates at the highest levels of Sector government."

She said it quietly, calmly, with no apparent emotion. Phillips searched her face for some reaction or attitude, but found nothing. He hadn't really expected to. Nobody rose to a position like hers without being exceptionally self-contained. Of course she had feelings—she would just never let anyone else know what they were.

He decided to ask the Colonel the obvious question. "Why come to me with this? This sounds like a purely Sec-For matter." His unasked question was, *Why not go to Rizlov?* He thought he knew the answer to that one.

"Because," she answered without hesitation, "General Malvasian has reason to believe that you are one of the targets of the plot."

"Indeed. And what am I supposed to do about this?"

"The General wishes to confer with you on the appropriate course of action to protect you and to thwart the conspiracy."

Phillips was impressed by Echeverria's disinterested treatment of such a matter. Even without the insignia and in civilian clothes, she would have stood out as Security. Still, he couldn't help wishing that she would unbend a little, at least volunteer more factual information. One brief answer per question was a plodding pace. He glanced at the pulsing clock. Nearly three o'clock.

"Why didn't General Malvasian come here himself?"

Echeverria leaned toward him and her voice almost took on a hint of concern. "He couldn't take the risk, sir. He has personally taken charge of security for Overseer Selius. She was the source for much of his information and is herself in considerable danger."

Phillips sighed deeply and rose to his feet. He was alert now, but still very tired. "I suppose you'd better take me to him then, Colonel."

Echeverria stood up quickly. "That's what the General was hoping you'd say, sir. Can I help you with anything to get ready?"

"No," Phillips said with a thin smile, wondering if he looked *that* old. "I'm as ready as I'm going to be. I just have to close up the house." He went over to the forest scene, pressed on the frame in three places, and said "All systems, full security." He then turned to Echeverria and said "Let's go."

He led the way, the doorways opening before him and reforming closely behind Echeverria. There was no floater waiting on the street in front of the house.

"It's around the corner to the right," the Colonel said quietly in response to Phillips's inquiring glance. "One moment, though." She kneeled down and reached under a shrub growing near the front door. "Now we can go," she said, hefting an energy pistol in her right hand.

He let her take the lead, and she moved steadily but cautiously down the walk to the street, where she paused momentarily, surveying the shadows along and on either side of the empty plasticrete roadway. Then she hurried on, not pausing again until they neared her floater, a dull gray model with Security's pair of silver stripes running around its circumference. There she again paused, motioning Phillips to remain where he was while she quickly ran along the sidewalk to the front of the vehicle, then jumped out to check the floater's street side. Then she hit the palm lock and waved Phillips into the floater as the opaque bubble lifted up on its back hinge.

Once they were both inside the floater, Echeverria seemed to relax. She keyed in some coordinates on the control unit and the vehicle's sudden acceleration pushed her and Phillips strongly backward in their seats. "We'll be there in about thirty minutes, sir," she said to Phillips, then turned her attention back to the scanning screen on the driver's side.

"Where exactly are we going, Colonel?" Phillips had assumed they'd be going to SecFor headquarters, but that was only ten or fifteen minutes away at even moderate speed.

"It's one of the special Security Compounds we maintain for sensitive cases, sir. They were built by former Director Caulston. Information about them isn't officially classified, but few people are aware that they exist, and even fewer know where they are. Much more secure than the Detention Center." Echeverria was half-turned toward Phillips, her attention divided between him and the vehicle's scanner. "The

Compound we're heading for is within the Baelric Forest, just inside the edge nearest the city."

"But that's nearly one hundred twenty kilometers!" Phillips exclaimed. He hadn't realized the floater was going *that* fast.

Echeverria nodded. "A little over, actually. It's one of our more remote locations."

Phillips settled back in his seat, leaving the Colonel to monitor their progress while he pondered the situation. As odd as it sounded, it made sense. The compounds had probably been constructed by the previous Security Director to facilitate prisoner abuse and illegal detention of political opponents—before he had been removed from office for unspecified offenses against the Union, Caulston's zealotry and intolerance had become legendary. Rizlov seemed mild by comparison. Whatever their original function, however, the compounds would serve Malvasian's purpose equally well. The Detention Center was immune to outside attack and escape-proof for an unaided prisoner, but a person with connections could easily locate and eliminate one of its inmates. They would have to be the right connections, of course, but if Rizlov were involved, the Detention Center would be no protection and for a large payoff, plenty of people would take the chance.

But with one of these isolated Compounds, Malvasian could much more easily monitor and control access to Overseer Selius. Even if Rizlov found out where she was being held, he would have little chance to get at her. And the more he thought about it, the more Phillips came to believe that Rizlov was behind the threat that Malvasian had discovered, and that Selius must have some information damaging to the Senior Adjudicator.

Why else would Rizlov have been so adamantly opposed to leniency for Selius? Even his normally conservative, authoritarian outlook couldn't explain his almost irrational hostility toward her and her counselor. Then too, who but someone of Rizlov's status and power could pose a threat to Phillips and Selius? A Triune Adjudicator and a Planetary Overseer weren't likely targets for small-time conspirators.

Phillips stared at the dim gray bubble curving over his

head. He wondered what the plain outside would look like, faintly lighted by the smaller of Drinan IV's two moons, now in half-phase. It was a sparsely settled area, he knew, with neither industry nor agriculture to draw people. The large farming operations were to the south and east of the city, with its heavy industry concentrated in the near northern districts. Out here to the west of Drinan there were a few communications and power relay stations, and little else.

Many years ago, Phillips had on a whim taken a trip across the Western Plain to the Baelric Forest. He couldn't remember why, although he supposed it had been to clear his mind and get some breathing space beyond the confines of the city. Then, in broad daylight, the plain had been a sea of faded yellow grasses, broken occasionally by islands of low tan scrub. Not really what he would call scenic. At night, traveling at nearly 250 kilometers per hour, he was mildly curious as to whether the terrain would look more tranquil or just more boring. He guessed the latter. Just scrub and grasses and grasses and scrub.

His head gave a minute jerk, and he snapped his attention back from his vague reverie, abashed that he had begun to nod off for the second time that night. In the faint red and yellow lights of the instrument panel, he could see that Colonel Echeverria's attention was still focused on the 360-degree scanner screen. Phillips dismissed Echeverria's behavior as habitual professional caution, no doubt keeping an eye out for any mysterious followers they might have acquired.

Although he didn't really believe there was any immediate danger, Phillips had to admit that the Colonel's and Malvasian's precautions were reasonable. Aldon Rizlov was a formidable opponent—clever, powerful and unscrupulous. Malvasian would need all the help he could get to stop whatever plot Rizlov had in mind.

Ultimately, the Central Council might well have to be called upon to intervene, and General Malvasian would very much benefit from having a Triune Adjudicator on his side. That was the crux of the matter from Phillips's point of view.

He was not particularly worried about his own or Lanya Selius's physical safety—he was confident that Malvasian could counter anything Rizlov might try in that direction. He was much less certain that the General could make a strong enough case against the Senior Adjudicator to convince the Central Council to act. And without such action, Rizlov would remain a threat to himself, Selius, Malvasian, and anyone else who opposed him.

Phillips rocked forward in his seat as the floater suddenly slowed. He caught at the armrests reflexively and tensed his legs.

"Sorry, sir. I should have warned you," Echeverria said without looking at him. "I programmed the floater for minimum trip time, so the deceleration is rather abrupt."

Phillips could feel the floater turn sharply to the left as it came to a near stop. A moment later all movement ceased and Echeverria raised the vehicle's bubble top. Outside it seemed at first absolutely dark, but as Phillips's eyes adjusted, he could make out faint patches of moonlight on the ground. Looking up, he saw pale splotches of silver in a pitch-black sky. He was puzzled briefly, then realized that they were under the dense canopy of the Baelric Forest, and the great trees were blocking out all but a few errant rays from Drinan IV's small moon.

He began to see their immediate surroundings in more detail. They were parked next to another SecFor floater on a small two-floater pad near the base of an enormous tree. Ten men could not have linked arms around its mottled and lumpy trunk.

"Well, Colonel, where's the compound?" Phillips asked after he had gotten out of the floater and looked around. All he could see was the floater, the slick dark pad on which it rested, and a suggestion of a path that must have led back through the thick forest growth to the main highway.

"Come this way and I'll show you," she said, walking over to the nearby tree. She was pulling on a pair of thin gloves.

Phillips wondered if they were going to have to climb the tree. It would be consistent with the rest of the night's bizarre doings.

Phillips joined her and they went around to the side of the tree opposite the floater and pad. There she pressed on a nondescript bump of bark and stood facing the tree, motioning Phillips to stand beside her. From somewhere nearby a man's voice spoke softly, "Identity and purpose, please."

"Deputy Director Echeverria and Triune Adjudicator Phillips to confer with Overseer Selius," Echeverria said to the tree.

"Very well, you may enter." The reply took longer than Phillips expected. He guessed that they had some system of verification other than a direct link to the government's central computers, probably to keep the operation more discreet.

He was about to ask the Colonel where they were going next when the ground they were standing on began to sink.

"The compound is entirely underground," Echeverria explained.

As Phillips's head dropped below ground level, a cover slid into place above him and the tube down which they were traveling began to glow, getting brighter as they descended. They hadn't gone down very far before they came to a gentle stop, but there was enough time for a small question to take shape in Phillips's mind. *Why did she say we were here to talk to Selius, and not Malvasian?*

He was about to ask Echeverria his question when a portion of the tube in front of them slid aside. They stepped out into what looked to be a reception area. A small desk faced them from the middle of the square room and there was a single door panel in the middle of each of the other three walls.

A large, well-muscled young man in Security gray rose from behind the desk and saluted smartly. Echeverria returned the salute perfunctorily and Phillips nodded casually. The young man—a captain judging by the insignia on his collar—relaxed and smiled pleasantly.

"Welcome to Compound Four, Colonel Echeverria, Adjudicator Phillips." His voice was the same soft one that had spoken to them aboveground. It was a nice voice, Phillips thought, with an unmilitary warmth to it. And the last words it would ever say had been Phillips's name.

The Captain had just taken a step forward, perhaps to lead

the visitors to Overseer Selius, perhaps to offer them some refreshments. Then it happened.

Phillips had gotten as far in his reply as "Thank you, Captain," when the young man stopped. His friendly expression twisted into an agonized grimace. He made a convulsive grab for his chest, then fell sideways across the desk and from there to the floor.

Phillips could only stare, numb and speechless, as the Captain came to rest on his back, his eyes startled wide open by death, a two-centimeter hole burned into his chest.

"What?..." He turned to Echeverria for an answer, and found the beginnings of one in the cold expression on her face and the energy pistol pointed at his midsection.

"It couldn't be helped. Captain Arvash was a very capable man and completely loyal to Director Malvasian."

Phillips glanced back toward the lift tube's doorway.

"I would rather not kill you too, sir," Echeverria said, each word so distinct, so deliberate. "But I will if I have to." She gestured with the gun. "Let's go find the rest of the staff, then see about Overseer Selius."

18. The Old Man in Action

With some reluctance, Grestahk Malvasian left his office in the Government Complex. Night had long since fallen over the city, but the problems of the day were still buzzing insistently in his mind. As he took the lift tube down to the parking level, he realized he wouldn't sleep for some hours to come, as much as he might need to.

For the past few weeks, General Malvasian had been busier than he had been for several years, and he loved every minute of it.

In addition to his normal duties, including overseeing the activities of his immediate subordinates, he had been dividing his time between checking on the Phillips-Reversionist connection suggested by Rizlov and investigating Rizlov himself. It meant a hectic schedule, more than a little subterfuge, and an average of four hours of sleep per night. He would just as soon have slept at the office, but he didn't want to call more attention to himself than necessary. Not even his top aides knew of his extracurricular projects.

His floater was not alone on the ground-level parking ramp. Still, he was somewhat surprised at how little company it had. He had always thought of Security as a round-the-clock operation rather than something that waxed and waned with the sun.

But then, he told himself, *the entire Sector is my concern, and it's always midday somewhere on every planet*. Even here at the Sector's center, nearly everyone else operated strictly by local time.

As he stepped into his vehicle, the General decided that he preferred being potentially "on" all the time.

The bubble top closed. Malvasian ran his eyes over the control console and the communications unit. A touch of his hand would put him in contact with Security personnel on any inhabited planet in the Sector. His informal connections, though less numerous, were even more widespread. He wondered how surprised Senior Adjudicator Rizlov would be if he knew what "his" Director of Security had been up to, and the conclusions he had drawn.

The sturdy old pro eased back into his seat with a sigh, punched in the coordinates for home, and smiled with satisfaction at the buildings flashing past the one-way surface of his floater's bubble.

It usually took less than twenty minutes to get from his office to his home, but Malvasian's nature and his responsibilities forced him to remain accessible even during that brief trip. The majority of messages coming into his office were routinely screened by his staff before reaching his desk, and could wait for his return if he was out. But those prefaced with a special coded signal came directly to his desk comm unit.

When he was not in his office, "Director Only" messages were routed automatically to his home and his floater. They were stored at each location for fifteen minutes, then erased. Only his palm print and password could release a "Director Only" message from his comm units' storage, and not even he could prevent its erasure.

The system worked well. Whenever a top-priority message arrived, the General's belt communicator received a special high-pitched signal. He was almost always close enough to one of his comm units to retrieve the message before it vanished. And fifteen minutes wasn't enough time for anyone to break the units' security.

It worked well, but it was seldom used, so it was always something of a surprise when the signal went off. Few people knew the proper code for the system, and those few resorted to it rarely.

Leaving the city's crowded center, Malvasian watched the buildings speed by a little faster as they began to thin out. He glanced down at the comm unit in the center of the floater's control console with a feeling akin to affection. It kept him in touch with key I.U. personnel in his Sector. It maintained contact between himself and the Security Directors of the other Sectors. It even allowed a small number of unofficial sources to reach him, and vice versa, when the need arose.

It *beeped* at him.

Surprised or not, he reacted quickly, pressing his left palm onto the identiscreen and tapping in the eight-character code for message release. It was a spoken message, and the General recognized the voice immediately, despite its strained tone.

"Director Malvasian, this is Senior Adjudicator Rizlov," *How like the man*, he thought wryly. *Insist on that full title.* "I have information that one of your top people is working for the Reversionists. We need to discuss this in person, tonight. Without calling attention to our meeting. I'll be at Power Station Six from midnight until one o'clock, two hundred meters south of the main gate. I'm trusting your assurance that this channel is secure."

How intriguing. Malvasian stared at the comm unit's speaker for some time after it had gone silent. *If he can accuse Phillips, he just might be serious about this charge too*. The Security Director didn't for a moment believe Rizlov's allegation, but he wasn't so sure whether or not the Senior Adjudicator himself did.

Malvasian brought his floater to a stop on the side of the roadway on the southern outskirts of the city. It was nearly midnight. Only one vehicle passed by as he sat, lights off and eyes closed, weighing the possibilities. After gnawing at the problem for a while, he concluded that he had no real choice. Not if he meant to keep playing the game. He had to meet Rizlov to maintain his cover. Either that or confront the Senior Adjudicator with charges of his own.

Another floater sped by, a large transport heading south toward the agricultural processing centers. The General shook his head slowly. No, he wasn't ready to challenge Rizlov yet. He would have to get to Power Station Six before one o'clock. *Besides*, he thought, *maybe I'll learn something I can really use*.

His mind made up, Malvasian canceled his original destination code and punched in a new one. Instead of continuing southward to his home on the northern fringes of the farming district, he spun his floater through a wide, flat U-turn and headed back toward the city. He stayed well below his floater's maximum speed, but few civilian vehicles could or would have matched him as he sped along the belt highway skirting Drinan City.

East, northeast, then north he raced. He glanced occasionally at the ETA readout, reassuring himself that he had a few minutes to spare, give or take a few seconds. The General ignored the residential and commercial buildings along his route, mostly dark now anyway. He focused his attention instead on Rizlov, and tried to anticipate what the man had come up with this time.

Power Station Six was located in the oldest section of the industrial zone to the north and northeast of the city. Contrary to the usual pattern, industrial development around Drinan City had proceeded inward from distant regions rather than outward from the city's center. As a consequence, the obsolescent and deteriorating facilities were on the outer fringes of the zone, with the efficient modern plants in closer. The perimeter highway had followed, shifting toward the city a stage or two behind the inward development.

Malvasian had always wondered why the Sector capital had adopted this reversal of the normal pattern of expansion and decay. In lighter moments, he sometimes imagined a future when the inward development progressed so far that it squeezed itself out of existence at the exact center of the city. What would be the result? A socioindustrial black hole? An economic singularity?

The buildings Malvasian saw as he entered the industrial zone were heavy, blocky creatures, dull, no longer in the shiny bloom of youth but still completely functional. Beyond them, outward, he knew, things became worse by perceptible stages. The stages were marked off by swaths of plasticrete that used to be the main highway and were now secondary or tertiary roadways or worse.

His floater swerved off the newest highway and down an exit ramp. This side road headed roughly northeast away from the city, Malvasian recalled. Very close to where it ended, trailing off into marshy wastes, was Power Station Six, in the last, outermost layer of industrial decay, where the once main highway had probably become little more than a rubble-strewn alley.

The road began to narrow. There was no street lighting and only an occasional gleam of light through a window suggested that the area wasn't completely abandoned. The buildings edged in closer, seeming almost to lean over the floater as it passed, moving more slowly now. A few buildings even straddled the road, creating short but pitch-black tunnels that sight alone couldn't penetrate. The floater dodged obstacles detectable by radar and infrared sensors. Malvasian left its powerful spotlight off. He could see no reason to advertise his presence, and could think of many not to.

The road came more and more to resemble a tunnel. Buildings on either side reached out to each other with conveyors, conduits, and enclosed walkways, weaving a ceiling beneath which the General's vehicle proceeded with increasing caution among fallen girders and half-cleared piles of rubble.

Rizlov's certainly picked an out-of-the-way spot for a meeting, he thought with sarcastic admiration, straining to see ahead through the unlit tangle. *I wonder if I'm even going to be able to find him in this mess.*

Malvasian glanced briefly at the floater's clock. Dim red numerals showed that it was nearly one. He called up a map of the area to be superimposed on the scanning screen. Very close now. No sign of another floater operating nearby. He came to an intersection cleared of debris and turned right. The street here was more open, and the General very quickly came to a high security barrier which ran along the road on his left. According to his floater's instruments, the barrier was energized. He had found Power Station Six.

The station was the last of the city's original fission generators. It was an immense facility, producing huge amounts of electricity for residential and industrial use. But its technology was fragile, vulnerable to even unsophisticated saboteurs. Thus the security barrier, stretching far ahead into the darkness.

Malvasian guessed that the station was the only thing in this area still serving its original purpose and still valuable to Drinan. Yet even here the street was unlighted, and the buildings across from the security barrier were as bad as anything he'd seen—dark, abandoned, some beginning to lean or crumble.

A few hundred meters down the street, Malvasian came upon a break in the smooth gray wall. A massive gate ten meters wide was recessed slightly from the barrier's surface, its shiny black a contrast to the barrier's dull gray.

"Main gate," Rizlov had said. As far as Malvasian knew, this was the *only* gate to the plant. The operation of these old plants had been largely automated, so the bulk of traffic into the place was to supply fuel and spare parts and to remove spent fuel and other "hot" materials. No need to provide a human-sized employees' gate; the few on-call emergency personnel could use the main gate too.

So. Main gate, but no sign of Rizlov further down the street. Malvasian slowed his vehicle to a crawl. Had Rizlov changed his mind and not shown up, or had he left already? The security barrier continued for nearly five hundred meters beyond the gate. A narrow walkway ran beside it, separating it from the street. Malvasian could see well enough on this stretch of road, wide as it was and open to the sky, but there was nothing to be seen. Street and walkway ran largely unobstructed at least as far as the end of the wall.

The General's scanner confirmed his eyes' message: Rizlov wasn't there.

Malvasian decided to drive as far as the corner of the barrier to see if Rizlov had parked out of sight down there. *Maybe he meant five hundred meters instead of two hundred, or misjudged the distance*, he told himself, not believing a word of it.

He had gone about half the distance from the gate to the corner when he noticed a faint blip on his scanner. He stopped his floater immediately, next to a pile of rubble from a partially collapsed building. A quick check showed the signal to be the characteristic radio "white noise" leakage from an operating floater's power plant. It was about fifty meters ahead and to the right—in an alley across the street from the power station.

"A low profile is one thing, but this is ridiculous," the General muttered. "Nothing drives this road but station transports every week or so, and even they probably don't come out here this late at night."

Malvasian set his communicator for tight beam transmission. "Sir, this is Malvasian. I'm alone. No one followed me and there's no one else on the street. Let's talk."

There was no reply. The floater on his screen stayed put.

"I repeat. This is Malvasian. I have not been followed. Please respond if you are receiving my message."

Still no answer. Malvasian turned off his comm unit and stared at the scanner screen. He knew the signal could penetrate the stone and metal of the nearby buildings and debris. If Rizlov were in his floater and able to respond, he surely would have done so by now. But why would he have left his floater? Was it possible that his suspicions had been correct, and that whoever he was going to accuse had followed him here, had gotten to him before Malvasian arrived?

The General had not survived nearly fifty years in his profession by being foolhardy. In situations with little to gain and much to lose, he usually listened to the tiny voice whispering in his ear, "Better safe than sorry." He respected the voice's judgment. It had been around as long as he had.

Working quickly, he recorded two brief messages for Rizlov and set his comm unit to transmit them alternately at slightly varying intervals. Then he programmed into his floater's control module a series of simple movements, to be overridden only by a homing signal from his belt communicator. He removed his energy pistol from its charging socket under the driver's seat and hooked it into his belt. The last thing he did before leaving was to set the floater's defensive shield to maximum power. Then he raised the bubble partway and slipped out the passenger's side.

He was in the shadow of the mound of rusting metal beams and cracked stone blocks near which he had parked. As soon as the bubble resealed itself, the floater began to move forward toward the alley where Rizlov's vehicle, or somebody's, waited. Malvasian crouched silently for a moment, listening, then half-trotted around the pile of rubble and into the shelter of the remaining portion of the building.

Somehow he had to cover the fifty meters to the alley without being seen by whoever might be watching for him. He wasted no time worrying. If his floater didn't draw sufficient attention to itself, he'd have to improvise. He scrambled through a partially blocked hallway to the rear of the ruined structure.

The back third of the building was intact. Malvasian reached a corridor paralleling the street out front and turned to his left. He ran past a series of empty rooms. At another time he might have tried to reconstruct their functions, imagining them bustling with activity as they must have been decades ago. Now, he only had eyes for the side door at the end of the corridor. It should open onto an alley separated by one building from Rizlov's floater. He hoped it wasn't locked or blocked shut.

When he reached the door, he paused briefly with his ear to its surface, but he could hear nothing. He peered through the door's smudged oval window. The alley seemed bright by comparison with the dark corridor behind him, and he could see so sign of danger. The rubble was scattered in piles too small to conceal a person. Still, he drew his pistol and set the beam for moderate dispersion before testing the door.

Whatever mechanism had once held it secure had long since crumbled. Malvasian pushed the door cautiously and, after a momentary catch, he heard a faint *snap* and it swung open. He crouched just inside the doorway, but he knew he couldn't wait very long. When nothing happened after five slow breaths, the General tensed himself, then sprang through the door and threw himself against the wall of the opposing building.

His quick dash had left a clear trail of footprints in the dust of the alley, but that same dust had muffled the sound. It was a good trade-off, he realized, glancing up and down the alley. Long-term detection was unimportant; short-term surprise was his concern.

Safe for the moment, he considered his next move. By now his own floater should have reached the mouth of the next alley. If his suspicions were correct, whoever was waiting wouldn't be fooled for too long by the recorded messages. And if Rizlov were there, Malvasian would have to appear quickly to allay the Senior Adjudicator's own suspicions.

The General had intended to work his way through the next building, but he could see no easy entrance to it on this side, and there was no telling how long it would take him to get through it once he was inside. The narrow street that ran behind this row of buildings offered a faster, if more open route. He decided the risk was worth taking.

At the end of the alley, he crouched low and peered around the corner of the building. Some thirty meters away, he could make out the dark gap of the next alley. A tumbled stack of large containers rested against the base of the building near the far corner, providing cover for himself and anyone waiting down there. But their attention ought to be directed at the other end of the alley, at least for a little while longer, he thought.

He kept low, below the level of the windows along the back of the building, and moved as quietly as his training had taught him. *Any minute now they'll realize something's wrong*. The thought surprised him a little. He hadn't consciously ruled out the possibility that it was Rizlov down there, but apparently something in his subconscious had. Or perhaps it was the small voice in his ear, since this was certainly the safer decision to act upon.

He reached the mound of containers and paused. They were large plastic barrels that had fallen when their metal shelving had rusted and collapsed. Malvasian crept around them as stealthily as he could until he could see the other side. The barrels had piled up against the building, but several had rolled away from the main stack and lay like dark boulders in the street and scattered across the mouth of the alley.

From his present position, he could see only a few meters into the alley. There was no one around, and the strange floater must have been further in, away from this end.

Oh, well, the General sighed mentally. *Even if they spot me, maybe they'll mistake me for one of the barrels.* With that thought to encourage him, he continued to edge around the pile until he was at the entrance to the alley. He hunkered down behind two barrels, one upright and one on its side, and peered between them. His eyes had dark-adapted to their maximum by now, and he was able to see the length of the alley.

At the far end, about sixty meters away, stood his own floater, idling in a barely audible hum, its defensive shield invisible. Thirty meters closer sat the second floater, its engine silent. It was somewhat larger than the average two-passenger model, a little more elongated, with the insignia of the Triune—three interlocking rings—emblazoned on its opaque bubble.

It looked like Rizlov's personal vehicle; therefore, Malvasian knew it was a fake. As obsessed as he was with secrecy, the last thing Rizlov would do was to take a floater identifiably his own to this meeting.

However, someone wanting to convince Malvasian that Rizlov was here might use just such a vehicle. Someone not expecting the General to be so suspicious. Someone like the two men crouching behind piles of barrels and rocks, one on each side of the alley. They were four or five meters on

Malvasian's side of the suspicious floater, their backs to him. And they were apparently becoming impatient, nervous, or both.

"Jarrett!" the man on the left whispered sharply. "It's, nearly one-thirty. We can't wait much longer."

The voice sounded vaguely familiar to the General.

"Shut up!" the other hissed, equally audibly. "His floater's got audio sensors, you know."

That one too. Ah yes. Malvasian nodded grimly. Barton Jarrett—a Security captain on special assignment to the Triune. The other must be Loren Roehrdanz, a sergeant under Jarrett's command. Malvasian made it a point to know his personnel. He was already mentally revamping Security's screening procedures.

"They won't be on—he's still trying the radio," Roehrdanz whispered a little more quietly. "Besides, we're pushing the timetable here. Rizlov insisted we get the General before Echeverria reaches Phillips."

That brought a sudden frown to Malvasian's face. He was not exactly stunned that Rizlov would plot something against Phillips, nor that Echeverria was involved—he'd suspected the nature of her loyalties for some time. But he hadn't expected to be on the Adjudicator's enemies list himself, and he was surprised at the deadly directness of the scheme. He'd been looking for something more along the line of political ostracism.

"You don't have to remind me about the damn timetable. If he'd just get the hell out of his floater, we could finish up here." Jarrett paused for a moment to pick up something from the ground. Malvasian couldn't see what it was. "I'm going to signal Carinan to use the disruptor."

The General didn't recognize this third name. He smiled in sour satisfaction that they'd had to recruit at least one conspirator from outside the Security Forces. Now, what to do about it? Carinan must be in Rizlov's floater, and the floater would have to be neutralized first. Whether or not the disruptor was powerful enough to overcome his own floater's defensive shield, it would easily eliminate any unshielded Security Directors it might be aimed at. Jarrett and Roehrdanz would have to wait.

Rizlov's floater had had no defensive shield up when Malvasian first noticed it on his screen. The General guessed that its shield had remained off. If not, the shield was certainly down now, since firing a disruptor from inside an operating shield would only destroy whatever was inside the shield, in this case Rizlov's floater and Carinan.

Malvasian heard Jarrett giving the order to Carinan as he set his own energy pistol to its narrowest beam. A floater would be crippled or destroyed by a single shot, if that shot penetrated to the core of the power plant. Even a microthin hole would do the job. You just had to find an unshielded floater and know where to aim.

With professional detachment, Malvasian raised himself slightly and rested his pistol on the fallen barrel in front of him. He held it firmly in both hands, sighted carefully down its length, and pressed the firing stud. A pale thread of energy sprang from the gun, thinner than a hair and nearly invisible. It touched a spot on the rear of Rizlov's floater, paused for a millisecond at the metal skin, then bored through to the power plant. It took perhaps a tenth of a second for the beam to penetrate the power plant's heavy metal casing.

Almost as soon as he'd fired, Malvasian was diving toward the shelter of the wall on his left. The explosion wasn't deafening, but it was loud enough to hurt, and the cloud of metal fragments and flaming debris that came flying out of the alley would have been impossible to dodge. Several chunks of metal sliced into the barrels behind which Malvasian had been hiding, nearly toppling the one and starting the other rolling slowly into the street. Dark thick liquid oozed out of the gashes, adding a sickly sweet odor to the acrid heat of the burning floater.

The General stood slowly and brushed some of the dirt and dust off his uniform. Then he glanced cautiously around the corner. The alley was filled with thin smoke and quickly cooling embers. Where Rizlov's floater had been was now a glowing mass of metal—the base and the heavier supporting struts had resisted being blown away, only to melt in the brief but intense secondary heat release from the disintegrating power plant.

Of Carinan there was not a trace.

Peering through the darkness and the smoke, Malvasian reset his pistol for maximum dispersion.

Roehrdanz and Jarrett were still behind their sheltering piles of debris, which had remained largely intact. Roehrdanz lay motionless and Jarrett was coughing and trying unsuccessfully to sit up. Malvasian looked up the walls of the alley, but could see no sign of anyone on the edges of the roofs or in the window openings. He stepped back and surveyed the street back the way he had come and ahead past the alley. There was no one.

A dull *bump* drew his attention to the far side of the street, but it was just the overturned barrel coming to rest against the side of the building. Nothing else was moving. Except for the faint hum of his floater, everything was quiet.

He sent the homing signal to his floater and waited as it moved tentatively into the alley. It sensed the barrier of the still smoldering wreckage and backed out to seek another route. Satisfied that it would reach him in a few minutes, Malvasian turned his attention to the two conspirators in the alley.

Jarrett was still floundering around, stunned but not knocked out by the explosion. The General approached him carefully, wary of any tricks. Jarrett looked up when Malvasian reached him, and his eyes seemed to struggle to focus on the General's face.

Malvasian prodded him with his foot. "Well, Captain. Are you seriously hurt?"

Jarrett blinked. "Huh? What?"

Malvasian rolled him over. "No wounds? No breaks?"

Jarrett rolled over again onto his back. "Carinan?" He still sounded dazed. "No. The fire?" He mumbled a few more words, then his expression cleared a little. "Who?" He raised himself up on his elbows and his eyes widened. "You! But the disruptor . . ."

"Has been disrupted, I'm afraid." The corners of Malvasian's mouth twitched slightly. "You just relax and I'll be back to ask you a few questions later." He aimed his weapon casually and fired. At maximum dispersion it had the effect of only stunning the average adult, and at this range it couldn't miss. Jarrett jerked once and collapsed.

The General's floater arrived at the back entrance to the alley just as he was turning to check out Roehrdanz. *At least I won't have to walk out of here with these two*, he thought with relief.

He went over to the Sergeant, who had not moved during his brief session with Jarrett. He reached the Sergeant's side, and the suspicion that had been growing in him became a certainty. Once he saw the thin shard of metal protruding from the man's temple, checking his pulse became a mere formality. He went through the motions anyway, then rose, shaking his head.

Killing an outsider was one thing, and it had been the only way to prevent this "Carinan" from using the disruptor. But to be responsible for the death of one of his own people was quite another matter, however unintentional the killing had been. The fact that Sergeant Roehrdanz had sold out to Rizlov didn't make Malvasian feel any better at all.

If the man had been shooting at me, he began, then firmly stifled that train of thought. He would study his regrets later, when he had the time. Now he needed to act, and quickly.

It was twenty minutes to two by the time the General was done wrapping the body in a plastic sheet and loading it into the storage compartment of his floater. After closing the storage hatch, he raised the floater's bubble and reached underneath the comm unit housing, where he pressed a button that wasn't supposed to be there. Then he straightened and turned to consider Captain Jarrett.

By now Rizlov would probably be expecting a report from this team. Fortunately, Jarrett seemed to be the leader, so it would be reasonable for him to make the report. And he would do so, Malvasian vowed, his face a lined granite mask in the dying glow of the ruined floater.

His boots crunched through ash and debris as he walked back to where the SecFor officer lay.

He pulled a small injector out of one of his belt pouches and pressed it against Jarrett's neck. The Captain moaned weakly, his breathing became more rapid, and his muscles began to twitch randomly. In less than a minute he was fully awake, though still in pain from the explosion and the General's shot.

Malvasian pulled him to his feet and pushed him back against the wall. He held Jarrett there with one hand around his neck. The other held his pistol directly in front of Jarrett's left eye.

"Captain," he said quietly, calmly, "I know about the plot. I knew of it before I arrived here, and Sergeant Roehrdanz told me the rest." He shifted the beam control on his pistol slightly. "You will report to Rizlov that your mission was successful, but that you had to use the disruptor. His vehicle sustained minor damage which you will have to repair before returning it to him. You should be able to return it this evening."

Jarrett stiffened his shoulders and said nothing.

"Come, come, Captain," Malvasian continued with a smile. "We both know how much good Rizlov's protection will do you now. Would you like to start this conversation over with one eye instead of two?" He waved the pistol toward his floater. "Sergeant Roehrdanz was smart. He didn't make me prove my sincerity and now he's resting comfortably in the rear of my floater. A Captain should be smarter than a Sergeant."

Malvasian raised an eyebrow quizzically. "Will you make the report now?" He pointed the pistol again at Jarrett's eye. "Or later?"

The Captain slumped and a look of resignation came over his face. "You win, General. I don't owe Rizlov *that* much." He swallowed hard. "I'll make the call."

"Wise decision," Malvasian said in a tone of hearty approval. He led Jarrett over to his floater and motioned him into the driver's seat. Keeping his gun trained on the Captain, Malvasian slid into the passenger's seat and switched on the comm unit.

"Your transmission will, of course, be audio only. An unfortunate result of the damage to Rizlov's floater, which you will explain should he insist on visual contact." The General kept one hand on the power switch.

"You don't know how much the Sergeant told me. Do what you're supposed to and everything will be fine. Deviate from your reporting procedure or try to warn Rizlov in any way and I will terminate the transmission." Malvasian's voice took on a steely edge. "And while Rizlov is waiting for you to repair your malfunctioning comm unit, I'll fulfill my responsibility to keep the Sector Security Force free from traitors. Do we understand each other?"

Jarrett looked from Malvasian's face to the gun still pointing at him and nodded slowly.

"Very well. Make your call."

Jarrett punched in the appropriate transmission code and Rizlov answered immediately. Malvasian congratulated himself silently. Obviously Rizlov had been awaiting just such a report. He listened intently to the exchange, but it was over in less than two minutes with no sign of suspicion on Rizlov's part, though the Senior Adjudicator was ill-pleased with the complication Jarrett reported.

Rizlov broke the contact, and Jarrett turned to Malvasian. "Now what?" he asked.

"Eventually a court-martial, but for now I'm going to have to keep you quiet. Sorry," Malvasian said with the slightest shrug of his shoulders as he shot the Captain again. A sedative injection would have been more merciful, but Malvasian was not feeling in the least merciful.

Now what, indeed? thought the General. Given enough time, he could find out everything Jarrett knew, but he didn't have time, and he suspected that Jarrett knew little more than he'd already revealed anyway.

He pulled the unconscious Captain over into the passenger's seat and strapped him securely in place. The shot should keep him out for hours, but Malvasian could see no reason to take any chances.

The floater's clock glowed a red two-fifteen. From what he'd overheard between Jarrett and Roehrdanz, Colonel Echeverria must have gotten to Phillips by now, unless she had run into complications too. But had she gone to Phillips's house or lured him somewhere else? Had she been sent to kill him, to detain him, or perhaps for some more subtle purpose?

Malvasian considered the possibilities. The Triune was in a three-day working recess, so Phillips would be home sleeping or working late. Even if Echeverria had intended to take him somewhere else, she would probably have had to go to his house first. At such an hour, a personal appearance would be far more convincing than a call, even from Security Headquarters. It would also minimize the chances that the message would be intercepted. Then too, if persuasion didn't work, she couldn't coerce him without actually being there.

The General strapped himself into the driver's seat, his fingers poised over the floater's control keyboard. It made sense. Phillips wouldn't have responded to a mere message the way he himself had to Rizlov's—their situations were entirely different. The trail had to at least begin at Phillips's house, and possibly end there.

In any case, the General thought as he tapped a command into the floater's control module, *what other leads do I have?*

19. Follow that Floater

Phillips lived in Green Hills, an affluent residential district on the western outskirts of Drinan City. It was a few kilometers beyond the perimeter highway, which had not moved inward there as it had in the industrial sector. Malvasian suspected that the name had been given in the spirit of irony or consumer fraud, since the area had originally been as flat as a landing field and covered by sand, rocks and brown scrub.

Over the years, Green Hills had become a haven for upper-level government officials and successful businessmen who wanted to live away from their hectic urban work environment. In the process, much of the city had moved out with them, including the electrical grid and the sewage system. And the central water supply.

Now Green Hills really was green, with trees, lawns and exotic gardens everywhere—a small protrusion into the dry expanse of the Western Plain.

Green Hills was also over 60 kilometers from the disintegrating neighborhood of Power Station Six. Malvasian pushed his floater to the limits of its navigational and drive systems, but he knew it would take at least twenty minutes to reach Phillips's neighborhood. His vehicle skidded through a sharp left-hand turn, then picked up speed, dodging obstacles he barely had time to see before they were past.

"Faster, damn it, faster," he muttered, knowing it was pointless but knowing he could do nothing more useful either. He was jerked back and forth in his safety harness as his floater swerved between an abandoned vehicle of some kind and a pile of rubble; then he was accelerating up the entrance ramp to the highway.

He wanted to call Phillips, but decided that that would only warn Echeverria if she had already arrived, and if she hadn't gotten there yet, she probably wasn't going there at all. He wanted to call SecFor Headquarters and issue an alert for Echeverria, Phillips, and their vehicles, but Rizlov might have other confederates in Security who could overhear such a call. One of the last things Malvasian wanted right now was to let Rizlov know his plot was unraveling.

The General knew that unless he gave himself away, he would be invisible to most official search procedures, thanks to the little device he'd activated back at the Power Station. A "nullifier" his unofficial consultant had called it. It broadcast at Security's radar frequency, ordering their scanners' input processors to ignore his vehicle.

So he was safe, but he could do nothing until he reached Green Hills. He leaned back in his seat, closed his eyes to the roadway blurring past him, and tried to forget about everything he had no control over, which at the moment seemed to be nearly everything of any consequence. The exercise was, as always, only partly successful, but it did ease some of his mental tension.

The Security Director's floater sped down the highway, unnoticed by the traffic monitors, too soon here and gone to

be of concern to the few civilians sharing the wide plasticrete ribbon. They had their own business to attend to, their
own homes waiting somewhere in the night. Inside his vehicle, a gentle vibration reached Malvasian, its whisper the
only reminder that he was moving at all.

He was sidling around the edges of true relaxation, its soft
orange glow warming his mental extremities, when he was
suddenly thrust forward and to the left against his safety
straps. Focusing his eyes beyond the floater's bubble, he
saw that he had just made the Green Hills turnoff.

Came up sooner than I'd expected, he thought, then
added, *but everything does at over 250 kilometers per hour.*

He brought the floater down to a manageable speed and
took over manual control as it reached the residential streets.
Caution was the byword now—the General had no intention
of surrendering his hard-won element of surprise. He would
scout around the area first, to see whether or not Echeverria
was here or had been here before deciding on his next step.

The streets were laid out in an unimaginative square grid
pattern, with one house per side of each large block. Lighting disks shone down at regular intervals, spreading a subdued glow from the tree-hooded walkways into the streets.
The houses were multistoried and expensive, set in immacu-
late lawns with exotic landscaping.

The whole area radiated respectability—not the sort of
place one would expect a Security Director to go on business. *Also rather boring*, Malvasian thought. *Not the sort of
place in which this particular Security Director would care
to live.*

When he got within a few blocks of Phillips's house,
Malvasian doused his lights and drove by the street lighting
alone. He traced the perimeter of a nine-block square with
Phillips's block in the center, carefully searching for any
sign of Echeverria. His floater's passive sensors were set for
maximum sensitivity, and his own internal sensors were on
the alert for the slightest anomaly in the sleeping neighborhood.

Of the twenty-four houses he passed directly in front of,
one had a light showing in a single window. The rest were

completely dark. There were no other drivers out at this hour, and only three floaters were parked on the streets.

Not a late-night area at all, he thought with mixed feelings. On the one hand, it made his presence stick out like a sore thumb to anyone who might be looking for him. On the other, it made his search much easier.

Phillips's house was set back from the street, but from a block and a half away the General could tell that some lights were on in the place, more than just night lights, suggesting that Phillips was still up and about. And the Adjudicator was not alone, judging from the Security floater parked on Phillips's block, around the corner from his house.

Still there, eh? Malvasian pondered the situation briefly. The conclusions seemed obvious: First, that Echeverria had not been sent simply to kill Phillips or to forcibly abduct him; and second, that she was unaware of the failure of the other half of Rizlov's plan. Otherwise, why would she still be here with so little concealment? Parking around the corner was barely going through the motions, probably for the benefit of the area's sleepy and unconcerned residents.

With his assumed enemy located, the General decided he could be equally casual. He brought his own floater to a rest behind some shrubbery on a side street one block down from Echeverria's floater and across from Phillips's block. He supposed that Colonel Echeverria intended either to "disinform" Phillips in some way regarding Reversionism and the need for some drastic response favored by Rizlov, or to talk him into accompanying her somewhere. Whichever, Malvasian figured he could wait until Echeverria left, on the one hand to set Phillips right, on the other to see where he was being taken.

"No need to go rushing in just yet," his tiny voice counseled.

It was approaching three o'clock—hours past bedtime for most decent citizens and late even for General Malvasian, but he was wide awake without having taken a single stimtab. This was the way it had always been for him—once he became fully involved in an assignment, he could keep going for days on end with little or no sleep, and even the most routine tasks took on an edge of excitement.

One of the keys to his success as a Security Agent had been his ability to talk himself into caring about every case he'd been assigned to, no matter how unpromising or mundane it might appear to be. In the present instance, he reflected, he didn't have to play such games. Attempted assassinations had always gotten his full and immediate attention, especially when he was one of the intended victims.

The last attempt had been five years ago, on Rovella, while he was on one of his rare vacations. A dreamdust smuggler had decided that his business would run more smoothly if Malvasian were dead. The man's first shot had missed, and the General had tracked him through the planet's jungles for four days and nights before finding his body already half-absorbed by a carnivorous slug bush. Alertness and persistence get results, the General always told his Agents.

So Malvasian sat in his floater, concealed by an untrimmed hedge of white-leafed Oromel bush-vine, studying Phillips's house through gaps in its tendriled branches. He kept a peripheral watch on his infrared scanner, but only the shapes of small nocturnal animals scampered occasionally across the screen. Jarrett remained unconscious in the passenger's seat.

The old familiar tension began to build in him, born of anticipation. He had won the opening skirmish, and now he had to endure the lull before action resumed. How many nights, how many years had he done this, waiting under the stars of untold planets for something to happen? Sometimes dangerous, sometimes risk-free, the waiting remained the same. Something would happen, and then he would act.

The General's only concern was not to miss the moment. He had little fear of being observed, with his power plant delivering a mere trickle to the passive sensors and with Echeverria apparently so complacent. *Stay alert. Be ready.*

Next to him Jarrett's breathing was deep, slow, regular.

The floater's interior was dark except for the pale images on the infrared scanner's screen.

Outside, the ghostly Oromel leaves waved in a slight breeze, alternately obscuring and clearing Malvasian's view of Phillips's house.

A small animal, probably a buzzball, rushed from the cover of the bushes in front of his floater and raced across the street, pursued by a much larger carnoct. Both disappeared into the shadowed foliage on the other side of the street.

The carnoct was a lethal hunter for its size, lots of teeth and long-clawed front limbs, but Malvasian's money was on the buzzball. The tailless, six-limbed little beasts could run or climb anywhere faster than anything else he'd ever seen. A carnoct chasing a buzzball was like a freefall wrestler grappling with a neutrino.

Just then another movement caught his eye. Through the gently weaving bush-vines the General could see Phillips's front door opening. Two figures emerged. They paused for a moment, and one of them stepped out of the circle of light by the doorway. When she reappeared, for Malvasian could see that it was, indeed, Colonel Echeverria, she had something in her hand. At this distance Malvasian couldn't be sure, but he had a very good idea what that something was.

His eyes narrowed in concentration. *Soon now. Very soon.* He slid his right hand over until it rested on the control console. Wherever she was going, Echeverria would almost certainly head back to the main highway first. The General had been careful not to place himself on the direct route between her floater and the highway entrance ramp. Still, if she did start to head his way, he would have to shut down his floater's power completely and hope for the best. Trying to dodge away would definitely attract her attention. Sitting still, his was just another unremarkable vehicle, not worth more than a casual glance.

Phillips and Echeverria walked down to the sidewalk, paused, and turned in the direction of Echeverria's floater. Malvasian watched them until they disappeared around the corner, then he shifted his attention to his scanner's screen, quickly lowering the instrument's reception frequency from infrared to broad-band radio.

In a moment, a bright blip showed that the Colonel had her vehicle operating at full power. The blip began to move rapidly in the direction Malvasian had predicted. When it neared the limits of his passive radio emissions detector, he switched over to his tracking radar and waited another minute before powering up his own floater and following.

Malvasian set his floater's controls to stay close enough to maintain radar contact with Echeverria's floater, but far enough back to be out of range of any other detection devices. His tailor-made unauthorized nullifier would take care of Echeverria's own radar.

Back along the empty residential streets he went, then up the ramp onto the perimeter highway. By that time Echeverria and Phillips were far down the road, well out of sight. The General's vehicle picked up speed, matching Echeverria's movements. Shortly, he could feel his own floater slow as the radar blip turned to the right, then he was pushed backward as his floater matched the blip's acceleration along its new course.

When he reached the turnoff point, Malvasian saw that it was the Western Expressway exit. His floater slowed only marginally as it took the slightly banked ramp, straining to match Echeverria's straight-line speed. The bright yellow blip nearly slid off the edge of the General's screen, then settled back a half-centimeter toward the center as his own vehicle hit the Expressway.

By then, Echeverria was several kilometers ahead, already past most of the local exits, and she wasn't slowing down. Just a few more minutes at this rate, Malvasian reflected, and she'd be on the edge of the Western Plain, with nothing before her but 120 kilometers of dry grassland. Nothing there but a handful of power relay stations and communications links, all automated.

Malvasian didn't have to strain to inventory Echeverria's possible destinations along the Expressway; there were very few. It marked a geometrically straight line from Drinan City over the Western Plain, through the Baelric Forest, and across the coastal desert, ending at Brinktown. Malvasian had traveled the Expressway enough to have lost all interest in the landscape through which it ran. He kept his eyes on the scanner, wondering whether Echeverria planned to take Phillips all the way to the coast.

Brinktown. How likely is it? The question pulled the General's mind along on a brief review of its tarnished history and that of the wide roadway leading to it. The expressway was nearly 1,000 kilometers of triply reinforced plasticrete that would probably outlive humanity on the planet, and had already gone a long way toward outliving its usefulness. It had been laid down to serve as the major transportation link between the two principal cities of Drinan IV.

Drinan City had fulfilled its part of the plan, becoming the Governmental Center not only of the planet, but of the entire Sector. Brinktown, on the other hand, had fallen considerably short of expectations.

Officially, on the maps, Brinktown was "Yengtzu City," named after one of the planet's first explorers. It lay on the eastern shore of Drinan IV's largest body of water, the Dantile Sea.

Over time, however, the planet's economy and technology had not developed in the predicted directions. The high hopes had been lowered, abandoned, or at least altered drastically, and Yengtzu City had not prospered.

Yengtzu City, Drinan City's sister jewel marking the coastal end of the wide white ribbon of the Western Expressway, had become a dump, figuratively and literally. Its intended functions severely diminished, it was now the site of the processing and disposal facilities for the chemical and radioactive wastes generated by Drinan City. As an added insult, the city had been designated as the planet's quarantine port, where ships carrying biologically dangerous or suspect cargo were to land, as well as those whose passengers or crew had contracted contagious diseases at a previous port of call.

The city had even lost its name, for all practical purposes. It was Yengtzu City in official communications, but only the most stuffed of shirts referred to it that way in casual conversation. Everyone else called it Brinktown. Balanced between desert and ocean, pollution and contagion, it was a dream gone nightmare.

Brinktown. How likely is it? the General asked himself again, sorting through the facts, weighing, analyzing.

He had visited there more than once on business. Its inhabitants included a disproportionate number of the hardened and the beaten down, those who would do anything for money and those who had no alternative. He could well imagine Rizlov finding plenty of willing accomplices in its alleys and bars, people whose scruples were determined solely by the inducement being offered.

But Malvasian could not imagine Rizlov actually recruiting there. The Senior Adjudicator was too suspicious by far to rely on people whose loyalties were so flexible. And too fastidious to associate with the place itself. Rizlov, with his passion for orderliness and control, would probably be appalled at the idea of entering the deterioration and chaos of Brinktown.

Then, too, Brinktown was an unlikely destination for another reason. Even if Rizlov wanted Phillips there, and even if Echeverria had persuaded him to accompany her on such a trip, they surely would not have driven the entire way. At her current high speed, it would still take over five hours to arrive. Flying would be the reasonable way to go, especially if the trip were based on some supposed urgent need, which the time of day strongly suggested.

No, Phillips would almost certainly expect to fly to Brinktown in a Security air shuttle. They weren't taking a shuttle, and he had seemed to be going voluntarily, so they probably weren't going to Brinktown. If they were, Malvasian was determined to stay with them, living on stimtabs if necessary.

And if not Brinktown, where?

The pale Expressway raced beneath Malvasian's floater. The scenery sped along with, slowing gradually with distance until it came to a near halt on the horizon. The General glanced outside occasionally, more from habit than anything else. One of the rules of the trade was never to rely solely on your equipment when you could use your own senses too. It's when your scanners fail that something's lying across your path or coming up from behind. So the General looked, and nothing was.

He himself would have been nothing more than a dull gray shadow, a rounded shape here and gone in the night, to anyone watching the Expressway so far from the city, so late. His spotlights were off, his sensors kept at very low-range power levels, just in case Echeverria should scrutinize the road behind her. As straight and level as the Expressway was, offering no concealment, Malvasian didn't feel sheepish in the least about his precautions.

He also didn't feel too much in doubt about where Colonel Echeverria was taking Adjudicator Phillips. With Brinktown a remote possibility at best, what else was out here? Most people would say nothing, and they would be almost right. Not even everyone in Security knew about the other point of interest, less than a kilometer inside the eastern edge of the Baelric Forest, reached by an unmarked and nearly nonexistent trail.

It was one of the four Special Security Compounds that Malvasian had kept in operation. They had originally been secretly constructed by former Director Caulston, whose notorious use of them had been a major reason for his removal by the Central Council. Malvasian had had them redesigned and put to quite different uses, but the Compounds were still highly classified items in SecFor's files.

Still, Echeverria knew about them, and Rizlov would know everything Echeverria did. Even Phillips, as an Adjudicator, might be aware of them in general, if not of their specific locations. And the one they were heading for was where Overseer Selius was being housed. Lanya Selius, whose case before the Triune Phillips was clearly supporting, and whom Rizlov was adamantly determined to see condemned.

When Malvasian had relocated her there, he had told only those who had absolutely needed to know. That meant Captain Arvash and Lieutenants Gammel and T'Kach, the entire SecFor staff of the Baelric Forest Compound. Even the commander of the Drinan City Detention Center knew only that Malvasian had chosen to transfer Overseer Selius to the "Omega Facility," which meant that it was confidential and there was no point in asking where.

So, was it just coincidence that Echeverria seemed to be heading for the Compound in which Selius had been secreted? The General shook his head firmly. No—he didn't believe in coincidences. Not when there was a reasonable alternative. Next to him, Jarrett swayed slightly as the floater swerved to avoid some obstacle on the Expressway. Actually, he could list several quite reasonable alternatives.

First, Arvash, Gammel or T'Kach could have let something of the plan slip in an unguarded moment. Second, one of them could be a confederate of Rizlov and Echeverria. Or third, Rizlov might have had a surveillance device planted where it could overhear Malvasian's plan. He had taken precautions, of course, but the only bugs that count are the ones you never find. The General preferred the latter explanation —he'd already discovered quite enough defections from Security for one night.

"Only one way to tell, Mr. Director," he grumbled to himself. "Get hold of your second-in-command and make her talk." Felice Echeverria was tough, even for a Security pro, but he was no amateur himself, and he'd never been more determined to get to the bottom of a case. His professional pride and his life were on the line, and perhaps the security of the entire Sector. Rizlov had to be stopped, whatever it might take.

Malvasian called up the location overlay on his scanner. Very soon now he would know if his guess was correct. As if reading his thoughts, his floater slowed suddenly, coming to a near stop before proceeding at little more than a crawl. On his screen, Echeverria's yellow blip had slipped to the left of the vertical line of the Expressway. It continued for a short distance in that direction, then stopped. So did the General's floater.

He waited two minutes, but Echeverria's floater stayed put, so he resumed manual control of his own vehicle and proceeded at a moderate speed. He entered the fringes of the Baelric Forest, attention now evenly divided between his scanner and the trees lining the Expressway.

When he came to a large boulder on his right, the General pulled off the Expressway and nudged his floater in amongst the undergrowth behind the massive pale rock. He slaved its controls to his belt communicator, leaving just enough power on so it could receive and respond to his commands. Before he left, he checked Jarrett's condition and gave him an injection that would keep him out even if the effects of the earlier energy shock were to wear off.

Shortly thereafter, a dark gray figure peered from behind the boulder, studied the line of trees opposite for a few moments, then scurried across the wide white expanse of plasticrete to disappear again into the shadows.

20. Why Don't You Do Something . . .

Echeverria pushed Phillips over to the left-hand wall and ordered him to lie face down on the floor. By straining his eyes till they hurt, he managed to see her slide open the door in that wall just enough to throw two small objects into the next room and shut the door quickly. She then backed away from the door and trained her gun on it, waiting.

It seemed like an hour that she stood there, though Phillips knew it couldn't have been more than about ten minutes. His head and neck ached from trying to watch her without moving. Finally, she stepped over to the door, crouched low, and opened it all the way.

Nothing happened. Echeverria straightened up and reached in to turn on the room's lights. One glance through the doorway seemed to satisfy her. "All right," she said, turning to Phillips. "You can get up now. They'll be out for a while."

Phillips stood slowly. He felt awkward, sluggish, and he knew the cause was deeper than a mere lack of sleep. .

"Come on, we can't stay here all night." With her gun, Echeverria waved Phillips over to the other side of the room.

He crossed the room slowly, carefully, not looking at the body beside the desk. "Why not just kill me like you did the others?"

"I had to kill Arvash—he saw me," Echeverria answered

from behind him. "The others are unconscious. A couple of crude nerve gas bombs of a type that radical Reversionists have been known to use."

"And Overseer Selius?" Phillips asked, trying to make sense out of what was going on.

"She's going to escape shortly with your help and that of a small group of Reversionist activists."

Phillips turned to face Echeverria. "But I'm not a Reversionist!"

"Of course you are," she said in a calm, patient tone. "Why else would you help them spring the Overseer? Only somebody in your position could have gained entry to this compound, and only the Reversionists would have scattered these leaflets around." With that, she pulled a sheaf of papers out of her jacket and threw them behind her. Some landed on the desk, some slid off onto the floor. A few even fell on . . .

Phillips looked at the Colonel with sudden comprehension. *You are really slowing down, Umberto.* "Why are you doing this?"

Echeverria smiled mockingly. "I'm not doing it—you and the Reversionists are." As she spoke, she reset the beam width on her pistol. "Oh, you mean this?" she asked, pointing the weapon at his face. "I'm setting it to stun. The broader beam will let me cover both you and Selius without killing either of you. There's no point in planning an escape if you die in the attempt."

"That sounds reasonable," Phillips replied sourly.

"Of course it does. Now let's collect the Overseer." She pointed with her gun. "Open that door, if you please. Any sudden moves or sounds you make will naturally be your last for a while."

Phillips tried to think of something clever to do, some way to distract Echeverria, to disarm her. The only thing he could come up with was to open the door quietly to keep from getting shot.

Beyond the door was a brightly lighted corridor some thirty meters long with three widely spaced doors along the right-hand side.

Gesturing with her gun, Echeverria directed Phillips to the first door and had him open it while she stood close behind him. The room was lighted by several dimly glowing ceiling panels. It seemed to Phillips to be a compromise between a detention cell and a hotel room.

It had a small food dispenser, two chairs, a table, two beds, and an enclosed area in the far corner, presumably the bathroom. Everything was functional and reasonably comfortable-looking, but not luxurious, and there was not a lot of room, especially if it was supposed to hold two people. There was no sign that anybody at all had been in there recently—no food, no personal items, no wrinkles on the bed covers. Nothing.

Echeverria had Phillips step back into the corridor and close the door. They went to the second door and repeated the procedure, with the same results. That left one more room, and Phillips felt himself tighten up inside as they approached it, which surprised him. He'd thought that he was already as nervous as he could get.

He pressed the small control plate and the door slid open. This time, the room beyond was dark. Phillips barely had time to wonder why before Echeverria shoved him roughly through the doorway and leapt in after him.

"Who's there?" demanded a woman's deep voice from his right just as Phillips stumbled against the room's table. He turned awkwardly, trying to ignore the pain in his left knee. Then the lights came on.

Selius apparently had much quicker reflexes than he. She was crouched in a combat stance at the foot of her bed, squinting against the light, set to spring at the intruders. In her place, Phillips thought, he would probably just be sitting up in bed and trying to rub the sleep out of his eyes.

As it was, his eyes were wide open. Some things, he realized, never lose their attraction. The Overseer obviously favored sleeping in the nude, and her present posture did nothing to conceal the fact. She was a large woman, but her body was not at all chunky or ill proportioned. Her smooth, sleek muscles and the alert, calculating expression on her face reminded Phillips of a natural predator, an ice cat in human form.

"Relax, Overseer." Echeverria's voice pulled Phillips back to the reality of the situation. "There's no point in trying anything. I could shoot you before you took two steps."

Selius straightened slowly, then looked from Echeverria to Phillips and back. "What do you want?" She wasn't afraid or embarrassed, just wary.

"Get dressed. We're leaving." Echeverria kept the gun focused on Selius, but she stood far enough away from both of them that a slight shift of her hand would put Phillips back in her line of fire.

The Overseer turned and pulled her uniform down from where it was hanging on the wall. Phillips noticed a slight discoloration on her right thigh, and that leg looked a little shorter, as if some of the bone had been removed. Instead of thinking about how to disarm Echeverria, he found himself wondering whether Selius's right leg had been injured in the line of duty, and how much pain she had suffered. Had Captain Arvash felt anything when Echeverria had shot him?

"Now, I don't want to have to carry you both, but I don't want you getting any ideas, either." Echeverria scanned the room quickly. "Overseer, take a sheet from one of those beds. Either one. Hurry up. Now go stand behind him, as close as you can. Closer. Good. Wrap the sheet around your waists and tie it tight. That's it." Selius followed the instructions while keeping an appraising eye on Echeverria.

"How much did Councilor Breglum offer you to do this, Colonel?" Selius asked as she finished tying the knot. She was speaking almost directly into Phillips's ear. "Considering the penalty if you're caught, it must have been quite a lot."

"I don't plan to get caught," Echeverria replied. "Besides, it isn't Breglum's idea. It seems Adjudicator Phillips and some of his radical Reversionist allies decided to help you escape."

"I see." Selius tugged at the sheet. "And his being tied to me like this is just a ruse to confuse SecFor's investigators?"

"Something like that." Echeverria waved toward the doorway. "Let's go. If we want to continue this conversation, I'm sure we can find a better place to do so."

They walked out the door and down the hallway slowly, clumsily. Phillips fought off the distraction of Selius rubbing against him and tried to figure out some way to stop Echeverria. If he and Selius could coordinate their efforts, they might be able to jump her as they entered the lift tube, or when they were inside it. But that would take perfect cooperation and he couldn't think of any way to communicate such a plan to Selius.

They stepped from the hallway into the reception area and Selius stopped suddenly.

"Did you have to kill him?" Her voice was as hard and cold as Norhaven's polar nights. Phillips could feel her muscles tense behind him.

"I can as easily make it three if I have to," Echeverria answered coolly. "You decide."

For a moment, Phillips thought Selius was going to do something. He tried to anticipate what that might be, but then she took a deep breath and pushed forward again. Still, he noted, she seemed as tense as before.

They reached the door to the lift tube without incident.

"Open it up, Adjudicator," Echeverria ordered.

Phillips reached for the control panel and pushed the sole button on it. This was evidently the lowest or the only level to the compound. Just as the door began to slide open, he heard a faint sound from somewhere behind him. Before he could turn his head to see what it was, Selius bent her knees and sprang backward, throwing both of them into Echeverria.

The Colonel might have been caught off-guard, but she was quick enough to twist aside and catch only a glancing blow from the pair as they crashed to the floor. Phillips saw that Selius's effort had failed even as he struggled to strike at Echeverria with his fists and his feet. She had fallen to one knee and was raising the gun to a firing position.

Our only chance! he screamed to himself in frustration, furious at his own stupidity and helplessness.

21. ... To Help Me

General Malvasian jogged silently down the floater track to Compound Four. The track took a sharp turn just before reaching the Compound, and there he stopped and moved into the trees. A quick reconnaissance of the area seemed in order. He believed very firmly in finding out what he was getting into before getting into it.

The Compound was virtually all below ground. A two-floater pad at the end of the track was the only sign that anything was out here at all. The entrance was a well-disguised lift tube with its controls hidden in the bark of a large tree. The communication antennas ran up through the same tree and spread out among its upper branches. Not the sort of installation one stumbled upon accidentally. Not even the sort of place one stumbled upon on purpose, unless one was a very good stumbler indeed.

Malvasian circled the entire area, staying as far back in the trees as he could. He had his pistol out, with its beam adjusted to a very narrow width and consequently high intensity—he wanted range and accuracy, and if he had to fire at anybody, he wanted them to know he meant business. Although he saw no one to use it on as he studied the area, he knew Echeverria and Phillips were there, somewhere. Echeverria's floater and the Compound staff's floater were both on the pad.

The tops of both vehicles were opaque and closed. It was impossible to tell if anyone was inside either of them. Malvasian leaned against a large tree and considered his alternatives. None of them was ideal. He could wait until somebody came out of the Compound or one of the floaters and then act, but that could take hours and might be too late.

He could try to break into the floaters or use the Compound's lift tube, which could surprise Echeverria or could expose himself to her or a confederate of hers. Or he could . . .

"General Malvasian, please don't move." The voice was a woman's, but not Echeverria's. It came from somewhere behind him. "I have a gun and I do know how to use it." The voice sounded very serious but not especially hostile. Malvasian quickly narrowed his alternatives to one: not moving.

"General," the voice continued, "I think I know why you're here, and if I'm right, we're on the same side. However, I could be wrong. What are you doing here?"

The voice was vaguely familiar, but Malvasian couldn't put a name or face with it. If only she would come out from behind him!

He was certain it wasn't anyone working for Rizlov or Echeverria—they would know he wasn't an ally. Who else could possibly be out in this unlikely spot at this unlikely hour? Perhaps a Central Council Agent? One might have been assigned to deal with Rizlov as Caulston had been dealt with twenty years ago.

He held onto his energy pistol, but he didn't turn around.

"Come, come, General. We don't have all night."

Finding himself on ground that was somewhat uncertain, Malvasian decided to take refuge in the truth. Not all the truth, but the part that related Echeverria to Rizlov and Phillips. Feeling the pressure of time, he described the events from his ambush near Power Station Six until the present moment. He spoke simply and economically. Embellishment had never been his style, and he couldn't see any advantage to it under the present circumstances, in any case.

It took Malvasian only a few minutes to explain the relevant details.

"I see." He could hear the woman behind him moving closer. "General, I'm going to trust you and I think you should trust me. If I were on Rizlov's side, you'd be dead right now, and I can't think of any reason you'd be working for him. I'm here primarily looking after Overseer Selius, and I think Echeverria and Rizlov are after her and Adjudicator Phillips."

The woman stepped around to Malvasian's right and, seeing her, he realized why the voice had sounded familiar. She looked at him warily. "Do we have a partnership?"

He breathed easier and kept his gun aimed at the ground. "I think we do, Advocate Chou. I don't know how you got here, but I can certainly use your help."

"Good." Chou smiled briefly and lowered her own gun. "Now then. Echeverria and Phillips went down into the Compound shortly before you arrived here. I'm pretty sure no one else was in Echeverria's floater. What are the odds that she has a confederate down there?" Chou's tone was calm and businesslike. It sounded to Malvasian as if she had had previous experience in such clandestine activities.

"There are three staff members out here, and they're as trustworthy as anyone I have," Malvasian replied. "I seriously doubt that any of them would work for Rizlov."

"They're all at risk too, then. Maybe Echeverria will slip up and they'll stop her, but we can't assume that. I don't think we should wait to find out." She looked up coolly at Malvasian. "It would probably be best if you were to go in the back way and try to surprise her. You know the layout and are more familiar with the people involved."

Malvasian gave her a sharp glance. "How did you find out about that entrance? Not even the Compound's staff know it's here." *For that matter, Grestahk, what the blazing quasars is a Level One Advocate doing out here in the first place? A dumpy female Advocate at that!*

"I have my ways, General. No one told me about it, if that's what you're worried about. I discovered it two nights ago while I was studying the layout here." Chou nodded back toward the clearing. "She's not going to be twiddling her thumbs while we discuss such minor details. What do you say? Do we go with my plan? I can stand guard by the main entrance just in case she gets away from you or leaves before you get down there."

It was as good a plan as Malvasian could come up with, so he agreed. A few minutes later he was lowering himself down a series of rungs set into the side of a narrow metal shaft. That shaft's cover had been buried under a foot of dirt and leaves, and the lock was keyed to his left palm print. The entrance was nearly a hundred meters from the Compound, to minimize the odds of someone discovering it by accident. By the time his foot touched the bottom, Malvasian had decided that he and Advocate Chou were going to have a very serious conversation when all this was over.

The shaft and the tunnel that connected it to the Compound were unlighted—the power needed to light them would have made them more detectable. Malvasian turned on his small hand light and hurried along the tunnel. He had constructed the tunnel himself several years ago, before he'd reopened the Compound, and he was pleased to see that it hadn't yet been invaded by anything larger than a few insects and a thin layer of dust. The air was quite stale, however, and he found himself panting somewhat before he reached the tunnel's far end.

He walked slowly the last several meters, partly to avoid making unnecessary noise and partly to catch his breath. The doorway into the Compound was hidden in the back of one of the closets in the staff's living quarters. Malvasian opened the heavy tunnel-side door carefully and pressed his ear against the thin closet-side panel. After two minutes of complete silence, he turned off his light and slid the panel aside with painful slowness. As much as he wanted to hurry, he knew speed would be useless if he gave himself away.

When the panel was fully opened, he slipped into the closet, feeling around to avoid tripping or knocking something over. He caught a faint sweet scent in the air and instinctively held his breath. It was a simple nonlethal nerve gas that had once been part of Security's arsenal. SecFor had abandoned the stuff over thirty years ago, however. The only people who used it anymore were some planetary independence fighters and scattered groups of radical Reversionists.

As Malvasian recalled, the gas decomposed in a matter of minutes, and the faint whiff he'd detected indicated a concentration well below the potency level. With some relief, he took a shallow breath, then a deeper one, realizing he had little choice in any case. *Why would Echeverria use that?* he wondered. She had access to far more potent weapons.

A light was shining in along the edge of the closet door, which was slightly ajar. The General pushed it open far enough to see most of the room. Lieutenants Gammel and T'Kach were sprawled across their beds, presumably knocked out by the gas. They would hardly have been sleeping with all the lights on. Captain Arvash's bed was empty.

Malvasian eased the closet door open all the way and stepped out into the Compound staff's living quarters. A quick glance showed him no one was there except for the two lieutenants. The door to the reception area was wide open. He approached it cautiously, reaching out with his senses and holding his gun in a firing position.

Crouching down next to the doorway, he tensed his muscles and slowly relaxed them, then stuck his head and gun hand out around the edge of the doorway. And froze.

Arvash had been one of his most capable and trustworthy people. If Malvasian had ever had a son, he would have wanted him to be like the Captain—strong, intelligent, good-looking, with an easy friendliness about him that was genuine and disarming. And there he was, lying dead in the middle of the floor, burned down with his gun still clipped to his belt.

Malvasian's fingers tightened convulsively around the handle of his own gun. Whoever killed Arvash was going to pay, and the law and his official responsibilities had nothing to do with it.

Just then he saw someone step out of the room at the far end of the prisoners' section of the Compound. He pulled back immediately, but he'd seen enough to know that it was Phillips and Selius, tied together somehow.

So Echeverria's got them both. His mind automatically analyzed the situation and determined the best course of action.

She hadn't killed Selius and Phillips, and she must know that Gammel and T'Kach would revive shortly. The logical conclusion was that she was planning to leave the Compound, taking the Overseer and the Adjudicator with her. Therefore, she'd have to use the lift tube. When she brought her two prisoners over to it, her back would be turned, and the General could take her out without endangering the other two.

He waited, breathing quietly, listening to the approaching trio. *Don't kill her*, he ordered himself sternly. *She's the strongest link to Rizlov. We need her alive*.

He heard them stop for a moment when Selius first saw Arvash's body. Then he heard them move toward the lift tube. They stopped again, in front of the tube's door, as far as Malvasian could tell.

Echeverria spoke. "Open it up, Adjudicator." Her attention would be focused on Phillips and the lift tube. Now was the time.

Malvasian shifted to where he had a clear shot at Echeverria. As he did so, his foot scraped along the floor. It wasn't a loud sound, but it was loud enough. Echeverria spun, Selius and Phillips fell backward into her, and Malvasian fired.

His shot went above the Colonel's head as she was knocked down. It burned a small hole in the wall near the now-open lift tube door. Echeverria brought her gun up and fired. Malvasian tried to duck back, but his right arm went numb as her stun beam hit it. His own gun dropped to the floor.

Now what? She's got you.

All Echeverria had to do was take two steps and fire again to incapacitate him. Instead, she grunted in pain as Selius landed a hard kick on her right side. Reacting instantly, Malvasian rolled across the exposed doorway opening, grabbing his gun with his left hand and firing in the same motion. He thought he caught Echeverria in the shoulder, although she didn't cry out. He didn't want to lean out and risk losing his left arm as well, so he waited for a moment.

"She's in the lift tube, General!" Selius called out. He leaped out into the reception room, but he was too late. The door was closed and she couldn't be stopped from reaching the top.

"We may still have her," he told Selius and Phillips, who had just managed to untie themselves. "Chou's waiting at the top, just in case things didn't go well down here."

"Chou?" Phillips and Selius asked in unison.

"I don't understand it myself," he replied, "but she is. To be on the safe side, I'm going to go back up the way I came, and one of you take Captain Arvash's gun and guard the lift door. I'll call down if everything's all right. If Echeverria comes down, stop her." His face was bleak as he concluded, "Take her alive if you can, but do whatever is necessary."

Five minutes later, the General called down over the Compound's intercom. "This is Malvasian. Chou got Echeverria. We're bringing her right down. Get the medkit from the staff's living quarters. The Colonel's seriously wounded, and we can't afford to lose her now. She's our closest link to Rizlov."

22. I Have a Plan

Two hours later, the sky was beginning to lighten in the east, though it was still as dark as night beneath the canopy of the Baelric Forest.

Belowground, sitting at the Compound's reception desk, Phillips wondered if the night would ever end. Lieutenants Gammel and T'Kach were lying in their beds, still recovering from Echeverria's nerve gas. Echeverria and Captain Jarrett were locked in separate cells, Echeverria sedated to relieve the pain of her shoulder wound. The bodies of Captain Arvash and Sergeant Roehrdanz were laid out in a cold-storage locker in the supply room.

Where will it end? Phillips wondered. He and the others —General Malvasian, Overseer Selius, and Advocate Chou —were seated around the desk, trying to make plans. As the long night turned reluctantly into day, they were all drinking strong synthecaff to keep going.

All except Chou, Phillips noticed. She seemed as bright and refreshed as if she'd just had a good night's sleep. He himself was on his third cup of the bitter caffeinated drink.

His head was buzzing faintly and his eyes had begun to slip in and out of focus. For the past twenty minutes or so, he had contented himself with being a listener while the other three discussed the situation. That discussion was taking a turn he didn't like.

"We're agreed, then, that Adjudicator Phillips is Rizlov's primary target, with Overseer Selius a useful secondary victim." Malvasian's voice sounded tired but nevertheless confident. Selius and Chou nodded their assent.

He continued, "Rizlov went after me to further confuse the situation and to allow Echeverria to take over as Director. That way SecFor's investigation would be certain to focus on Reversionists rather than on himself." Malvasian paused and tapped firmly on the desktop. "Since he thinks I'm already dead, I'm the logical one to go back, quietly, of course, and keep an eye on him until we get Council approval for arresting him. Besides, I've had more experience at this sort of thing."

"Begging your pardon, General," Selius responded, "but I've had more years in Security than you, and I could move more freely in Drinan City, since my face is much less familiar than yours."

The General shook his head. "You've had an exemplary career, Overseer, but it's been spent away from the capital. Besides, Rizlov may actually be looking for you and Adjudicator Phillips, since he hasn't heard from Echeverria." Malvasian was polite but firm.

Chou spoke up. "If you want somebody who knows Drinan City and whose presence will not alarm Rizlov, General, I am clearly the person to send." She smiled apologetically. "I know you still have questions about me, and I promise to answer them as I can. But for now we need to act quickly without putting Rizlov on his guard. Besides, I'm *supposed* to be in the city—Rizlov ordered me to stay there. You could contact some of your people from out here, and I could be our group's personal eyes and ears on Rizlov."

Malvasian, Selius, Chou. Each had some sort of reason for going back to keep an eye on Rizlov. Each thought the others ought to stay out of the way and safe. None of them seemed to even consider Phillips as a possible agent. The more he listened to the discussion, the angrier Phillips became at their casual disregard.

He could almost hear their unspoken reasons: He's too old. He's not a military man. He's too recognizable. He's Rizlov's primary target. *You bet your asses I'm Rizlov's primary target*, Phillips thought. *If Malvasian's right, Rizlov and Albing have been killing me slowly for almost twenty years.*

The other three talked on. Phillips tuned them out. He was sure they thought him too old, falling apart. Phillips seethed. Who did these people think they were, dismissing him that way? He outranked them all, had lived in Drinan City longer than any of them, understood the Senior Adjudicator better than they ever would, and had a much stronger motive for dealing with Rizlov. The man had not only plotted to kill him, but had nearly ruined the past twenty years of Phillips's life. Damn it to dust, this was a target that was going to shoot back!

"I'm sorry, General, but I can't let you do this." The words were out of his mouth before he'd realized he was going to speak them.

"What?" Malvasian asked, startled. Chou and Selius turned curiously to look at Phillips.

Phillips raised his voice. "I can't let you take the responsibility for dealing with Adjudicator Rizlov."

"But sir, we haven't decided yet. We're still trying to come up with the best course of action." The General's voice was calm, reasonable.

"Don't patronize me, General," Phillips said sharply. "I know what you're discussing, and it's quite clear that you *have* decided that one of you three should watch Rizlov to make sure he doesn't flee while you wait for the Central Council to remove him." He took a quick deep breath and let it out as quickly. "I can't accept that plan."

"May I ask why not?" It was Selius this time.

Phillips smiled and nodded at her. "I'd be surprised if you didn't ask." He was feeling light-headed, buoyant, and he didn't think it was because of the caffeine and fatigue.

"I have two reasons. The first is that I don't think it will work. You don't really think Rizlov's just going to sit around waiting to hear from Echeverria, do you? He'll send people out here to see what happened, and he'll check whatever spot she was planning to take us to. Maybe somebody's on the way right now." He looked at Malvasian. "Do you know when Echeverria was supposed to contact him?"

The General shook his head. "No, but we can assume . . ."

"That the time has already passed," Phillips concluded. "Therefore, Rizlov knows his plan has failed in some way, and there's no telling how he'll react. The man's truly convinced he's protecting the Union from a serious threat. He's obsessed, but he's not stupid. We can't afford to wait for the Council to act. We don't even know if they *will* act."

"And why would they not?" Chou asked. Her voice was soft, but the look she gave him was direct and penetrating. Phillips had the feeling that she knew the answer and was just testing to see if he did too.

"Our case against Rizlov is relatively weak right now— one admission under duress and several inferences General Malvasian has drawn from his own investigation. We find it convincing, but the Council might not. Then too, the Council might even share Rizlov's views about the political situation in this Sector. They might even see *us* as the conspirators, out to sabotage Rizlov's leadership."

The room was silent for a moment as the others considered Phillips's argument. They had seen Captain Arvash's body lying on the floor next to the desk they now sat around. They knew Echeverria had shot him. They were convinced Echeverria had acted on Rizlov's orders. But would the Council see things that way?

Malvasian shifted uncomfortably in his chair. "But without Council approval, we can't take any direct action against Rizlov."

"That's the advantage of my plan, General. With Adjudicator Doriani's agreement, I *can* remove Rizlov from the Triune and have him confined pending a Council hearing." Phillips took a drink of his now cold synthecaff and waited calmly for the storm.

Chou, Selius and Malvasian all talked at once.

"But that would mean placing yourself . . . "

"How can we be sure that Doriani would . . . "

"What if Rizlov were to . . . "

Although they all voiced objections, Phillips knew they were reaching for straws. He could see the lack of conviction on their faces.

How wonderful, he thought, taking another drink of the bitter liquid. *I'm actually winning this argument.*

He set his cup down and held up his hand. "Please, let's not waste time. You all agree we have to do something quickly, and that we're all at risk until Rizlov is stopped. I'm the only one who can legally stop him without Council approval." He looked at each of the others in turn. "Unless you'd rather take Rizlov's own approach and assassinate him." He paused. His companions shook their heads silently, reluctantly. "No? I thought not."

The plan was simple. Chou, who could move freely in Drinan City, would return and meet with Adjudicator Doriani as soon as possible. With her she would take a Restraint Order signed by Phillips and witnessed by Malvasian. She would also take a holotape of Phillips explaining Rizlov's actions and asking for Doriani's support. *Kia won't let us down.* Chou would then go to her apartment and wait.

In the meantime, Phillips would drive back to Drinan City and contact Rizlov. He would set up a meeting for the following morning in some safe public place. After that, he would call Chou and tell her where the meeting was to be. At the arranged time, Phillips would meet with Rizlov, and Chou and Doriani would show up with the necessary legal documents. Taken by surprise, Rizlov would be in Phillips's custody before he could do anything about it.

"Are you sure you can get him to meet you alone?" Selius asked, sounding concerned and skeptical.

"I don't know that I can, but I think I can." Phillips shrugged tiredly. "You see, in Rizlov's mind I'm already beaten. This scheme of his involving you and the General is just his way of building a really damning case against the Reversionists while also opening up a few key spots in Sector government for his own people to move into. I'm pretty sure I can play on his arrogance to get a one-on-one meeting." *Why shouldn't he be arrogant?* Phillips thought. *I haven't exactly been shining lately.*

Malvasian shook his head slowly, looking down at the table. "I don't like it, sir. You're taking an awful risk. But I can't think of a better plan." He raised his eyes to stare into Phillips's own. "I do have one question."

"Yes?" Phillips prompted when the General hesitated.

"You said you had two reasons for rejecting our plan, despite the fact that our 'plan' was no more than the roughest of outlines. Your first reason was that our plan wouldn't work. What was the second reason?" Malvasian continued to stare at Phillips, challenging him, demanding the truth.

"Fair enough, General." Phillips returned Malvasian's gaze. "My second reason was that this is my fight. You three have become involved in it, I realize, but Rizlov has been killing me for twenty years, and I've been letting him get away with it. It's time I fought back." He looked around fiercely at the others and back to Malvasian. "And if you think that's too emotional, I don't give a spacer's damn."

Phillips stood up, hiding his unsteadiness by keeping one hand firmly on the back of his chair. "Advocate Chou, we should leave for the city in a few hours. I suggest we take this opportunity to get a little sleep." With that, he turned and headed for the staff's quarters, willing his feet to step one ahead of the other in a straight line.

23. Reckoning

Night did not fall evenly on Drinan City. As in most colorfully illuminated large cities throughout the Union, it settled in irregular patches, wherever the lights would let it.

The circular perimeter highway, the feeder lines, the major city streets shone brightly. The Government Complex was a never-sleeping glow in the center. Gleaming oases of hotels, restaurants, bars, nightclubs and sensyntheaters marked the intersections of well-traveled routes. But among all these lights, night sifted down, filling the spaces between—a building here, an alley there, an entire block across the way.

One of the night's largest, darkest refuges was the sprawling Drinan Botanical Gardens.

The gates of the Botanical Gardens had closed behind the last departing visitors a few minutes before sunset. Now Phillips waited under the cover of dense shrubbery for night to fall. He was alone in the vast expanse of vines, bushes and tree-covered paths. There were no guards to worry about, no evening workers. The entire grounds were surrounded by a high security barrier, and the especially rare and valuable specimens were well protected in their own enclosures. No inside patrols were necessary, so the paths were unlighted.

As the glow of twilight was blotted from the sky, the Gardens became a labyrinth of formless shadows. Phillips was glad he'd brought his night-sight goggles along.

He had entered the city earlier that day, and had contacted Rizlov soon thereafter.

"Hello, sir." He'd used a public vidphone near the Gardens. Even if the call were traced, he'd be gone and in the Gardens before Rizlov could send anyone after him.

"Phillips?" Rizlov peered closely into the screen.

"Alive and well. And I'd like to stay that way." He was dressed in casual dark civilian clothes. He doubted that passersby would recognize him.

"What do you mean?" Rizlov asked calmly. Phillips had to give him credit. The man had a lot of self-control.

"I mean a deal."

"Deal? What are you talking about?" The Senior Adjudicator sounded interested, his confusion feigned.

"Oh, let's say I were to retire and agree not to become a consultant to the Central Council. Do you think I could get a guaranteed pension?" Phillips thought that was vague enough to protect the conversation from eavesdroppers.

"Possibly. We'd need to discuss details." As far as Phillips was concerned, Rizlov had just admitted everything.

"I thought so. The Botanical Gardens. The fountain

straight in from the main entrance. An hour after sunset." He wanted to wrap it up quickly, to get ready for the evening's meeting.

"Wait a minute. How do I . . ."

"See you then." Phillips cut the connection and walked over to the Gardens, where he paid the regular admission without identifying himself.

He checked his watch nervously. Nearly ten o'clock. Rizlov should be arriving soon. Phillips took a quick swallow of water from his canteen to wash away the cottony feeling in his mouth and throat. *Keep your eyes open.* Rizlov had to come through the small entrance next to the main gate—it was the only one his identicard would open without setting off any alarms. *Don't let him slip past you.* He considered taking another stimtab, but rejected the idea quickly. As keyed up as he was now, another of the small white pills would have pushed him over the edge.

He felt a brief pang of guilt over not sticking to the plan he and the others had agreed to. Facing Rizlov by himself might be a mistake, and it could backfire, but he had taken too much for too long to let this opportunity pass. Win or lose, the only way Phillips could prove himself to himself was to confront his long-time enemy personally. He thought of the others now involved in Rizlov's machinations—Malvasian, Selius, Chou, possibly even Doriani. He hoped they would understand.

Then he saw it—a slight movement near the main gate. In the smaller entrance doorway, someone crouched, shadow within a shadow. Whoever it was remained there for a minute or two, then crept off to Phillips's left, staying close to the gray security barrier, still crouching. Even in the dark at nearly 100 meters, Phillips could tell it wasn't Rizlov. He unclipped his pistol from his belt and smiled grimly, keeping one eye on the furtive shadow. Of course Rizlov hadn't come alone, despite their agreement.

Phillips waited until he saw the diminutive Senior Adjudicator step cautiously out of the doorway's shadow. He probably had somebody else waiting for him outside, but that didn't concern Phillips. Rizlov started walking slowly along the dim path that ran straight out from the entrance. They had agreed to meet where that path first crossed another. A fountain marked the intersection. Even a stranger to the Gardens could find it.

Once he was sure that Rizlov was heading for their rendezvous, Phillips slipped off to his left to deal with Rizlov's guard. When he met Rizlov, it would be just the two of them. He pulled his night-sight goggles down over his eyes and the world became a light grayish green. It wasn't as bright as day, but it was bright enough so that he could see into all but the darkest shadows. Assuming his quarry was wearing goggles too, he stayed low and hugged the available cover.

As he moved through the undergrowth, skirting open spaces, he felt something awaken in him for the first time in ages. His eyes began to notice where dry branches would crack underfoot, and his feet automatically avoided such obstacles. His ears became sensitive antennae, able to hear the other man far away brushing against leaves. He himself slid through the trees and bushes silently. All his father's lessons came flooding back into his awareness, all the hard-learned skills from Norhaven reasserting themselves, forcing his body into the motions of a hunter.

In his mind, Gregor's voice whispered, "Bush squirrel or ice cat, it's all the same, son. Stalk the one just as you'd stalk the other." Breathing as quietly as the grass beneath his feet, he considered the remembered maxim. "Maybe so, Father," he replied silently, "but the price for failure isn't the same at all." Tonight, in this pocket of wilderness in the midst of Drinan City, Phillips knew he was facing his own ice cat. He moved closer to Rizlov's hireling. His nerves tingled.

Everything was so natural, so easy. Thought, feeling and action were one. He flowed through the darkness. Soon he was a mere five meters from the man, then four. His unknowing opponent seemed intent on circling around to come at the meeting place with Rizlov from behind. Three meters. He could see that the man was wearing night-sight goggles and had a gun in his right hand. The prudent thing to do would be to stun him now, before he turned around. Closer.

The perfect stalker can actually touch his prey before it knows he's there.

Less than two meters, *Don't breathe—absorb air through your skin, be a plant, a part of the forest*. The man stopped. *Still your heartbeat, quiet your thoughts—be a rock, a log, the unmoving air*. Suddenly the man turned, began to raise his gun, but Phillips's hand was already coming down. Before his quarry could cry out, the handle of Phillips's gun connected solidly with the other's head, and the man collapsed silently.

Rizlov paced back and forth by the fountain where their meeting was to take place. He looked around at the impenetrable shadows surrounding the clearing. The Senior Adjudicator was out of his element here, and he seemed anxious. Phillips watched him for a while as he let his eyes adjust to the removal of his goggles. It boosted his confidence to see his ruthless foe's icy demeanor wavering, however slightly.

Rizlov appeared to be unarmed, but Phillips kept his hand near his gun as he stepped out onto the walkway circling the fountain. He was a few meters behind Rizlov, who was looking down the path that led toward the front gates.

"Good evening, sir," Phillips said in a cheerful tone of voice. He was rewarded by a sudden jerk of Rizlov's shoulders. The Senior Adjudicator turned slowly to face him.

"Phillips." He said the word as if it were something foul-tasting that he was spitting out.

"Who else?" This close, he could see that Rizlov had no weapons. *Always let somebody else do the dirty work,* Phillips thought scornfully. He allowed himself to relax a little, though adrenaline was still charging through his system.

"Who else, indeed?" Rizlov's gaze wandered toward the shadowed undergrowth, then refocused on Phillips. "So. You wanted to talk. What about?"

"When I called you this afternoon, I wanted to make a deal." He unclipped his gun and adjusted the beam control. "Now I'm not sure that's necessary."

"Meaning?" Rizlov walked over and leaned against the fountain.

Phillips smiled at him. "Meaning the Sector would be a lot better off with you dead than alive."

"Don't be stupid." Rizlov's voice was as crisp and cool as ever. "What do you think the Council would do to you?"

"I don't know. Maybe they'd thank me, maybe they wouldn't find out." He shrugged. "It doesn't really matter. You must know my rejuvenation treatments aren't working anymore. I'll be dead in a few years regardless of what the Council does."

Rizlov started to say something, then stopped, eyeing the gun Phillips held casually in his right hand. He began again. "I, um, may know something about your treatments." He took a deep breath and hurried on. "Listen, damn it, you've got a lot to lose. Your treatments can be corrected."

Phillips stared down at his pale-haired nemesis. "Corrected? What do you mean? How?"

"I don't know the details, but you have to believe me." Rizlov looked up at him then and reached out with one small hand. "I can talk to Director Albing. I'm sure she can restore the viability of your treatments."

Phillips took a step toward Rizlov. "You mean to say that you and Albing . . . for all these years?"

"Yes, yes! But listen," Rizlov licked his lips nervously, "she can undo the damage!"

So Malvasian's hunch was right! Phillips felt a glow of satisfaction at having gotten Rizlov to admit to the sabotage. Still, it wasn't enough.

"How do I know you're telling the truth? You could be lying just to save your own life."

Rizlov ran his hand through his hair, trying to think of an answer. "How about this? I could make a call to Albing with you listening in. I've called her before to check on your status, so she wouldn't have any reason to be suspicious. Just a few minutes would make it clear that what I've said is true."

"That might suffice," Phillips said dubiously. Inside, he was shouting, *It wasn't in my mind! It wasn't me at all!* But then his mind swung back to an earlier thought, one that had moved him to speak out back at the Compound. *I owe this scheming bastard for twenty years of self-doubt, twenty years of watching death creep closer and closer.*

"But then again," he said, glaring at Rizlov, "maybe it just doesn't matter." With that, Phillips raised his gun and fired.

Rizlov jerked back, his eyes widening in surprise. Then he looked down at the rim of the fountain. Next to where his hand had been resting was a small hole, charred around the edges.

"Somebody's going to wonder where that came from," Rizlov said with a slight quaver in his voice.

"Let them wonder. You have more important things to worry about, such as why I shouldn't kill you here and now."

"I thought we'd been over that already." The Senior Adjudicator moved over to the fountain again, carefully avoiding the hole Phillips's shot had made. "Besides, there are people who know I've come here, and why."

Phillips sighed regretfully. "I suppose you're right." *Sometimes, Umberto, I wish you weren't so damned reasonable.* He strongly suspected that if their roles were reversed, Rizlov would already have shot him. "Make me an offer that sounds better than taking my chances with the Central Council."

Rizlov smiled confidently. "How about the offer you alluded to this afternoon? You retire and agree not to file a complaint with the Central Council, and I'll undertake to guarantee your personal security, as well as Doriani's. I'll even consult with you on your replacement."

"And my rejuvenation treatments?" Phillips asked tightly.

"But of course!" Rizlov agreed quickly. "I would speak to Director Albing as soon as possible."

"Hmm." Phillips tapped his fingers on the fountain's stone rim, considering. After a minute or two, he said, "Tempting, but not good enough. How about this? You resign from the Triune and I'll agree not to press charges with the Council."

"And leave you and Doriani in control?" Rizlov asked harshly. "I think not." He looked past Phillips, toward the encircling green-black shadows. "I believe our conversation has reached an impasse, and it has definitely ceased to be amusing." He raised his voice to a near shout. "You can come out now. Adjudicator Phillips will be leaving with us."

Phillips smiled. "If you're talking to that fellow who came in ahead of you, you'll have to speak louder. I persuaded him to lie down back there a ways. He probably hasn't come to yet."

"Oh, him." Rizlov didn't seem surprised. "I figured something of the sort had happened when you showed up. He was supposed to get to you beforehand." His voice took on a tone of mocking admiration. "Stopping Glessup was quite a feat for a man of your age. He was good at this sort of thing. I didn't think you had it in you."

Phillips accepted the compliment with a slight nod.

"But actually," Rizlov continued smugly, "I was talking to Zhuria, the man who came in *after* me. It would have been stupid of me to get rid of Doriani and leave you free to cause me problems."

Get rid of Doriani! Phillips clutched his pistol tightly. "What do you mean?" he asked, feeling himself go cold inside. "What have you done to her?"

"I? Nothing. The man I sent over to her place had complete discretion regarding methods." Rizlov smiled, taunting Phillips. "But I'm sure it was quick—he's a professional."

Kia! Phillips recalled her brave defiance of Rizlov, the twinkle in her green eyes. "If you've hurt her, you bastard, I won't wait for the Council to hear your case." He raised his gun, pointing it at the Senior Adjudicator's head.

Rizlov's gaze shifted slightly to the right. "Don't do anything rash, Phillips. My man Zhuria is an excellent shot."

Phillips heard somebody moving in the bushes behind him, where his short foe was looking. *Rizlov's not going to win this time*, Phillips vowed. He spun around and fired into the darkness, falling to the pavement as he did so.

"Adjudicator Phillips! Don't shoot!"

What the . . . Phillips froze, his finger pressing the firing stud not quite hard enough for the gun to discharge again. *What's Chou doing here?*

The stocky Advocate emerged cautiously from the shadows. "I caught the man who was going to ambush you. He won't be bothering anyone for a while."

Phillips heard a noise behind him and twisted around in time to see Rizlov disappear down one of the paths. Chou started to go after him.

"Wait!" Phillips scrambled to his feet. "I don't know how you got here, and I'm glad you did. But this is my fight."

Chou looked at him searchingly for a moment, then nodded. "I guess it is at that. Go. I'll follow in a bit, just in case."

"Thanks." Phillips turned and ran down the path Rizlov had taken.

In a few minutes he was panting. The energy that had carried him this far was rapidly draining away. Two days with virtually no sleep and a surfeit of stress had taken their toll. Still, he'd caught sight of Rizlov and was determined to go on. Rizlov was no great physical specimen. Phillips was certain he could catch up to the smaller man, despite his own shaky condition.

Ahead, he could see Rizlov turn off down a side path. The Senior Adjudicator seemed unwilling to leave the paved walkways, so Phillips decided to take a chance. Rizlov's new path headed in a long unbroken curve toward a display area for exotic plants. By cutting through the trees on his right, Phillips would get there at about the same time as Rizlov.

Phillips's side ached as he pushed toward his meeting with Rizlov. He tried to move quietly without slowing down, but he was feeling clumsier with each step. The shadows seemed to be deeper than before, the trees and bushes thicker.

He burst into the clearing just as Rizlov rushed into it from his left. Phillips was trying to catch his breath and stop his head from spinning. The Senior Adjudicator was running frantically while looking back over his shoulder. They collided. Phillips's gun flew off into the undergrowth and they both went down hard.

Rizlov screamed inarticulately and began swinging his fists wildly. One blow caught Phillips's left eye and another bloodied his nose before he managed to grasp Rizlov by the throat. He felt numb, exhausted, but he pushed Rizlov off him and rose to his knees, still holding the smaller man at arm's length.

Gasping for breath, his legs shaking, he began to squeeze. Rizlov struggled, but he couldn't reach Phillips and couldn't break Phillips's grip. Soon Rizlov would be unconscious, then he would die.

"This is too easy for you, you damned waste-sucking little tyrant," Phillips snarled. "You're going to pay for killing her."

Phillips looked around at the nearby exhibits. Yes, there it was! The perfect executioner for Rizlov. It would be slow and painful.

"Come on," he muttered through clenched teeth. His heart was pounding, threatening to burst out of his chest as he struggled to his feet. He hauled Rizlov upright, glaring at him through a dim red haze.

"Over here. This will be perfect for you." He half-carried, half-dragged the semiconscious Senior Adjudicator over to a low stone wall surmounted by a head-high metal fence.

It was too dark to read the plaque attached to the fence, but Phillips had visited the Gardens often enough to know what was on the other side—a large carnivorous slug bush from Rovella. "It's only justice, sir," Phillips breathed into Rizlov's ear. "You've been eating people alive for years. Now it's your turn."

His lungs burned. *Get him up on this ledge first. There*. Phillips's head throbbed. Somewhere far away someone was calling his name. *Now, if I can just lift him up*. He raised Rizlov slowly, halfway up the fence. The voice came nearer, became distracting. *What? Who?* Chou was just below him, telling him something important. *No, I have to administer justice*. Her voice became clearer, more insistent.

"I said, Doriani's alive. She's unharmed." Chou looked up at him, held out her arms.

"Huh?" He stared at her dully.

"Come down from there. Rizlov's assassin failed."

"Kia's alive?" He let go of Rizlov, who dropped unceremoniously to the walkway below.

"Yes, yes. She's fine. Now step down here." Phillips

stepped. "Careful. There. Take one of these." She handed him a large dark pill.

"What is it?" Phillips asked as Chou set him down with his back resting against the rough stone wall.

"Just something to help you get your strength back." She looked at him severely. "Sit still for a few minutes. You pushed yourself too hard tonight."

The pill seemed to dissolve as Phillips was swallowing it. Almost immediately a soothing warmth spread from his throat and stomach outward, until his whole body felt relaxed and calm. He even found himself thinking more clearly. The warmth began to fade, leaving him rested and alert. His breathing was slow and even, his pulse normal.

He looked at Rizlov, remembered what he'd been about to do. He shuddered and turned wide, shocked eyes back to Chou. "Spacer's damn! I was going to feed him to that plant!"

Chou squatted down beside him and took his hand. "You were under a great deal of strain. And you didn't go through with it." She squeezed his hand. "Remember that—you didn't kill him."

He nodded. She had kept him from committing murder. She had also prevented Rizlov's second man from killing him. "What now?"

"That's easy," Chou said with a smile. "We go with the original plan. I got Adjudicator Doriani's signature. Let's do this legally." She stood up and helped Phillips to his feet. "Feeling better now?"

"Better? I feel wonderful." He looked down at the pale form sprawled at his feet. "Sorry, Senior Adjudicator," he said, "but I think we're going to be taking this to the Central Council after all."

Then he turned to Chou. "Not that I'm ungrateful, but how did you happen to turn up here at such an opportune moment?"

"Well," the stout woman began, resting her hand on his arm, "What you said back at the Compound made sense, and we all agreed that your plan was the best way of dealing with Rizlov. But General Malvasian wanted to reduce the risk of something happening to you." She looked down in what Phillips could swear was embarrassment. "So he planted a tracer on you, in the lining of your boot, just in case."

Phillips's mouth quirked in a half-smile. "Just in case I decided to do something stupid like going after Rizlov by myself?"

Chou looked up at him with no trace of amusement on her face. "It wasn't stupid, Adjudicator. You were very expressive in our discussion at the Compound, and I've watched you during Overseer Selius's hearing. I think this was something you had to do. I'm just glad I was able to help."

"That makes two of us, Advocate." He hadn't felt so good in years. Regardless of what the Council decided, he had beaten Rizlov, and Doriani was still alive. "Speaking of things that need to be done, we'd better get Rizlov and his friends out of the Gardens before the morning crew comes in to open up."

"Agreed." Chou looked down at Rizlov's motionless form. "Can you handle him?" Phillips nodded. "Good. I'll get the one I ran into, and we can come back for the one you ambushed. Adjudicator Doriani said she'd wait up for us at her place, and we can file formal charges first thing in the morning. I think the General and the Overseer will want to be there for the occasion."

With that, Chou turned and disappeared into the bushes. She returned shortly with a large man draped over her shoulder. She walked as lightly as if she were carrying a small child.

Phillips bent down and heffed Rizlov up onto his own shoulder. When he got the dead weight situated as comfortably as he could, he turned an appraising eye on Chou. "Have you ever heard of a place called Seelzar?"

"Seelzar?" She considered for a moment. "That's not on any of the maps, is it?" She gave him a wink and led the way briskly down the path to the main gate.

"I thought so," Phillips mumbled, struggling along after her.

24. Loose Threads

I

Malvasian watched the three figures disappear through the hatch of the courier ship. He shook his head. Somehow, Rizlov still managed to look arrogant, even though he was dwarfed by the two huge Special Operatives. The hatch closed. Several minutes later the ship's drive ignited. The old General squinted against the blue glare as the silvery ovoid lifted, slowly at first, then with increasing speed until it disappeared into the pale sky.

That should be the end of it, he thought. Rizlov's plotting had been uncovered and the Council had stepped in. True, there was still the formal hearing to go through, but the evidence was overwhelming. They'd acted decisively against Caulston years ago on less evidence.

And yet . . .

People arrived and departed, moving along pedramps through the spaceport's observation lounge. The sun moved across the sky. Malvasian continued to lean against the railing, staring across the landing field.

Off to his right, a bulky freighter rose from behind its blast shields. Its aging drive system spewed yellowish white flames in an irregular pattern.

The General sighed heavily. Rizlov had been power-mad and maybe a little paranoid, but he hadn't been all wrong. There was something odd in Phillips's past.

Malvasian had investigated Phillips, though not with Rizlov's purpose in mind. He had used every official and unofficial channel at his disposal, and still the truth had eluded him. The incident on Wehring's Stopover twenty years before was still a mystery. There were people involved who couldn't be identified. There were two Special Operatives whose deaths had never been adequately explained. There were rumors about a planet called Seelzar that wasn't anywhere within the Union.

A group of tourists passed through the lounge, jabbering in a language Malvasian couldn't quite identify. *From somewhere in Sector One,* he thought, giving them a cursory glance. The pedramp carried them down a tunnel toward the departure gates and out of sight.

Malvasian turned back toward the window. Two passenger shuttles were landing at opposite ends of the field.

"Busy day," he muttered to himself. *Busy week,* he added silently. Rizlov's plot had been uncovered and his accomplices arrested. Rizlov himself had just now departed under guard for Bandura, and his day of judgment before the Central Council.

And still the General wasn't satisfied. Adjudicator Phillips's past was one mystery, and Advocate Jarnice Chou was another. Malvasian was certain that her defense of Selius and her opposition to Rizlov had been genuine, but he was also certain that she was more than she seemed.

Ever since the night at the Security Compound in the Baelric Forest, he'd known she was not just a Triune-certified Advocate. At first he'd thought she was a Council agent, or someone working undercover for Phillips, but he'd found no evidence for either possibility. She was, on the face of it, a novice Triune Advocate.

Except . . . Malvasian frowned. A group of tourists arriving from Rajnesh rode the pedramp through the lounge, heading for Customs. The General registered them in his mind, then dismissed them.

Except that Chou's biography begins twenty years ago, and she's supposed to be thirty-five. Nothing before that date on her file could be verified. No reliable documentation could be found. Twenty years ago was when the incident involving Phillips had occurred.

Five days ago, Rizlov's plot against Phillips had been foiled, in part by Chou. Now Chou had disappeared. Malvasian had been trying to find her for two days, and there was no trace of her anywhere.

The General believed in coincidences only when he had to. By now, he had accumulated too many questions for coincidence to answer. What had happened twenty years ago when Phillips was on Wehring's Stopover? Who was Chou? Where had she come from? Where had she gone? And where was Seelzar?

A passenger shuttle took off, its drive glowing a clear blue-white. In orbit far above, the shuttle's mother ship would be preparing to move out to its jump point, to continue its h-space trip around the Inner Systems.

Somewhere on Drinan IV, Jarnice Chou was hiding, or so it seemed. Somewhere, in the Union or Beyond, a planet called Seelzar may have been orbiting a nameless star.

Malvasian watched the shuttle rise until it was out of sight. He didn't know where to begin looking for the answers.

2

Phillips stood in the bright sunlight streaming through his bedroom window. In his right hand he held a small round bottle. The bottle glowed a deep blue in the morning light.

They should help until you can get a rejuvenation treatment, Chou had said.

I can only hope so, Phillips thought, looking down at the bottle of pills.

Albing had been replaced as Director of Rejuv. Center Seven, and Phillips had every reason to believe that his next treatment would start to undo the damage she had done. One more visit to the Center might well have killed him if Albing's sabotage had remained undetected.

Fortunately, General Malvasian had uncovered the connection between Rizlov and Albing. Now Albing was under arrest, Rizlov was on his way to a hearing before the Central

Council, and everything was back to normal. More or less. Until a replacement could be found for Rizlov, Phillips and Doriani were acting as the full Triune. So far, there had been few points of disagreement between them.

Phillips sat down in a contoured recliner and let the sun's warmth soak into him. Kia Doriani was becoming less of an enigma to him, now that he wasn't preoccupied with Rizlov. She was more than a potential ally—she'd become a real person, someone with whom he could work and someone to talk to. He wondered what it would be like not to live alone anymore.

Of course, he realized, there was no way the Council would approve two Adjudicators living together, especially two who had been involved in such a spectacular shakeup. One of them would have to step down.

Maybe retirement wouldn't be so bad, he thought half-seriously. *I could relax for the first time in years, do a little traveling without Rizlov having me followed.* . . . Idly, he turned the small bottle this way and that, watching the blue refractions play along the walls.

Phillips smiled to himself at the thought, but he knew he couldn't retire now, even if an acceptable replacement could be found. He'd finally beaten Rizlov. He finally had a chance to direct the course of Sector government, and he wasn't about to pass it up. With Doriani's help, and Malvasian's, he could move Sector Seven away from repressiveness, and maybe away from such strict obedience to the Central Council.

Still, he very much wanted to pick up the thread he'd been forced to abandon twenty years ago. He wanted to visit Seelzar.

Out beyond Morin's World, Kirowa had said.

That's not on any of the maps, is it? Chou had asked with a wink.

Now Phillips was in a position to help protect that unseen planet, if only he knew where it was and what its people needed.

Chou was the logical person to ask, but she was nowhere to be found. Immediately upon Rizlov's suspension by the Council, Doriani and Phillips had issued a decision clearing

244 • STEVE MUDD

Selius of all charges. The next day, Chou was gone. For two days Phillips had tried without luck to locate her.

Is she back there already? He wondered how to contact someone who didn't want to be found from a planet that might not even exist.

The blue bottle felt heavy in his hand, and cool despite the sun's warmth.

Interlude

"We're going to catch her in a Brinktown bar?"

"As good a place as any, I suppose. Ready, Gen?"

"As ready as I'll ever be. I do wish we had the SpecOps with us, though."

"They're too obvious, and I doubt that force would work anyway. Besides . . ."

"What?"

"I don't trust them. I think they might be reporting directly to deMarnon or the Council."

"So that's why you sent them to check the old Baelric Forest Compound."

"Uh-huh. I feel much better with them out of the way."

"John, you're sure about this? The Council has already officially executed John Caulston once. There's nothing to prevent them from doing it for keeps this time."

"I know that, Gen. But we've both been in that position for almost twenty years anyway. The only difference is that now we have a chance to find out what's really going on, what they haven't told us."

"It *would* be nice to get out from under the Council's thumb. And don't forget, I've been there even longer than you!"

"How could I forget? You got me into this in the first place."

"And now we're going to get ourselves back out?"

"Maybe. Gen, if anything goes wrong, I just want you to know that I . . ."

"Me too, John. Now come on before she leaves or somebody else shows up."

"Right. I'll go in the front and you watch the back."

"You get all the fun."

"Well, if you'd rather . . ."

"No, no. Just be careful. And slouch a bit more—remember, you're in Brinktown."

25. What's a Nice Girl Like You?

A vagrant stream of narcosmoke wafted past her face. Chou waved it away, wrinkling her nose at its cloying aroma. She told herself one more time that she wasn't running out on them, that they had the situation well under control. For the most part, she believed it.

She tried to analyze things calmly and objectively, but the Wasters' Choice was not conducive to concentration, or indeed to thinking of any sort. It was a typical workers' hangout in Brinktown, full of loud music, louder customers, and smoke-laden air. It was a place where wasters—workers in Brinktown's reprocessing plants and disposal fields—could come to forget for a few hours the stress and monotony of their jobs.

It was also a place where no one would expect to find a Level One Advocate. Chou had done her best to blend in with the crowd, wearing a worker's stained jumpsuit, clipping her hair shorter and smudging her face. To all appearances, she had just come in from the fields. *I just hope Rythmun recognizes me when he gets here*, she thought. Keena Rythmun was an experienced Agent. He was also her only link with home, and she found it impossible not to worry.

"So's yours!" A hoarse shout nearby broke into her musing. The heavyset laborer sounded drunk.

"I'm going to make you eat that, waste brain!" rejoined another. The second worker's thin face was red with anger.

"Come and try it, mutie!"

The two shouters, one tall, one stocky, lurched out of their chairs and started swinging at each other. Soon they were rolling on the floor, kicking and gouging, goaded on by a circle of cheering spectators.

That's one way to handle disagreements. As violent as it was, at least it was more honest and less dangerous than the games Rizlov had been playing back in Drinan City. Chou took a drink of her beer and grimaced as it went down. It was a foul local brew, but it was the least noxious thing available in the Wasters' Choice.

As the fight moved away from her, she comforted herself with the thought that the Central Council had, in fact, agreed to uphold Rizlov's suspension until they could hold a full hearing. In his absence, Phillips and Doriani were empowered to issue Triune decisions on cases where they were in agreement. As a consequence, Overseer Selius had been cleared of all charges, and Advocate Jarnice Chou had no more responsibilities to fulfill.

Phillips and the others were perfectly capable of concluding the business with Rizlov, she told herself. They didn't need her around anymore.

Across the room, the fight ended as suddenly as it had begun, when the taller, thinner contestant threw the other into a wall. The loser slid down to the floor in a heap, and the winner swaggered back over to her table to finish the drink she'd left there. The spectators dispersed.

In the relative quiet that followed, Chou decided that Sector Seven was in pretty good shape right now. Niala and Urtloew had chosen well—Phillips and Selius were clearly favorably disposed toward Seelzar's interests. Malvasian, too, seemed approachable, but that would be her successor's decision. It was time for Advocate Chou to disappear.

She had maintained her cover for several years without

arousing even a hint of suspicion. There was no sense pressing her luck anymore. As soon as Rythmun showed up, she would make arrangements to go home for good. *Let someone else take the chances for a while.*

For eighty years, Jarnice Chou had enjoyed life as one of the Wellborn of Seelzar, raised in the green glow of the alien Wells. Then one day she had volunteered to be an off-planet Agent, partly to satisfy her desire for adventure, partly to fulfill her responsibility as a citizen. Since that decision some twenty years ago, she'd only been home four times, and then only long enough for brief revitalizing visits to the Wells.

She knew she could still be useful as an Agent in the Interstellar Union. But she wasn't irreplaceable, and she was tired of looking over her shoulder, of never being able to trust anybody fully. She needed to be back among her friends, among her own people.

Chou looked at her watch. He should be here in a few more minutes. She downed the rest of her beer and wondered whether she should take a chance on a glass of Brinktown wine. Just then, someone stumbled drunkenly over to her table and dropped down into the chair across from her. He was a tall, seedy-looking character who'd clearly seen better days. *Just what I need*, she thought with disgust. *Maybe I'll wait for Rythmun outside instead.* She pushed her chair away from the table.

"Just a minute, Advocate Chou." She stopped abruptly. The man's voice was firm and concise, with an authoritative tone completely out of keeping with his disheveled appearance.

"Do I know you?" she asked, trying to sort her impressions of him, searching her memory for some recognition. It definitely wasn't Rythmun. *How does he know who I am?*

"Not personally," he replied, his yellowish brown eyes staring at her with shrewd calculation. "My name's Caulston, and there are some things I'd like to discuss with you."

She frowned in thought. "I've never heard the name before." It did sound vaguely familiar, but where . . . ?

"Oh, I think you have." The man smiled. "But I can understand your not remembering. You see, I've been dead for nineteen years."

Suddenly Chou recognized the name. John Caulston was Malvasian's predecessor as Security Director in Sector Seven. And the Central Council had sentenced him to death for a multitude of crimes, including murder. Nineteen years ago.

"And as much as I'd like to go into the details now," he continued, "I think it would be better if we left here quickly."

Caulson stood up and Chou hesitated, considering.

He leaned down toward her. "I can't make you come, I realize, but you'll find it in Seelzar's best interests to do as I say. We could turn out to be allies."

Seelzar? Chou barely managed to hide her shock. She sighed and stood up. "Very well." She couldn't afford to call his bluff. That one word changed everything.

They walked toward the door, Caulston leading the way. Chou looked up and down the street as they left the bar, but she saw no familiar faces. She had never felt so far from home.